T0106148

Praise for SEA ESCAPE

~ *Entertainment Weekly* Top Ten Summer 2010 Book Pick

~ Indie Next List Notable July 2010

~ Amazon July 2010 Recommends

~ *Greater Boston,* WGBH, Summer 2010 Book Pick

"Struggles, secrets, insecurities, and passions . . . a deep family mystery makes *Sea Escape* a fully engaging read!"

—*Booklist*

"A multigenerational novel that plucks the heartstrings like Django Reinhardt."

—*Entertainment Weekly*

"A perfect summer read, especially at the beach."

—*Hudson Valley News*

"*Sea Escape* is an extremely touching and nostalgic work of art with an enlightening surprise ending."

—*Fresh Fiction*

"Lynne Griffin's *Sea Escape* is a tender, heartfelt portrait of mothers and daughters: the attention we crave from each other, the secrets we hide, the unexpected ways our wishes are sometimes answered and the walls come crumbling down."

—Jenna Blum, author of *Those Who Save Us* and *Stormchasers*

"Lynne Griffin adroitly weaves the separate truths of two women, a mother and daughter, into the singular, moving story of one family. Peopled with characters who are delightfully complicated and divinely flawed, *Sea Escape* becomes a novel of faith and resilience as both women risk disillusionment and heartache to unravel a legacy of entrenched secrets. Griffin spins their journey with literary grace and a keen sense of human nature, building to a climax that makes both her characters and, indeed, her readers reassess what it truly means to be a family."

—Carol Cassella, author of *Oxygen*

Praise for *LIFE WITHOUT SUMMER*

"A spellbinding tale of loss and hard-won redemption . . . Griffin's carefully crafted characters ring heartbreakingly true and her finely wrought plot will snare readers from the first page."

—*Publishers Weekly* (starred review)

"This stirringly believable epistolary novel . . . {is a} strong addition to women's fiction."

—*Booklist*

"An insightful, honest book about the nature of grief, loss, love, marriage and divorce . . . Lynne Griffin has given readers the gift of a compelling novel of character and of life."

—Jeanne Ray, *New York Times* bestselling author of
Julie and Romeo and *Eat Cake*

"A remarkable debut novel."

—Kristin Hannah, *New York Times* bestselling author of *True Colors*

"Part whodunnit, part psychological portraiture . . . always involving. Griffin is a master of the crisp and telling detail, and her troubled main characters are wonderfully human."

—Martha Moody, national bestselling author of
Best Friends and *The Office of Desire*

"There are many deep satisfactions in this absorbing and deftly plotted novel, but what I most admired was Lynne Griffin's wonderfully complex characterization of her two heroines. . . . A sparkling debut."

—Margot Livesey, author of *Eva Moves the Furniture* and
The House on Fortune Street

"Griffin's sensitive debut reveals how loss can tear people apart yet be the same force that binds them again with strength and love. Many readers will find comfort and healing through this heartfelt, genuine story."

—Ronlyn Domingue, author of *The Mercy of Thin Air*

"I could not stop reading. . . . The epitome of smart women's fiction . . . a deeply satisfying book that pulls us through the lives of two very different women, any one of whom could be ourselves."

—Patricia Wood, Orange Prize–nominated author of *Lottery*

Sea ESCAPE

lynne griffin

Simon & Schuster Paperbacks
New York   London   Toronto   Sydney

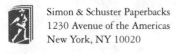

Simon & Schuster Paperbacks
1230 Avenue of the Americas
New York, NY 10020

First Simon & Schuster trade paperback edition June 2011

SIMON & SCHUSTER PAPERBACKS and colophon are registered trademarks
of Simon & Schuster, Inc.

For information about special discounts for bulk purchases, please contact
Simon & Schuster Special Sales at 1-866-506-1949 or business@simonandschuster.com.

The Simon & Schuster Speakers Bureau can bring authors to your live event.
For more information or to book an event contact the Simon & Schuster Speakers
Bureau at 1-866-248-3049 or visit our website at www.simonspeakers.com.

Designed by Akasha Archer

Manufactured in the United States of America

10 9 8 7 6 5 4 3 2 1

The Library of Congress has cataloged the hardcover edition as follows:
Griffin, Lynne Reeves.
    Sea escape : a novel / Lynne Griffin.
        p.   cm.
    1. Mothers and daughters—Fiction. 2. Parent and adult child—Fiction.
3. Cerebrovascular disease—Patients—Fiction. 4. Family secrets—Fiction.
PS3607.R5484 S43 2010
813'.6—dc22   2009048691

ISBN 978-1-4391-8061-7

In loving memory of my parents,
John William Reeves &
Patricia Grace McGrath Reeves

For whether it be a strong wire rope or a slender, delicate thread that holds the bird, it matters not, if it really holds it fast; for, until the cord be broken, the bird cannot fly.

—Saint John of the Cross

Sea
ESCAPE

1

Letters are windows casting light, illuminating the ties between two people. I could've sneaked a peek inside my parents' romance by reading his letters to her, but I respected my mother's love of curtains. At forty-five, the details of their marriage remained a mystery to me; I had no desire to confirm what I already knew. Even dead, she loved him more than me. My mother spent her days drenched in memories of safe arms and sweet music, reading his precious words, faded ink on yellowed stationery. I looked for ghosts around corners, certain I was running out of time to find a way to be enough for her. An inability to live in the present was one thing we had in common.

"Are you okay in there, Mother?" Well aware she startled at loud noises, I knocked lightly on the door nearest the driveway. No answer. By the fourth rap, I couldn't stop myself, I was pounding.

The first pinprick of worry jabbed me as I wondered if this was the day I'd find my mother dead in her double bed, cold, even though she was covered by her wedding quilt of interlocking green and pink floral circles. Juggling two grocery bags and reminding the kids to stop at the end of the boardwalk leading to Anaskaket Beach, I jiggled the lock, but she'd bolted and double-bolted the place as if Sea Escape sat on a main street in the city instead of on waterfront acreage south of Boston.

"Henry, will you run around back and peek in the window? See if Nana's in her chair. She probably can't hear us."

"Mommy, I have to go to the bathroom," Claire said as she cupped her mittened hands down low, crossing her legs at the knees.

"Yes, honey. I know, I know. Didn't I tell you to go before we left?"

As soon as I gave Henry permission to run, he was off. And as soon as he was out of view, I regretted asking him to help. What if my mother had slipped on her bathrobe and tumbled to the bottom of those twisting, turning stairs? For once I hoped he would be lured from me by the dunes he loved so much. Who lets a ten-year-old do a grown-up's job? I should be the one to find her lying there, arms and legs akimbo. I should be the one to tend to her shattered hip or broken pride.

I dropped the bags filled with baking supplies and birthday gifts down on a lonely Adirondack. Digging in my knapsack for her keys, I cursed myself, and the ocean like a jackal jeered at me, pitching its sea spray the distance from shoreline to wraparound porch, chiding me for leaving her keys at home. The last time I'd let myself in, she'd lectured me for twenty minutes about her right to privacy, reminding me I didn't live there anymore.

Worry stalled when everyone shouted at once.

"I have to pee."

"She's not there."

"It's far too oily for all this commotion. Can't you people hold your houses?"

I remained silent as my mother admonished me through the barricade of a door; the only sound I made came from a breath of fresh relief. Lock after lock clacked—one, two, three—and the door creaked opened. The frail woman who was forever giving me a glimpse into my future stood at the entrance, her slight frame no match for the breadth of the grand room she'd once shared—and in a way still did—with my father. Her beloved Joseph.

Claire kicked off her shoes and scrambled past her grandmother, heading toward the bathroom. My mother reprimanded my five-year-old with a commanding whisper. "No running."

Even wearing a flannel robe, her wavy bed hair dancing, my mother was intimidating. Beyond those scolding, dark eyes, she was as pretty as ever. Smooth skin, patrician nose, her face the shape of a valentine. If only she didn't wear her unhappiness like an unflattering dress.

I grabbed the bags off the porch chair and placed them on the inside bench. "You don't look a day over sixty," I said, trying to start the visit over. I hung my parka in the front hall closet, ignoring her curious accessories: the legendary strand of pearls and a pair of flat black dress shoes. My tact over her mismatched getup didn't stop her from staring at my lazy one.

"You worked," she said.

Neither a question nor a conversation starter, my mother's simple statement was intent on drawing attention to either my job, which she didn't appreciate, or to the fact that I'd forgotten to change out of my uniform. I placed one hand on my chest, remembering that while I'd rushed to finish writing progress notes in my babies' charts, a sleep-deprived intern bumped into me at the nurses' station. Coffee sloshed, dotting the front of my scrubs. It mixed with the formula splotches burped up on me by Baby Boy Forsythe, a child I silently called Seth. Looking worse than usual after my twelve-hour shift in the newborn nursery, I'd made a mental note to change, but when I got home, the current that drags me through my life whisked me away from my need for clean jeans and a warm sweater. No time for Laura to shower. Christian was in a rush to get to the Magnolia town meeting, where his design pitch for the park renovation was the only item on the agenda. Henry and Claire kept at me to hurry. It was Nana's birthday after all, we shouldn't be late.

I didn't tell them there was no real reason to rush. Duncan Hines and three meager gifts did not a gala make. My mother's seventy-seventh birthday would be celebrated at home. Our party of four would dine seaside.

"Hey, Nana. Happy birthday!" Henry came out of nowhere, wrapping both arms around her trim waist. If she hadn't been holding on to the door, she may well have been laid out flat.

My arrival hadn't unpursed my mother's lips, but Henry's happy-go-lucky entrance charmed a smile right out of her. My brother's rare appearances would have too, though I couldn't recall a single time when Holden hugged her like that. I would've bet money he hadn't picked up the phone to wish her happy birthday either, but I didn't dare bring up the subject of Holden. It mystified me how a man responsible for trying big cases couldn't remember to call his own mother. For her sake, I should've reminded him.

"Easy, honey. You almost knocked her over. Take off your shoes. You know the rules."

"I didn't mean to." The hurt in Henry's voice should've moved me to compassion. If only I'd looked at his face first, I might have seen his quivering chin and misty eyes. His uncombed hair with its cheerful cowlick and his shirt buttoned unevenly would've reminded me. Being inside Sea Escape, with its lush carpets and fine fabrics, each with its own name, overwhelmed Henry. He was an outdoor boy.

My mother closed her eyes briefly, using the door to find her balance. "I'm fine. He's excited is all."

I gave him a look, motioning for him to grab a bag and carry it to the kitchen, where I started to unload things.

"I'm going to go watch TV in Nana's room." He tried to duck out of helping me, though at least this time he knew enough not to ask to play on the beach alone. We were there to spend time with his grandmother.

"Not right now, I need help putting these away. I'm tired from work." I handed him a jar of preserves and a package of English muffins.

My mother followed us into the kitchen area. She stood behind the butcher block island, gripping the edge as she watched. The first sigh came when I pulled a quart of chocolate milk from one bag. I knew how she felt about Claire's refusal to drink regular milk and about me for giving in to my daughter's finicky habits. She drummed the fingers of her right hand on the counter, something I did when my hand fell asleep. Something she did whenever I annoyed her. She sighed again when Henry pulled a bunch of bananas from one bag.

"For heaven's sake, I'm not a chimpanzee," she spoke under her breath. "I'll be back," she said. "I'm going to finish dressing."

I perked up and shouted *"great"* a little loud, relieved that her outfit was interrupted, not intentional.

Watching her travel in slow motion through the large room, which included her oversized and underused kitchen, her elegant living and dining areas—my mother was a pioneer of the open floor plan—I realized there was something else we had in common. Morning, with all its to-dos, was daunting to both of us. I grew more exhausted the more I stood still; she, the more she moved.

I shouldn't have agreed to take the extra shift in the nursery. Saturdays were reserved for my mother. But when one of the other nurses wore her marital status like a name tag, pleading with me to take her Friday night so she could go out on a date, all I had to do was think about a temp in the nursery trying to cope with those sixteen infants, and the word *no* couldn't slip from my lips. Three hours after shift change, twenty hours since the last time I'd laid my head down, I was pulling cake mix and eggs from a shopping bag, hunting down pans in a cavernous cupboard, and preheating an oven I was afraid to get dirty. By the time I made the cake, cooled it, frosted it, and served it, I'd be asleep standing up.

All I wanted to do was sneak by my mother up those stairs,

so I could climb into her bed and pull the covers over my head. Christian warned me that baking a cake with the kids at my mother's was trying to do too much. Never mind that she might not live to see another birthday after the stress I'd cause by making a mess of her kitchen. I had to remind myself this was her day and celebrating it wasn't about what was convenient for me. Besides, Christian knew as well as I did that a store-bought cake might well have saved time, but it would be served up with sighs and eye rolls. I could almost hear my mother saying, *Doesn't anyone make anything with their own hands anymore?*

"I should help her," Henry said as he watched his grandmother place her hand on the sturdier of the two banisters.

She couldn't possibly have heard him from that distance, yet without turning around, she called for him.

"Joey, come, come. Give me a hand. I'll freshen up, and you can take care of a few things for me upstairs."

Henry looked at me, his expression a request for approval. I wanted to remind her his name was *Henry.* Instead I did nothing but nod, wishing she would've asked me for help.

He ran to her. My mother's shoulders tensed as both of Henry's feet hit the first step with a clomp.

"Nana, can you show me how—"

"Hush now. Remember where you are, young man," my mother said.

When Claire returned from the bathroom, she interrupted what was likely the beginning of a sermon on indoor versus outdoor behavior. It was as though my daughter had never been in a hurry. I knew she didn't have an accident, because she's as fastidious as her father. Had one drop landed on her pants, she'd be insisting we go home to change. Thank God for young muscles and small miracles.

Claire plopped down in the middle of the living room next to the perfectly packed backpack she'd placed there. Out came Josefina, the Latin doll that came into the family as a result of one of my mother's good days. Before Christmas, she'd told me *to buy the girl one of those ethnic dolls,* one she'd seen in a catalog. She thought my daughter would like a doll that looked like her. Claire adjusted Josefina's fiesta dress and white stockings as if she were our fifth party guest. While Henry had a way of misplacing things like homework and time, library books and purpose—or anything else he needed to remember in favor of what lay before him—Claire was as neat as my childhood home.

As a gift for my mother, Christian forced a collection of amaryllis bulbs, arranging them in a terra-cotta planter. While I waited for Henry and my mother to come back down, I positioned the flowers on the table by her wing chair, next to the morning *Gazette.* I read the headline—CHILD OF STAR REUNITES WITH HER FAMILY—then turned the paper facedown, thinking maybe I could buy time before hearing my mother's familiar lament: *If your father still wrote for the paper, tabloid news would never take the place of war reporting.* My eyes shifted to the chair beside the table and the envelope and letter abandoned there. She must have been lost in it until I pulled her back to the present with my banging. I knew I shouldn't pick them up. I wanted to look away from his words, but I couldn't stop myself.

My dearest Helen,
   I don't know how to tell you this

"Mom! When can I make the cake?"

I ripped a corner of the envelope's flap when Claire startled me. Folding the letter, I placed it back inside. Addressed to Mrs. Helen Tobin, postmarked September 1966, the letter was sent to her the year after I was born. I ran my hand over the penny stamps, wondering why they were affixed upside down. Smoothing it out the best I could, I laid it on the side table where she usually kept it. I got an uneasy feeling after I'd put it away. I didn't want her to think I'd read it.

"We might have to go buy one, honey," I said. "Nana doesn't have any pans."

"I want to bake. We can go get our pans and come back here to make it." Claire was a master at voicing her opinions and good at offering up solutions. I envied my daughter for being better at both than her mother.

"We'll see," I said, brushing a wisp of hair off her forehead. "I'll ask Nana what she wants us to do." Neither choice appealed to me since both required me to get back in the car and drive when all I wanted to do was curl up on the sofa.

Arranging the brightly wrapped gifts on the coffee table, I second-guessed Henry's present to my mother. A beginner's book on sewing didn't seem right, but he'd ordered it through his school's book club and paid for it with his own money. He'd insisted she would love it. I didn't have the heart to tell him she wouldn't. I remember the exact date my mother stopped creating her works of art. Henry's childish gift wouldn't be powerful enough to persuade Helen Elisabeth Tobin to begin again.

Just as I started to worry she was taking too long, I heard a thud come from the floor above me. I made for the stairs, but before my foot hit the first step, my mother appeared at the top landing. I should've guessed the source of the noise: Henry. My mother, more appropriately dressed in slacks and a boiled wool jacket, seized the railing and made her way toward me.

"Why don't I run up and get you another pair of shoes?" I asked. "Those soles can be very slippery." Her flats couldn't have been any safer than Henry's stocking feet on her polished hardwood.

"Stop fretting, Laura. I'm perfectly capable of choosing good hose. Now what's this about my cake?"

If she grumbled about my lack of preparation and planning, birthday or no birthday, I'd blame her. For years now, Sea Escape appraised higher on form than on function.

"I'm having trouble finding what I need," I said brightly, covering up my annoyance the best I could. "If you want, I could make a quick trip to my house for pans or pick up a cake at the bakery."

I wasn't surprised when I presented my mother with our options and they elicited a complaint about Mass. No matter what topic we started out discussing, she and I would land in church.

"Either way, at this pace, I'll miss the four-thirty," she said, looking at her watch.

"Maybe I could—"

She looked me up and down. "I don't suppose you were planning on going," she said. "Never mind. Father McNamara says the ten on Sunday. I'll go tomorrow."

Claire insisted we make the cake, which made it easier for me to convince her to come with me to get pans. I decided Henry could stay at Sea Escape to keep my mother company. Ever since I'd left him there the day of the hospital Christmas party, they'd shared a stronger connection, moving in close to whisper, smiling at each other. No scowls or smirks between those two. A little over a month ago, during one of our regular Saturday visits, he'd complained he was too old to visit Santa, and my mother had surprisingly offered to watch him so I could bring Claire. How could it be that my baby boy no longer believed in fairy tales?

So with eyes wide open and the car windows rolled all the way down to force a stay-awake cross breeze, I made my way from her house to mine for cake pans. The ten-minute drive from Anaskaket to Magnolia became a twenty-minute detour, jammed with ripped-up roads and slow-moving pedestrians; even a portable radar sign challenged my need for speed.

Once inside my house, I went as fast as my weary body would go. I grabbed the pans from under the stove and a clean sweatshirt from the laundry basket hidden behind the couch.

Back in the car, birds were chirping. I thought my lack of sleep was getting the better of me until I saw Claire playing with my cell. Once again she'd changed my ring tone.

"How many times have I told you not to touch things that don't belong to you? My phone is not a toy."

After crossly ordering her to get back in her booster seat, I threw the pans and my sweatshirt on the passenger seat. Missing, they landed on the floor with a muffled thud. When Claire held out the phone to me and started to cry, I felt guilty for being a shrew. In seconds, her red face and frightened look told me she wasn't upset with me for yelling.

"Henry said to hurry. Nana fell down. She's acting funny."

I didn't know what Claire meant when she parroted Henry. When I took the phone from her, the call had been lost. "Tell me exactly what he said. Honey, try to remember." Turning away from me, Claire clutched Josefina and stared out the window. I could see there was no point in pressing her.

No longer could I convince myself that my mother's earlier verbal hiccups meant nothing. I couldn't write them off as the results of a lousy night's sleep or her advancing age. Her choice to walk up the wrong side of the stairs had nothing to do with a loose handrail. Looking back over the morning, each symptom was a flashing light, collective warning signs of trouble that should've tickled my nurse's instincts. Yet I'd been a visiting daughter.

Finally the day I'd feared would come had a date. It was her birthday when I got the call. Never once did I think Claire would take it from Henry. On one of my more optimistic days, I imagined my mother accepting me reaching out to her. She'd forgive the sins she believed belonged to me. Or, maybe so tired of being alone, she'd admit to needing me. Mostly I dreaded coming upon her in one of her treasured rooms at Sea Escape, sprawled on an Oriental rug or collapsed across the damask sofa, and it would be too late to make things right.

For most of my life, I'd been consumed with worries of how I might lose my mother completely. I had no way of knowing she was in the process of being found.

Driving back to Anaskaket, I was wide awake.

2

March 1951

Helen stood on the station platform, pressing her slouch hat to her head as the incoming train's wind threatened to ruin her appearance. While she waited for Joseph to purchase his ticket, she smoothed down the collar of her smoke wool jacket and adjusted her skirt in order to get the side seams straight. Hoping she still resembled the impeccable Ingrid Bergman in *Casablanca,* Helen imagined a farewell kiss more romantic than any between two movie stars. If only Joseph's parents and hers weren't standing off to the side, eager to get in their own good-byes before he headed back to Sampson Air Force Base.

"You look like a little dream standing there, Helen. You're making it impossible for me to get on that train." Joseph tucked his ticket into the top pocket of his standard-issue khaki uniform as he made his way from the window toward her. In one smooth motion, he dropped his duffel bag at her feet and took her in his arms. Helen peeked to her right, hoping his mother was deep in conversation with hers; the only parent of the four keeping tabs on the couple was her father. She felt a pinch of discomfort with Joseph's public display. Then, lost in his arms, she disregarding her father's stare, her hat and suit, and let her boyfriend of four months kiss her, right there in plain sight.

"Time to board," Helen's father said, clapping Joseph's back hard with his palm. "Wouldn't want you to have to wait around for the next one."

Joseph's lips lingered on Helen's cheek, he whispered in her ear. "I could stand here, looking at you, forever." He gave her one more squeeze before moving on to dole out the rest of his good-byes.

Joseph took both of her mother's gloved hands in his and thanked her for inviting his parents over for Sunday dinner. Her mother pulled him in for a hug, which he heartily returned, and then he moved on down the line to his father.

"Dad. Thanks so much for coming. This is one heck of a send-off." The firm handshake he gave his father ended in an embrace. The one with Helen's father did not.

Finally Joseph held close his own mother, taking his time to reassure. "I'll be home in no time." He used his index finger to wipe a stray tear. "Don't get me started, now. You don't want me to look like a sissy in front of my girl, do you?"

Taking in each exchange, Helen could see Joseph's charm. He had an exceptional way of singling out each person, acting as though he or she were the only one standing on that platform wishing him well. That's exactly how he'd made her feel, right from the beginning.

After Thanksgiving, Helen had taken a seasonal job at Denholm & McKay department store. The paycheck she received working for her father at McIntyre Insurance didn't allow for sundry spending, and though he'd offered her some pin money one week following his afternoon at the track, she'd felt uncomfortable taking his lucky bills. Something about them was dirty to the touch. And a girl couldn't take money from her parents to buy them their own Christmas gifts, now could she?

The man with beach boy looks and city style walked right up to Helen at her gift wrapping station, ignoring Gertrude Birdie, who was clearly free to wrap the Betty Crocker cookbook he carried. As he plunked it down on the counter, Helen forced herself to look away from his Tab Hunter eyes and Gregory Peck chin. He had to be married, though she'd already noted the absence of a wedding ring. At the very least, he must be spoken for. He certainly didn't look the type to dabble in cooking his own meals. Then Helen registered that he was there to have his purchase gift-wrapped. She tried to cover her unease but ended up sounding like a fool.

"Bells, Santas, or trees?"

"Why don't you wrap this in your favorite paper, Miss McIntyre? I can tell you're a girl with good taste."

Helen realized she'd made a curious face only when the man with movie star looks pointed to her department store name tag.

"I'm Joseph Tobin," he said, tapping the cover of the cookbook in an attempt to bring her back to the task at hand. "And this is for my hopeless-in-the-kitchen sister. I think even I could make some of the things in here."

Helen fumbled with the roll of tape she clutched, cursing her awkwardness in the company of this confident stranger. She wished he wasn't staring at her so intently. He'd never know the talent she had for all things presentation if he judged her by the way her hands trembled. This is silly, she told herself, get the job done. She stepped into action by choosing the silver Christmas trees on the rich burgundy background.

"Your sister will like this. The recipes are simple and delicious," Helen said, commanding her hands to fold one crisp corner after another, taping, turning, taping.

"Well, if you say so, I'll bet she will. Hey, it doesn't seem very busy for a Saturday afternoon. I'll bet Miss Birdie here wouldn't mind if you stepped over to the fountain to share an order of Denholm's famous cheese toast with me. Would you like that?"

Fumbling with ribbon, fighting to make a perfect bow, she didn't wait for Gertrude's reply. Helen kept her eyes down as she accepted Joseph's offer.

Four months later, she was gaping at him as he said farewell to his family, imagining him as her devoted husband. Her mother always said if you want to know how a man will treat his wife, look at the way he treats his mother. Helen stopped fantasizing about life as Joseph's wife when she started picturing him holding a child. She was getting way ahead of herself. They'd been dating only since December, and he'd yet to speak of his intentions.

Joseph saved his final good-bye for her. Keeping things light, he tried to put Helen at ease. "Chin up, brown eyes. On my next leave, we'll really burn a hole in that Totem Pole dance floor, but you'll have to be patient with me. I imagine I'll be a bit rusty. Promise you won't have too much fun without me."

Helen couldn't string the words together to tell him she had little desire to go out with their pals without him, and none to dance with another boy. The ache in her chest swelled after he kissed her one last time. He held her hand as long as he could, hesitating to put one foot on that train. After he did get on, she watched him walk down the aisle in search of an empty seat on the platform side.

As the train pulled away, he leaned his body out the window. Even at a distance, Helen could see his eyes set on her alone, though his wide smile disappeared when he swallowed hard, the way he did whenever a subject turned serious. She told herself to hold on to her emotions. She mustn't lose her composure in front of his parents. Joseph's wavy hair caught the last light of day, and in that shining moment it hit Helen: this wasn't a directed scene from a movie. Joseph was really going back to New York, his next leave date unknown.

Helen kept waving until the train was a dot in the distance.

Once it was out of sight, she hugged the Tobins good-bye, not sure when she'd see them again. In the car on the ride back home, Mother tried to lighten her mood by tuning the radio to WTAG, but even some toe-tapping Tommy Dorsey couldn't change Helen's frown to a smile. It didn't help that Father sighed every time he looked in the rearview mirror, checking to see if she'd stopped dabbing her eyes with her hankie.

The minute she got back to her room, despite the early hour, Helen changed into her nightgown. In her humble opinion, without Joseph to talk to or gaze at, it was time for bed. Out of the corner of her eye she spied the brand-new sewing machine Father had given her for Christmas. Still in its square black box, it leaned aloof against her dresser. Blowing the dust off its case, Helen lugged the machine up onto her bed and opened it. She felt a tad guilty for not having used it yet.

At the holidays, she'd been miffed with Father for writing off her newest dream of going to interior design school. Day after day she watched her father play with life, death, and money at McIntyre Insurance Agency. Calculating risk on paper didn't interest Helen, nor did sorting paper after boring paper from the mounds he parked on the edge of her desk, usually right after she'd finished filing a weighty stack. But brightening a home with handiwork, now that was an intriguing occupation.

It really was a swell machine. She wished she weren't still annoyed with Father for dismissing her career plans. "You're already a competent secretary," he'd said, his motives impossible to miss. He'd appeased her with the gift, encouraging her to have what he called "a useful hobby," while his stern face and round black eyes told her he had no intention of letting go of his plans for her life. Lee McIntyre expected her to work for him until a suitable match could be made with the son of a wealthy business associate from Worcester. He acted as if going steady with Joseph Robert Tobin were merely a passing fancy.

Helen's father underestimated her determination to orchestrate her own affairs. Men had a way of doing that. Looking at that smart machine, she knew he'd misjudged her ambitions. Certain she'd need something to keep her mind off missing Joseph, Helen decided it was time—whether Father approved or not—to enroll in that course she'd been daydreaming about: Introduction to Home Sewing.

A few days after she'd said good-bye to Joseph at the train station, she left the office right behind her father. He worked a shortened day on Thursday afternoons in order to take his stuffy colleagues to Suffolk Downs, where they'd watch those poor horses race to the finish. Helen gathered her purse and coat, locked the office, and walked three blocks over to State Teachers College. She would pretend to have forgiven Father his stubbornness. Her mother would be proud of her for keeping the peace. Yes, she'd take her secret course and start a project whose aim it was to stay focused on the things she could control with her hands. She could get what she needed without making a fuss. Joseph would be gone a long time, with no predictable schedule of visits, and who knew if or when he'd be shipped out to Korea. She simply refused to feel blue, and she wouldn't allow herself to pine for him like those silly girls at State did over boys they'd known for far less time than she'd known Joseph. Helen prided herself on being a sensible girl.

The day after her class commenced, Helen started in on her very first sewing project. Sitting in front of it now, she realized it hadn't done the trick. She'd learned more about how to dismantle seams than actually sew the curtains she'd use to brighten her life on Fiske Street in Tatnuck Gardens. She gripped the cotton ticking stripe cloth in one hand, using the seam ripper to lift the thread with the other. Making a pair of curtains was a lot harder than it looked in the pattern book she had perched on the corner of her desk, next to her never-been-used sewing machine. Maybe it wasn't the way the directions were written or her beginner sewing skills that were the problem. It had to be Joseph who was distracting her from stitching the rod pocket in a straight line.

Each time she stared down at her Singer Featherweight with its slant needle moving up and down through the material, all she could see was Joseph's face and his lackluster wave out the window of that train.

She found that while she ripped, she counted. It had already been four days, twenty-two hours, and eighteen minutes since she'd last seen Joseph in person at the station and only three minutes since she'd seen him in her mind's eye.

Her mother's singsong voice drifted up the back stairs. "Helen. There's a letter from a certain someone. Addressed to you."

Dropping the cloth and nearly tripping over the sewing machine cover she'd left lying on her floor, Helen crawled over her bed to get to the door, messing up her spread. In a far from ladylike manner, she took the stairs by twos.

"Don't tease me. Is it really from Joseph?"

Maggie, Helen's mother, held the letter up to the Tiffany-style lamp sitting on the phone table in the foyer.

"It certainly is. He has lovely penmanship, you know. It's all straight and full of sharp angles."

"Are you trying to read through the envelope?" Helen attempted to snatch it as her mother playfully attempted to keep it out of her reach.

"Only because you're probably going to read the whole thing to Mary Pat, and not tell your poor mother a thing about what's in it. Why won't you say how you feel about this boy, Helen? I think he could be the one if you'd stop playing hard to get."

A smiling Maggie handed the envelope over. Helen took it from her mother's delicate hand, savoring a glance at her name and address, running her own palm over the writing.

"You are every bit a best friend to me as Mary Pat is. I tell you everything, truly I do." Helen looked longingly at the letter as she rested her head on her mother's shoulder. "I'm afraid to admit how much I care for him because any one of his letters could be the Dear Jane. Maybe I'm not his one and only."

Maggie rubbed one hand up and down Helen's arm. "Oh, honey," she said. "All you have to do is take one look at that boy to know he's gaga over you. You go enjoy your love letter. Maybe later you'll throw your old mother a romantic tidbit or two." She placed both hands on her hips, smoothing out her cinch-waisted housedress. "Dearie, do keep that sewing book under wraps, won't you? It's best if your father thinks you're only dabbling. That class will be our little secret."

Maggie moved to the front hall mirror to primp her hair-sprayed coif. Helen stared at her reflection as she held the letter to her chest, her foot on the first step. Would Joseph one day fail to notice her looks in the same way her father seemed to have lost interest in her mother's?

"I love the new color; it's none too dark," Helen said. "You look simply swank."

"Thanks, hon," her mother said. "Oh, do ask Mary Pat to join us for dinner, won't you? Your father's got a bridge game after work. We'll have another girls' night." Maggie turned to look at Helen languishing on the stairs. "Well, don't just stand there, go read your letter."

Helen agreed to invite Mary Pat, hoping she'd have the chance to do so. Her best friend had an uncanny knack for showing up in Helen's bedroom unannounced, at inopportune times, having entered by way of the trellis and the broad arm of the maple tree. In fact, just yesterday Helen nearly died of fright when Mary Pat rapped on the glass. Without realizing she was there, Helen had stuffed a bed pillow under her blouse and turned sideways, inadvertently giving Mary Pat a glimpse of what she'd look like pregnant. Her face turned red as her friend's laughter rang out.

Helen dashed back upstairs to her room. She reached into her desk and pulled out a silver letter opener. Sitting down on the end of her bed, she sliced the letter open with care.

March 20, 1951
My dearest Helen,

I arrived back at this prison called Sampson AFB, and needless to say, the first thing I'm doing is writing to you. I'll never be able to describe how it felt, leaving you behind. Oh, Helen, I'm going to have to finish out my time in the service like a person who takes bad-tasting medicine, hating every minute of it.

During every mile back to camp, I thought about what I'd write to you, so I'm not just sitting down ripping this one off. I was sure of myself before I picked up the pen.

I'll never be happy until I have you by my side forever. So right now I have to ask. Will you marry me? When I'm through serving, I'll work hard for you. I want to give you everything you desire. As soon as I get things squared away as far as bills go, I'm going to start saving for a house. Maybe someday we can afford our dream home by the ocean, our very own sea escape, where our life together will be perfect.

I haven't got much of anything now, but I'll stay in the bar-racks and even refuse furloughs if it will help me save so I can give you everything. All I want in return is you, for my very own. I love you for the very sincere person you are, for the very wonderful Catholic you are, for the way you make me feel important when we're together, and for the thousands of sweet things you do to show me you love me. I love you, Helen, for the beautiful girl you are.

I had to put my proposal down in writing. Please don't laugh at my sentimental ways. Know that it would crush me to think that you and Mary Pat would read my words and, giggling like school-girls, think them insincere. Promise me, for as long as you own these letters, meant for you alone, that you will keep them private.

I love you, and until I can take you in my arms I will not rest. Write soon to tell me what you think of my proposal.
All my love always,
Joseph

After the first tear hit the page, Helen was careful not to let any others mar his words. He loved her. He wanted to marry her. Her mind began to race.

Father would disapprove of his daughter settling for what he called a shanty Irish beau. Maybe if Helen and Joseph waited out his tour—until he was out of the service with savings in hand—Father wouldn't object to her being twenty-two to his mature twenty-five. For goodness' sake, by then Father would probably be thrilled, fearing all of Worcester would think his daughter unclaimed treasure.

First things first: Helen needed to accept Joseph's proposal. Out of her desk drawer she pulled her linen writing paper. She wished she could pick up the hall phone and call him, but those silly Air Force people wouldn't allow it. He could call her once a month, and she could call him only in the event of an emergency.

She couldn't keep him waiting until the monthly call. Sitting back at her desk, Helen pushed aside her Singer, the cloth, and thread. She didn't go ask her father for permission, or confide her plans to her best friend or her mother. With fountain pen to paper, she began her reply.

March 25, 1951
Dear Joseph,
    Yes! Yes! Yes!

3

The emergency room with its punch of alcohol was as far from my sheltered postpartum nursery ten floors up as my mother was from me. This part of the hospital pounded with an army of staff, filled with the gritty need to control life rather than simply make way for it.

I'd been here before with my mother, though it was years ago and I was the one lying still, oblivious to all that went on around me. I tried to imagine her back then, hovering over me in worry, when more likely she stood back, repulsed. I forced my recollections away from that awful day, choosing instead to focus on the times I'd been here with Henry, for minor things that didn't change how my mother felt about me. Like the time he needed three stitches in his lower lip after playing with the neighbor's puppy. And then again last fall, when he was dehydrated after a bout with a virus that followed him home from school.

Unlike Henry's visits, which included hours of sitting in the waiting room, my mother was triaged to a stretcher parked against a wall in the hallway. Her assignment said urgent, but not urgent enough to get a coveted bay. I hated my private wish to be important enough to get some attention, because it was tied to the reality that it could only happen if she invited death to pull up a chair.

Sprawled out for the world to see, her diminished form lay still under a single white sheet. Her red wool jacket poked out of the patient belongings bag at the bottom of the stretcher, an ominous contrast to her skin tone.

My mind raced back and forth between concern for her and sympathy for Henry and Claire after what they'd just been through. One minute I was struck by my mother's ghostly appearance as she lay unmoving on that hospital stretcher, the next minute a slow-motion replay of finding her down for the count at the bottom of those stairs pushed its way into my consciousness. It was as if experiencing the morning over and over again would help me understand how I'd landed here.

After Claire handed me the phone in the car, I timed the trip back to Sea Escape by counting how many times I hit my mother's number on speed dial. Twice I let it ring through to voice mail so I could listen to her curt message, full of proper words and pleasantries, allowing it to convince me she had to be all right.

Worried about my mother, and poor Henry—all alone—I'd never been happier to maneuver my Forester down that dirt road lined with its soaring cedars and scrub pines. When my tires began chewing the clamshell driveway, I leaned up to the windshield, searching for any sign of life through the walls of glass surrounding three sides of the home named by my father. Nothing stirred.

Panic rising, I begged Claire to obey me. To stay in the car. I wanted to shout, *Don't go down to the beach,* but I didn't want to give her any ideas. Leaping over the sagging porch steps in one stride, I ran the length of the porch, dodging Adirondacks. The bank of windows that brought the living room front and center with the Atlantic Ocean revealed a picture I knew I'd never erase from my mind. Wind whipped around the corner and slapped me in the face at the exact moment I saw her lying facedown on the Berber. Henry was holding her hand.

Sitting in my visitor's chair in the emergency room, I shook the image of my mother unconscious on that rug from my mind and tightened my grip on the purse I'd taken off the secretary desk at Sea Escape. I wouldn't get through this if I rested on the memory of Henry in a catatonic state, his back straight and unyielding, staring at the lone shoe on the third step.

Needing something to do while we waited for medical attention, I opened my mother's bag, knowing the first order of business in any emergency room was for someone to ask for insurance cards. It wasn't the first time I'd made excuses for rummaging through her things.

When my hand came in contact with the same delicate paper I'd handled earlier, I knew straightaway that another letter had been stashed there for safe reading. I half expected to look over to find my mother staring back at me, a scornful look having replaced her dreamlike expression. Absent was the tick list of things she'd done to reject me that morning. I would've welcomed one of her lectures on her right to privacy.

Nurses rushed past us wearing their crisis faces. Keeping their eyes on distant focal points, their practiced expressions said, *Don't stop me to ask how much longer you have to wait, someone else is sicker.* Ordinarily, I would have had no problem staying put in my metal chair searching for insurance cards and waiting for someone to tell me what was going on. It's true I considered stealing the chance to read the letter I'd found in her bag. But instead I closed the purse with a loud snap and stepped in front of the nurse in charge.

"I know you're busy, but can you find out how much longer till my mother's CT scan?" My voice echoed off the walls, coming out louder than I'd intended. Her eyes went from my makeup-free face to my stained top and back again. If my scrubs and my jargon hadn't told her I was a nurse, she might never have picked up the clipboard hanging over the foot of my mother's stretcher.

Without saying a word, she flipped the pages. Then the nurse without a name repositioned the oxygen prongs further into my mother's nose and tightened the strings under her chin. "I'll be right back," she said.

I knew *right back* in hospital time is pain that goes from manageable to intolerable, or the quiet slipping away done by a patient tired of waiting for a hand to hold, so I took my seat, resigned to keep watch over my mother.

I stared at her lying under those fluorescent lights, a spotlight on her rigid body. Staff rushed by. Machines beeped in syncopation. I felt like a stranger in my own land. Picking up her hand, I hoped to find comfort in the thready pulse that ticktocked against my fingers. About to place my hand on her forehead like a mother checks for fever, I remembered Henry brushing aside her gray curls as we waited for the ambulance to make its way toward the sea and my mother.

In hospitals, time is an elastic, stretchy thing. It extends on forever when the patient or family member waits for anything from a glass of water to a lab result to the answer to a simple question. Then it snaps back into place when nurses and doctors finally decide to take action. Suddenly everything happened at once.

A doctor at least fifteen years younger than me appeared out of nowhere. He pulled a penlight out of his lab coat. I got up and moved out of his way.

"Can you open your eyes?" he asked. Without waiting to see if she would, he peeled back one lid and shined his light, then repeated it with the other. My mother blinked, a good sign.

"Can you tell me your name? Do you know where you are?" He rattled off his questions, his neuro exam an exercise in going through the motions. His Middle Eastern tone was aristocratic; he raised his eyebrows and tightened his lips as he recorded his findings on her record, telling me he agreed something was wrong with this picture.

A heavyset girl in a navy smock, a pencil behind her ear, came up to me and pointed at my mother's bag.

"She got a Medicare number?"

Suddenly more protective of the letter tucked in the side pocket of the purse than I was the petty cash my mother likely had in her wallet, I reached inside and pulled the cards from their protective sleeves.

A radiology escort released the brakes on my mother's stretcher. "Kate, you got a req for Tobin." The girl barked her orders at the charge nurse now stationed behind the reception desk, giving me at least one name to work with.

The girl grabbed my mother's wrist, checking her ID band against a slip of paper she carried. My mother shuddered and moaned as the stretcher's wheels shimmied into place, pointing toward the double doors. It was the first sound she'd made since we'd landed there. Clutching her belongings, I started to follow.

"You can't come," the girl said, putting one hand out to stop me.

I didn't object or make the case that I might be able to help. Instead I ducked into the nearby conference room and flipped open my cell phone. All I wanted to do was talk to Christian. He would know what I should do next.

"How is she?" he asked before I had the chance to say hello. Hearing his smooth accent, I wanted him to keep talking. Christian grounded me. He never confused movement with action.

Barely able to get the words out, I told him I was fine but my mother was still unconscious. Saying out loud what was happening made the whole awful thing more real.

"I'm coming in there. You shouldn't be alone," he said. "And as much as I hate to bring it up, have you called Holden yet?"

I knew my husband had already begun to make mental lists of what needed to be done, and he'd execute them in the time it took me to remember my brother's phone number.

Christian stepped into take-charge mode as easily as I backed away from it. The minute I'd pulled into the parking lot of Coastal Landscapes to drop the kids off, he was out of his office, making his way toward us. I waved my shell-shocked children away from the car, and in the time it took the siren on my mother's ambulance to go from a shriek to a whine, I could tell he'd put the story together.

"No, you stay with the kids. I'll call Holden when I hang up with you. Claire was amazing, you know. The way she climbed in that window to let me in."

Stuck on the back porch with no conceivable way inside—I'd tried kicking the clapboards to shake Henry from his trance. No matter how much I yelled or knocked on the glass, he wouldn't budge. Breaking into the life my mother shared there with my father, severing the iron grip she had on Sea Escape, had proven impossible before. The fortress I'd once loved was colluding with my mother to keep me from getting close to her even after she'd let go.

"Laura, are you still there? You all right?" Christian asked.

"Sorry. How are the kids?"

"Claire doesn't really get it. She cried at first; now she's acting like nothing happened, just won't let go of that doll. Henry's a lost puppy. He keeps asking when he can see her."

"I never should've left him alone with her. When I finally got in, I went to check her pulse and accidentally broke her pearls. I'll never forget it, Christian. Henry did nothing but watch them spill and roll."

I imagined Christian, home now, comforting our children after what I'd put them through. Cleaning up my mess. He'd have wiped off my cluttered counter and placed milk and cookies there. When he said the words *Nana's very sick, but Mommy will help her get better,* Claire would climb into his lap and snuggle into his muscular neck. Henry would ask question after technical question. And while Christian held our daughter, he'd lay one of his hardworking hands over our son's and with the patience of Christ himself he'd answer every question in the way little children can understand sickness and pain, fear and suffering.

I wished then that I hadn't discouraged him from coming to me. Christian, who could sit in the family room focused solely on designs for a client's garden while Henry and Claire squabbled over a board game. Their arguing never got to him like it did me. I wanted everyone to be happy. He could sketch, arranging and rearranging plants, shrubs, and trees, all the while keeping his composure, and eventually the kids would figure something out. Christian was quick to remind me, no harm came from minor tiffs, no irreparable damage was done when feelings were allowed to come out.

Christian would be the perfect person to help me figure out how to be in this hospital as a daughter. I was about to change my mind, telling him, *yes, please come,* when my mother's stretcher rounded the corner and Kate redirected the radiology escort to a bay. My mother had arrived.

"She's back. I'll call you as soon as I know something."

Kate became the nurse I'd wanted her to be when we rolled into the place. We worked in tandem to settle my mother. She put up one side rail and clipped the nurse's call button to her johnny, though we both knew my mother wouldn't be pressing it. I tucked in her sheets and sat down on the edge of her bed. I wanted to touch my mother like Henry had back at Sea Escape, but my hands couldn't remember how to comfort her. Straightening the neckline of her hospital gown, I would have given anything for her to reprimand me for breaking the pearls my father liked to call her "South Sea beauties."

When the doctor's face appeared in the doorway, I knew he was there to give me the test results. Out in the hall, he looked at the radiology report instead of me.

"Your mother had a significant neurologic event caused by a blood clot."

I didn't need him to keep pointing to different parts of his head to know this was worse than I'd expected. He went on to say what no child, no matter how old she is, wants to hear about her mother.

"There's been considerable brain damage, though it's too early to know the full extent of it. We plan to fight this with our most powerful pharmaceuticals. Still, you should prepare for the worst."

I knew before he finished delivering the bad news that my mother would need more than strong medicine—or me—to pull her through. She would need the man who grounded her. My father.

4

❧❧

My thoughts skittered between images of a glassed-in room with rows of infant bassinets and a wrack line dotted with the ocean's castoffs: abandoned shells, snarls of seaweed, an array of pebbles splashed with color. Two very different places appealed to my need to flee my mother's bedside. I secretly wished I could slip away to glimpse the newest arrivals in the nursery upstairs or take a brisk walk on Anaskaket Beach, the backyard of my childhood. One space confined, the other expansive. I was good at working through and walking out my demons, surprisingly at home in either of those places. But my mother, the anchor, moored me to my visitor's chair. The babies and the beach would have to wait.

Early in our visit, I didn't dare follow the green line that led to the hospital cafeteria to get a cup of coffee. I knew the way without the primitive directions taped to the floor, laid down like bread crumbs. I stayed because I was afraid that, if I left, my mother might slip away from me for good. Instead I sat by her bed, waiting on a transfer to the intensive care unit, tempted by the letter in her purse.

In the midst of our lives changing, my mother did nothing but lie there accepting the medicine that would dissolve the blood clot lodged somewhere in her brain, while I wondered how in the world I would connect with her now when I hadn't been any good at it when she was at home, awake and talking. After hours of being despondent over her unending silence, I asked myself what Christian would do. I decided to make use of my father's voice, thinking maybe I could trick my mother into waking up and choosing life.

Paying reverence to the heirloom, I slowly exposed the letter to light. Overwhelmed with the urge to read it in my head, I forced my lips and tongue to speak his words out loud, reminding myself, I'd opened it for her.

April 28, 1951
My dearest Helen,

Well, five months ago I made the biggest mistake of my life. I went out with this girl, just to the movies mind you, and I've been hooked ever since. I don't know how to escape her. Do you have any ideas as to how I could give her the brush-off? I don't want to do it sudden-like. I'd rather do it gradually, over a period of a hundred years or so. You see, I'd never want to hurt her feelings. She has this strange idea that I love her, but frankly, I can't stand being with her more than thirty-six hours a day, eight days a week.

I guess I'd better get serious or you'll think your honey flipped his lid. As you must know by now, the day I met you was the luckiest day of my life. The world is upside down for me since you accepted my proposal. Even the weather's lost its head. It's spring, but there's snow falling here. I took a walk earlier, and it was as if I could be strolling down any street back home, though my life there with you seems so far away.

It wasn't long before I reached a church, and the line to go to confession was so long I decided to kneel down and say some prayers. It really is quite hard to explain, but there, away from the girl I love so much, I suddenly realized that, as lonely as I am, I am the happiest I have ever been in my life. Right then and there, I asked God one favor. That you wouldn't change your mind about marrying me, finding someone who could give you more than I can. Someone your father approves of.

A light tap-tap on the wall outside our bay announced the arrival of a man with a name tag; it read "Dion." He said he'd been assigned to take us up to the fourth-floor ICU. He was tall and thin, and moved like a reed in a breeze. He wore the same hospital garb as the last escort, but unlike her, he pointed to my mother's identity poking out from under the sheet, asking before he checked her wristband.

"May I?"

"Sure." I slipped the letter back into her purse, embarrassed at being caught dipping into her privacy and a bit unsettled learning my grandfather hadn't approved of my father.

Together we wheeled her down the blue line toward the elevator that would take us upstairs. Before leaving us there, returning to his job of guiding the next patient to her destination, Dion moved up beside me. He spoke in low tones.

"She will be fine, your mother. And so will you."

Before I could respond to his kindness, he slipped out of the room and, without haste, pushed the empty stretcher back toward the bank of elevators. The hurricane that was my mother's next nurse provided my diversion.

"I'm Molly. I'll be taking care of your mother for the rest of tonight. And lucky for you, I'm on the next two nights. I hear you're a nurse. That means we'll need to get a few things straight."

Without taking a breath or a pause, she talked on as she recorded information on the portable laptop affixed to the top of a table placed at the end of the bed. She pushed buttons on the monitor to get pulse and blood pressure readings, dialed up the oxygen, and checked the contents of my mother's IV. She didn't look like a Molly. A Molly should be lighthearted and warm, co-operative, like a Heather or a Holly. Our Molly was all business.

"You can ask me whatever you want. I won't hold anything back. Don't ask a question you don't want an honest answer to. You can stay in here as long as you don't get in my way. If I tell you to go, no matter what, you go. Number one priority is Helen."

As Molly said my mother's name, she reined in her energy and ran a hand over her cheek. She spoke directly to her. "We've got a lot of work ahead to get you well."

My mother's eyelids fluttered, and her heart rate went up a few beats per minute. I wondered if she'd done that while I'd been reading to her. I'd been so captivated by my charismatic father that I hadn't taken the time to notice her reaction.

"I have a question," I said. "When you have a minute can we step outside?" I gestured to the hallway, where more nurses were in perpetual motion.

"Shoot. There's nothing you can't say in front of Helen. She's the one who has to do the healing." Pulling the side rail up, Molly stood on the window side of the bed.

I lowered my voice. "Can you call the chaplain on duty? My mother would want, you know—"

"She religious?"

I nodded, and Molly leaned down to my mother, speaking to her as if she were wide awake. "The sacrament of the sick will put you in an optimal state for recovery. Sure, I'll call down to Chaplaincy," she said to me. "Anything else?"

There were a thousand things I wanted to know.

"No, that's it," I said.

Ten minutes later, I went back to the letter. Reacquainted with my father, I wished I knew more about him. His words were so soothing, I fought to keep my eyes open. Thirty straight hours awake and I would've paid more for an ounce of sleep than an addict would his meth. I was about to settle for a vending machine cup of coffee when my real remedy came in the form of Candy.

Candace Iverson, my best friend since fifth grade, strolled through the double doors of the unit with the confidence I envied. Wearing pressed trousers and a crisp white button-down, she was the only person I knew who looked put together in a crisis. Keeping all her attention on me standing on the threshold to my mother's room, she walked straight for me. Her short hair bobbed as she gave a nod to the unit secretary manning the desk. I could see he was about to tell her she couldn't come in when she whispered *family.*

I fell into her arms and let myself cry the way I only dared do with her, though I didn't give way to sniveling or bawling as fully as I had when I was ten or seventeen. In the years since then, I'd become an expert at keeping my emotions in check, not wanting to do anything to further upset my mother. I merely turned the release valve on my feelings enough to take the pressure off. Candy rubbed my back the way she did when one of her daughters was upset. Once inside the hospital room, she moved right to my mother's side, gesturing for me to pull up another chair.

She lifted my mother's hand to her face and kissed it. "Hey, Mrs. Tobin, it's me, Candy. I'm here to help, and I'll look after Laurie too." Turning to me, she tipped her head and made a sad clown face, telling me she was heartbroken to see my mother this way. Not moving. Not talking. Not reprimanding us for ignoring one of her many rules.

I wondered if she was trying as hard as I was to remember the younger, happier version of my mother. The slender woman with jet-black hair like mine, who in the early days of our friendship was content to be with us, fully engaged in our childhood preoccupations.

On the warm September day we met, I brought Candy home from school to Sea Escape. I knew my mother would be happy I'd found a friend to invite over. Giggling about a boy in our class named Pete—a boy Candy was sure she would marry—and gabbing about how much we liked our teacher, we climbed the stairs to the second floor. I knew to look for my mother in her sewing room. No doubt she'd be working on a new creation.

"Well, who do we have here?" my mother asked, able to keep running her machine over yards of fabric covered with flowers while still giving us her full attention.

"This is Candy. We're in the same class. She lives at the end of Coast Road, but only five houses away if you walk from here on the beach. We're kind of neighbors," I said, talking so fast I almost forgot to breathe. "It's hot, can we go swimming?"

My mother glanced out the window toward the beach as if she'd suddenly realized the day had gotten away from her. "Yes, I've done enough for this afternoon. I can finish the other panel tomorrow."

"What are you making?" Candy asked, touching a corner of the fabric. "This is real pretty."

"Every fabric has a name. This one's called Peony Sky in Jade. I'm making a pair of curtains for our special guest room."

"Who's the special guest?" Candy asked.

"No one for right now. You just never know who'll come into your life," my mother said, taking a deep breath and turning her gaze back out the window.

I remember feeling proud of my mother's talent, the cavalier way she lifted the presser foot and cut the thread, leaving things set up for a new day and a new job. Without neatening one more thing—as if I were her first priority and welcoming Candy the only thing she'd planned to do that afternoon—she kissed my cheek and took our hands. The three of us walked out of her sewing room together, right by the room she'd been intent on decorating.

"You'll need to call your mother to see if it's all right to take a dip," my mother said. "Tell her I'll be right there to watch you girls."

"I don't have my bathing suit," Candy said.

"You can borrow one of Laura's old ones." My mother stepped inside the special guest room. Opening the second bureau drawer, she pulled out the only swimsuit she'd ever bought me. Mostly, mine were handmade by her.

After Candy and I were dressed with towels in hand, we found my mother in the kitchen packing a canvas bag with treats. Without her usual book or magazine, she was content to sit on Anaskaket, her legs outstretched on a hand-stitched blanket the colors of rainbow sherbet, watching the two of us race into and out of the icy surf.

Seven months after I'd attached myself to Candy, my father died, and my mother was no longer satisfied to spend her afternoons with two young girls. She had trouble carving out time even for me. Instead she'd plant herself in the wing chair by the bank of windows overlooking the sea and spend her days with him, reading the love letters over and over. Letters she never let me read. And that was the beginning of me not being enough for her.

All these years later beside a bed in a hospital room, Candy and I whispered about the events of another memorable day in my life.

"How did you find out we were here?" I asked, tapping the chair next to me, encouraging her to come sit.

"Pete was working when your call came through dispatch," she said, rubbing my shoulder. "Were you there when it happened?"

Candy nodded in all the right places. I told her about missing the signs my mother was having a stroke and how I'd left Henry with her to go get cake pans. She laced her hand in mine when I told her what it was like to find the two of them at the bottom of the stairs. Every once in a while she looked over at my mother, pressing her lips together, shaking her head each time she registered no change in her position.

Watching Candy stare at my mother in that bed, I knew she couldn't help but see the person my mother had become. The distant, lonely woman who became lost in her perfect love. A woman who, right then, was moving further away from her imperfect daughter.

In that moment, I wanted to shake her awake so she could scold us for gossiping or staying up late like she did when we were teenagers and she still had scraps of energy left to deal with me. I wanted to drag her back from where it seemed she was inevitably going.

"When is she going to wake up?" Candy asked, trying to curl into a more comfortable position, the rigid chair and the size of her hips making it impossible. She settled for angling sideways, crossing her legs at the ankles, but she never let go of my hand.

"I don't know. I'm torturing myself with all the unknowns. I can't believe I left her—"

A chill ran through my body, so I wrapped my arms tight around me. I didn't want my mother to stay the way she was, and I didn't want her to die. I looked at her lying there as if she could be sleeping, and the irony of my mother being any more locked in than she already had been wasn't lost on me. I couldn't say which would be worse, getting her back or letting her go. I didn't dare utter the thoughts rolling around inside my head. I felt guilty enough for thinking them.

"What *exactly* did the doctor say?"

"He said the stroke was huge and awful, and that there's a chance she could stop breathing. He asked me to sign a do not resuscitate order."

"Did you tell him she made you promise, practically every other week, not to fill her up with tubes or park her in a nursing home?"

I didn't tell Candy that I'd intended to but found I couldn't go through with it. My mother was still in the emergency room when I'd finished reading her the entire letter a second time through, smiling both times when I came to the end. My father had closed the letter with: *P.S. I put my stamps on upside down, because they say that means I love you.*

Her doctor, Hasani, came out from behind the nurses' station and put the consent form in front of me as if it were paperwork I handled every day. Didn't he know we never made promises *not* to revive patients where I came from? My mother was in a coma, tethered to her high-tech glass cubicle, and I knew she'd never forgive me if I let him put a tube down her throat, connecting her to artificial air. But my hand refused to take his pen.

"I need more time. My brother is on his way from Chicago. I want to talk to him first."

"Without the order, you realize I'll have to admit her to the ICU," he said. "And intubate her if she codes."

I couldn't believe Dr. Hasani was being so clinical, and even in the face of his brutal honesty, I couldn't touch that form. I wasn't ready to let her go.

"Every time someone comes to do something to her and doesn't say their name or talks to me like I'm working instead of waiting for her to wake up, I feel like I could scream," I said to Candy, leaving out the part about not signing the consent when my mother and I were back in the ER. "I hate this."

"You have a right to be upset. And not just at this whole thing." It was the first time Candy took her hand away from comforting me. She put her fingers to her lips, hesitant to keep going.

"She hasn't been very . . . easy on you."

I felt myself bristle. A daughter's allowed to gripe about her mother's tetchy ways, but that doesn't mean anyone else can.

"People say even when someone's in a coma she can hear things," Candy said. "I never broke my promise. I didn't tell her. But I know you. You'll regret it if you don't. This might be your last chance."

I knew about hearing being the last sense to go. That's what I'd been counting on when I'd decided to read my father's letter to her. What I couldn't believe was that Candy was pushing me to heal old wounds when I was surrounded by a batch of fresh ones.

"Leave it alone. This isn't about me. What difference would it make now anyway?"

"You don't have to tell her what happened at the jetty, just the part—"

My mother turned her head toward me and moaned as if she were going to remind the two of us that this was neither the time nor the place to argue. I lurched out of my seat, leaning in so she wouldn't have to speak up.

"Oh, thank God, you're awake. It's me, Mother—it's Laura. Can you try again? I didn't hear you." I lowered the side rail with a bang that made her grimace. My mother didn't repeat what she'd said. Candy did.

"Laurie, I think she said *Joseph*."

5

December 1952

Helen ran both hands down the length of the champagne dupioni gown. As she turned back and forth in front of the wall of mirrors in Priscilla of Boston's bridal shop, the fabric shimmered, changing colors as it caught the light. To create an illusion of height, she'd asked to try on only those gowns in the princess silhouette style. This dream dress had a sweetheart neckline, long sleeves that ended in points, and covered buttons stretching all the way up her back.

"Joseph would drop his jaw if he could see you in that getup. You look exactly like Carole Landis in *Four Jills in a Jeep*," Mary Pat said.

Mary Pat Finlayson, maid of honor, sat in a Chippendale chair off to the side of the bride to be, swinging one leg and twirling a thick curl of red hair. Helen's freckle-faced friend compared her to a glamorous movie star with each dress she tried on.

"I think that one's prettier on you than the Elizabeth Taylor from *Father of the Bride*. If you don't go with it, I might have to put it on layaway for my big day. I could have it paid off by the time Warren asks for my hand, don't you think?" Mary Pat tossed the curl over her shoulder, twisting her face into an exaggerated pout. She'd become overly concerned of late about her boyfriend's reluctance to make any sort of commitment.

"Warren's an old slowpoke, that's all," Helen said. "He'll propose and you'll have your own swish wedding."

"So tell me, how'd your fiancé pop the question?" asked Miss Kirk, the seamstress who mumbled through the common pins she held between her teeth. "My job offers more romance than a dime-store novel."

Mary Pat plopped both feet on the floor and placed her elbows on her knees. Dramatically resting her chin in her hands, she answered for Helen. "You want romance? Get this. Helen found her true love at the gift-wrap counter of Denholm and McKay's department store, of all places."

"I did," Helen said, caressing the bodice of the gown Miss Kirk continued to pinch and pin. "And four months after we met, he proposed in a love letter posted from Geneva, New York."

Joseph had made their engagement official on his four-day leave the following December, one year to the day of their first meeting. Dancing to Eddie Fisher's "Thinking of You," he whispered the words to their song in her ear while they swayed to the big band music. When it ended, Joseph ignored the crowd that had gathered on the dance floor of the Totem Pole. As he pulled the square box from his tweed jacket and got down on bended knee, Helen bowed her head but could only utter the words "Oh, Joseph."

Back in the bridal shop, Mary Pat claimed her role in Helen's fairy tale. "When he asked for her hand, the orchestra started up a rousing version of Goodman's 'Sing, Sing, Sing,' and I motioned for the crowd to make a circle around them. You could barely hear the music for all the applause."

Helen smiled whenever Mary Pat told this part of the story, though all she could remember was Joseph asking her to be his bride.

"Well, I don't care which movie star you favor. I have a feeling your Joseph won't see anyone but you walking down the aisle if you choose this dress," Miss Kirk said. "It's easy to understand why explorers crossed land and sea for silk, it's like butter. Did you know that Korean silk is famous for this brilliant shine?"

"Korean?" Helen asked. The dreamy mood in the shop turned foul as she pulled the dress from her shoulders, revealing her brassiere. She paid no attention to the other mothers assisting their daughters, trying on dresses. "This dress was made in Korea?"

Helen's mother, Maggie, walked back into the salon, holding a china cup. It made a delicate clink as she placed it down on a side table. "Oh, honey, don't take that one off yet. It's so flattering on you."

"It wasn't made in Korea," Miss Kirk said. "It's the silk that was produced there is all." She stepped back from Helen and the dress, stabbing a cloth tomato with her pins.

"I don't care how pretty it is. I want nothing to do with it." Lifting yards of fabric, Helen stepped off the raised platform and marched toward the dressing room, where she could rid herself of the gown.

Mary Pat had jumped to attention once she'd heard the dreaded word *Korea*. As Helen brushed past, she heard her friend whisper to the seamstress, "The wedding isn't until next year, but her fiancé wants everything ready to go in case he gets his orders to ship out. She's on pins and needles, poor thing."

Helen's mother stepped in. "Mary Pat, be a dear and hand me that one, will you?"

Dress in hand, Maggie slipped in through the curtain of Helen's fitting room, holding a duchess satin. She hung it on the rack and, with two fingers, wiped the tears from Helen's solemn face.

"Try this lovely number, honey. Your father wouldn't approve

of the pink in that dupioni gown anyway. You know how traditional he is, and a nice bright white will keep your old aunties
from gossiping."

Helen dutifully tried on a few more gowns, chosen by her
mother and her best friend, two women who knew her taste almost as well as she did. Mary Pat selected wonderful wedding
dresses made with the finest organza, faille, and chiffon silks. Each
trimmed with Alençon lace, a delicate French floral pattern that
lay on a sheer net background. None of them fit right. In fact, the
entire outing was wrong.

Almost a full year after her storybook proposal, she was engaged to be married to Air Force Staff Sergeant Joseph Robert
Tobin. Shopping for her wedding gown, she should have been the
happiest girl in town. Instead, Helen was preoccupied with the
faceless, nameless people of Korea, fighting over goodness knows
what. She didn't understand why North and South Korea couldn't
manage their own problems and, more to the point, why the
United States had to stick its nose in another country's business.
Why should Joseph fight their war?

And then there was Father. At least he'd conceded it was
pointless to continue bringing young men home for dinner, hoping Helen would change her mind about marrying Joseph. Still,
every chance he got, he'd bring up Communism and something
called the Thirty-eighth Parallel, as if all he wanted to do was
make Helen worry. She wouldn't let Father know he'd been successful. Every time the phone rang, she feared it was Joseph calling to say he'd have to go over there. And what if he did and then
didn't come home?

Maggie unbuttoned the dress Helen was trapped inside and
held out a strapless one for her approval.

"Maybe we should go home," Helen said as she looked at the
gown. "I'm afraid I'm not very good company."

"I'll bet you'll feel better after the mail comes. There's bound
to be something from Joseph," Mary Pat said.

Helen loved Mary Pat, the romantic. Always one step ahead of her, she knew before Helen did that she wanted to go home in the hope a letter rested inside the mailbox. Each page, with his distinctive penmanship, would be the reassurance she needed that Joseph loved her and that things would turn out fine. They would have their pie-in-the-sky wedding in Blessed Sacrament Church, with its striking crucifix and rich mahogany pews. Everyone they held dear would bear witness as they declared their love and placed their intentions before God. And honeymoon or no honeymoon, Joseph would stay right here in the good ole US of A.

That afternoon, Helen checked the post once more, thinking perhaps she'd missed the delivery when she'd gone back in for a jacket. Some of his envelopes were small, the size of a thank-you note or postcard. Perhaps hers was tucked inside the lid of the mailbox, playing hide-and-seek with her feelings.

When Helen was once again certain there was no letter, she pulled her swagger coat tight, took a seat on the front stoop, and waited for the postman to arrive in hopes it was a red-letter day.

"Helen Elisabeth, you'll catch your death sitting there. Not to mention what you'll do to that coat your frivolous mother insisted on buying for a small fortune." Father, with his eyes like coal and his harsh tone, reprimanded her through the crack in the front door. "And the two of you wonder why I play the ponies."

"I'll be right in. I see Mr. Gilpin down at the Finlaysons'. Be back in a jiffy."

Helen tried to walk down the street with dignity, knowing Father was watching. He'd disapprove if she ran.

Murray Gilpin, the postman who'd walked the same route since Helen was five, did indeed have a letter from Joseph. She opened it as she made her way back to 11 Fiske.

December 1, 1952
My dearest Helen,
One year and counting until our big day. And only six more

months and I'm out of the service and home with you for good. Just think, the next time I see you, it will be summer. I bet the Totem Pole is really swell on a warm night. Of course then I won't have to keep your nose warm, so on second thought that might not be so great. I'm kidding, Helen. We won't need to make up reasons to kiss.

Sure would've been nice to dodge this business altogether or to be stationed closer to home, but it wasn't in the cards. Though I'd rather be writing for the hometown paper, I guess I don't have a right to complain about drafting all these memos and reports. I'm luckier than most of the guys who come in for a few weeks to train, only to fly right out again. Oh, I'll find a way to stick it out up here, because no matter how tough life is on base, or how hard it is to be away from you, it's a lot better than being in some foxhole in Korea.

"Now will you come inside? Phone's for you." Her father's annoyed voice interrupted Helen's reading.

"Please take a message. If it's Mary Pat, tell her I'll call her back in a few minutes."

"It's long distance."

Helen's eyes opened wide as Father held the door for her. Her mother reached out the receiver as far as the cord would go and whispered, "Give him my love." She retreated into the living room, where Father had gone, leaving Helen alone in the hallway to take her fiancé's call. Out of respect, her mother closed the French doors without a sound.

"It's not our monthly call—" Helen said, sitting down in the Queen Anne chair with its attached telephone table, twirling the cord with her free hand.

"Bum luck, Helen. I got my orders to ship out. I'm joining the Eighteenth Communications Squadron at Osan Air Base in South Korea. It's not all bad news, though. I'll still mostly be doing office work, writing briefs. Won't be as dangerous as you might imagine. And I think I've got a way we can make the best of it."

Helen shook her head, wondering how in the world Joseph

could see a silver lining in this news. How could he be so optimistic?

"What could possibly be good about you going over there?" she asked.

"I don't deploy until New Year's Day. They're giving me a four-day furlough to start in less than a week, at which time, my dear, you and I can tie the knot. That is, if you'll still have me."

"Of course I want to marry you," Helen said, staring at the familiar hall wall. The antique mirror, the fleur-de-lis wallpaper, her parents' wedding portrait. All of these things inconsequential in the face of Joseph's spur-of-the-moment proposition. "How to pull it off on such short notice is the thing. I don't have a dress. We haven't booked a photographer or chosen flowers. It won't be anything like I planned."

"Ah, come on, Helen. Don't tell me you can't whip up a wedding. I know my girl. You can do anything you set your mind to."

Five days later, standing in the intimate chapel of Blessed Sacrament Church, to the right of the sacristy off the main church, Helen kept telling herself she hadn't needed another full year to plan her dream wedding. Joseph was right. Who needed a church filled with relatives from all over New England and friends from State and the Totem Pole? Bridesmaids in a rainbow of colors and a flower girl in taffeta weren't really necessary. Mary Pat was there, wearing the emerald dress she insisted brought out the color of her eyes. Trumpet Voluntary had easily been replaced with Mendelssohn's Wedding March.

Helen knew that the only real detail that should matter was right there in the flesh. Her groom was standing in front of her before an altar. His loving stare told her that, together in silence, they praised God for bringing each to the other.

Joseph slipped the simple gold band on the ring finger of Helen's left hand.

"I pledge to love, honor, and cherish you, all the days of my life."

The light from dozens of candles—there only because of Mother's ability to sweet-talk Father Sweeney—illuminated the sanctuary and deepened the color of Joseph's dress blues.

Helen, in a cream-colored sheath, her hair clipped with a beaded tiara, repeated similar promises, her throat tightening ever so slightly around the word *obey.* Once their union was sealed with a kiss, they posed for the only picture they would have to hark back to December 8, 1952, the feast day of the Solemnity of the Immaculate Conception, a holy day of obligation.

6

Thirty-six hours after my mother had a stroke, she was tucked in, plugged in, and admitted to a bed in the neuro ICU. She'd opened her eyes a couple of times and moved her left arm and leg, but she hadn't spoken another word. I kept asking Candy if she thought Henry would be traumatized because he'd watched his grandmother fall down the stairs, landing in an unresponsive heap at the bottom. After the tenth time, she insisted I go home. She would sit with my mother while I went to see if he was okay. My mother was the best she'd been since we landed there, but she wasn't out of danger or the ICU. It didn't feel right to leave her.

"I should stay. She's my responsibility," I said.

"Let me help you. I promise not to leave her." She handed me my parka and knapsack. "Get some sleep too. I'll call if anything changes."

A catnap in the family waiting room certainly wouldn't replenish the energy I'd need to deal with Holden, who was due in later that afternoon. So with eyes half-shut, I left the hospital and drove to Magnolia. My house, in a quintessential New England town as pretty as its name, was located fewer than ten miles from Sea Escape. It didn't take any longer to drive the coastal roads home when the sun was shining. I'd forgotten the back streets would be thinned, piles of snow spilling over into driving space after last week's nor'easter. Still, it was worth it. Diamonds sparkled off the ocean, making it look warmer than it could possibly be, and the waves took their sweet time rolling toward shore. The view infused me with a dose of serenity and beauty, a sharp contrast to the drugs of silence and despair found in my mother's hospital room.

Turning onto my street, I started to have second thoughts about what I'd say to the kids about my mother. Maybe going home was a bad idea. I knew that once Claire saw me, she'd have a horrible time letting me leave again. A five-year-old clinging to my leg wasn't something I could handle on top of everything else.

Christian must have told Henry I was on my way. I'd been thinking about how great it would be to return one of his enthusiastic hugs when the vision of my son met reality. Ten seconds after I'd stepped out of my car, he barreled into me, slamming me against the car door. He squeezed me tight and asked, "How is she?"

"Whoa, let me catch my breath, you knocked the wind out of me." I gave him a halfhearted, insincere hug, blaming my irritability on the tedious drive and his grandmother's health. What kind of mother shakes her head at her child?

"Henry, come in here," Christian said. "I told you not to go out there in your slippers. And you don't have a coat on." Christian stood holding the door ajar, shouting through a crack. He gestured for both of us to hurry. I knew he saw ten-dollar bills, like magic carpets, carrying the heat out to the driveway.

"He just came to give me a hug," I said. "We'll be right there."

Once we were inside, Christian's irritation vanished and he

gave me a gentler version of Henry's welcome. With the side of my face resting against his chest, I heard him whisper, "Mi amor." And then, "Can you believe Claire's napping?

It felt like I'd been gone for a month instead of two days. When I'd been in charge of our home, there were laundry baskets and toys creating an obstacle course in the family room. No one took naps on my watch. The day before, the kitchen counter had unsorted piles of to-dos, RSVPs, and please files, in no particular order. Now wiped clean, there was a bowl of fresh fruit and a plate of Mexican sweet bread made by small hands. In the center of everything, a huddled crowd of trumpetlike flowers poked out of a ceramic pot, undoubtedly from Christian. I should've been grateful for his gift of paperwhites. Instead, my first reaction was *Oh, great, another thing for me to take care of.* A pungent tang came off the blooms and mixed with the sugary smell of the bread, assaulting me. I wanted my other, messy life back.

"When is she coming home?" Henry's voice shook with his question. I hadn't realized he was standing right behind me. When I turned to see him holding the sewing book he'd bought his grandmother, it broke my heart. It was unwrapped, so at some point it dawned on him my mother wouldn't be opening her birthday presents.

Henry was a shade lighter than Christian, as though my genes were the dash of cream stirred in at the last minute to top off his already perfect looks. I never tired of Christian's mother, Ria, showing me pictures of my husband at Henry's age. My favorite was the one of him standing in his family's bakery in Spanish Harlem, proudly holding a tray of the fruit-filled empanadas he'd made himself.

"I could stay with her at Sea Escape," Henry continued. "I would take good care of her. It wasn't my fault she fell."

Completely incoherent, I couldn't think of one thing to say.

"Cariño," Christian said, as he motioned for me to sit down on one of our kitchen stools. With a gentle nudge and an endearment, he could usually sway me to do anything by simply moving me forward. He and Henry moved in sync with each other. Once seated, they crossed their arms in exactly the same way, one resting directly on top of the other. Both wore sad faces. Henry's was the more serious and resembled the one he had on most days when he got off the school bus. The sewing book, not far from his elbow, was the only thing out of place on the counter.

"Nobody thinks you're to blame for Nana being in the hospital," Christian said.

"It's all my fault," I said. "I shouldn't have left you alone with her. I'm so sorry, Henry."

Though Christian had pulled out a stool for me, I resisted the urge to sit. Standing across from them, I was afraid if I sat down I'd never get back up. I broke off a bit of sweet bread, intending to feed my noisy stomach. Thinking about how sick my mother was tickled my anxiety. I put the piece back on the plate. Suddenly I couldn't believe I'd left the ICU. What was I thinking, running out on her so that I could come home to rest or indulge in Christian's pastry?

"Did she say she felt sick before she fell?" I asked. "Where were you when it happened?"

Christian leaned back so Henry couldn't see him shaking his head and scrunching his eyes, mouthing the words *He doesn't want to talk about it.* Henry pulled the sewing book closer to him, clutching it to his chest.

"Is Nana going to die?" he asked.

I never answered his question, because as soon as he said the word *die,* Claire came running into the room wailing, *"Mommy."* I scooped her up, and she wrapped her arms and legs around me like a baby octopus.

"Come, Henry, you can help me pack a few things for Mom to take back to the hospital. Remember, she has to go help Nana." Christian's remark was as much to reassure Henry as it was to prepare Claire that I'd be leaving again. Though he wouldn't admit it, part of him hated that she didn't attach herself to him like she did me. He patted Henry's back in an encouraging way, but it jarred our son enough that he lost his grip on the book. It landed, pages splayed, open on the floor. All of us stared at the letter lodged in the gutter of its spine.

"Where did you get that?" I asked. I put Claire down and tried to beat Henry to it. Lunging for the letter, we banged heads. My forehead throbbed, thwarting my attempt to get to it before he did. He held it in his hand, making no effort to stuff it back into the book or keep it from me.

"Did you take that from Nana's?" I knew it was the letter from the table next to her wing chair. The tear I'd inflicted on the envelope the day before—the telltale sign—was visible even at a distance.

"She said I could."

"Don't lie. My mother would never give one of her letters to you. No one's allowed to read them."

Christian, without expending much energy, took the letter from Henry and handed it to me. "What does it matter, cariño? You have it now. It can be returned to Sea Escape."

Claire stuffed a big hunk of sweet bread in her mouth. Tiny crumbs flew from her lips as she spoke. "Is he in twouble?"

Henry shot her a look.

"No one's in trouble," Christian said, moving the plate out of her reach. "We're all upset about Nana. Let's each take a deep breath and give Mommy a few minutes to rest."

I wanted to be offended by Christian telling the kids their mother needed time to pull herself together, but I had to agree with him about Henry. What difference did it make that he took the letter? My mother certainly didn't know or care that he had it. He was only trying to do what she'd always done, hold on by clinging to tangible things.

Looking at Henry standing there holding the book, I realized tragedy, though never welcome, insists on bringing gifts. I headed back to the hospital, well aware that my mother's demise brought my father back to me, and that my son's need to make sense of his grandmother's fall put a new letter in my possession.

I might have been happy as I pulled out of my driveway if the last thing I heard hadn't been Claire screaming my name and the last image of home hadn't been Henry's face pressed against the living room window, his little hand waving good-bye.

7

June 1953

Helen could have been content with the first valance she sewed to go over the curtains for their bedroom. The panels themselves looked marvelous, hanging an inch above the floor, held open with matching fabric tiebacks. The only problem with the embroidered shantung fabric was how hard it was to match the hummingbirds and delicate bee balm flowers of the valance with the curtain fabric. Mother said no one except Helen would notice if it were mismatched. Perhaps she was right, but Helen didn't want a single thing to mar the home she was making for her new husband. Joseph would see it for the first time in eighteen days.

The rain drumming down on the roof and the potency of the wind let her know, in no uncertain terms, she wouldn't be gardening around the cottage today. It was the ideal day for sewing. Before cutting the leftover material she would use to start another valance, Helen cut six perfect squares. These remnants would make a nice addition to the ones she'd been collecting. She had a swell idea for a baby quilt, one she hoped she'd be sewing sooner than later.

One more pair of curtains and she'd have them all wrapped up. New café curtains already hung on the tiny kitchenette window. The hourglass sheers filled in the glass doors that faced her parents' driveway. She loved the names of the curtains—swag, tab, and pinch pleat—almost as much as the fabric names themselves. She'd chosen Esplanade Rouge, a sturdy duck fabric, to re-cover the cornices she'd found in her parents' basement. Its name reminded her of the walk she and Joseph took along the Charles River in Boston the day after they were married. Exactly six months ago. And how could she resist covering the windows of their very first bedroom with a material called Paradise Garden Sage?

Everything about the cottage would be a surprise to Joseph. The last time he saw it, it was an ordinary garage. Helen hadn't told him about the disagreement she'd had with Father over where they'd live when he was discharged from the service. She didn't believe a wife necessarily had to share everything with her husband, especially upsetting things.

That unpleasant father-daughter conversation happened one Sunday in February, when Helen was leafing through the *Boston Daily Gazette.* To take her mind off Joseph being stuck goodness knows where in Korea, she kept her focus on their future.

Looking through the Homes section, she gathered information on the kinds of rentals available on a shoestring budget. She wouldn't let the week's overpriced listings put a damper on her daydreams about the quaintness of their someday love nest. She chose to focus on how thrilled she was that Joseph had a lead on a job as a stringer for the paper. He wrote to thank her for being willing to take in sewing jobs on the side, though he didn't think that would be necessary. After all, hadn't they agreed to begin trying for a child as soon as he returned?

Helen loved the time she spent designing her sewing projects, but nothing compared to the anticipation she felt about someday being a mother. She imagined a carefully constructed life, her home filled with beautiful things she made, and happy, healthy children born of their deep and abiding faith in God and each other. She didn't dare tempt fate by saying so out loud—but oh, how she longed for a girl. A child she could eventually share her talents with. Yes, Helen was eager to start their family, and she knew that, coupled with their monetary wedding gifts, their love was all they'd need to make ends meet.

"You'll live here," Father had said. "You're welcome to take over any of the three unused rooms upstairs. I suggest the back bedroom." He spoke as if he could still make a married girl's decisions. "And I won't take no for an answer about coming back to McIntyre Insurance. Your young man doesn't have two nickels to rub together, so there's no plausible way the two of you have enough money to afford the lifestyle to which *you've* grown accustomed. Never mind an apartment."

"We'll see, Father. Joseph and I have a lot to consider. We'll let you know what *we* decide." Helen folded up the newspaper, took an apple from the fruit bowl on the table, and headed into the living room. She'd left her job at the agency on the day she'd returned from lunch to see Father handing over wads of cash to an unseemly man with a missing front tooth and dirt beneath his nails. Quite out of place in the proper establishment. Father apologized, insisting this would be the last time he'd ask his daughter to conceal the extent of his gambling from her mother. Helen, unnerved by the man and for the first time fully aware of where Father's money was going, had refused.

So, gone was her job and, soon, gone would be her place of residence. She would not be one of those girls who got married only to live at home with her parents. Certainly that made sense while Joseph was still serving his country, but she wouldn't live under her parents' roof with her new husband when he returned for good.

Curled up on the divan, out of the corner of her eye, she saw the perfect compromise. The freestanding building with its blocky shape and peaked roof had been sitting right there. No one but Helen could've seen marital bliss in the form of a garden hideaway masquerading as the family garage.

Days later, she presented several design sketches to Father, telling him this was the only way she and Joseph would remain on Fiske Street. Before agreeing to the renovation, he'd bullied her into working two days a week at the agency. Reluctantly, Helen accepted the deal, though she insisted on revamping the inside of her new home all by herself. On this point she refused to budge.

Now, the second week in June, she was about done redecorating. As she laid out the remaining fabric to cut the valance, she saw her mother looking in through the glass door of the cottage. Helen slipped the quilting squares into the drawer of her sewing table. Maggie attended to her windblown hair as she closed the door. Her vinyl raincoat dripped water onto the braided rug.

"Here, let me take that," Helen said. "You've got to promise me you won't tap and peek once Joseph gets home." Helen kissed her mother on the cheek, her own light mood instantly dampened by Maggie's serious expression.

"Honey, we have to go to the house. The storm's expected to get real bad. Your father and I heard on the radio that there's a severe thunderstorm watch in effect."

"What's that?" Helen asked.

"The Weather Bureau in Boston issued a warning. They want folks to take cover. I'm sure it's nothing we can't wait out with a pot of chamomile and a game of rummy. I just want you to be with your father and me. You've got plenty of time to put your finishing touches on the place. Have I told you lately how inviting it looks?" Maggie asked, glancing around before pulling Helen's slicker from the mounted rack by the door. She held it out for her daughter to slip on.

"You tell me ten times every day, Mother, and I never tire of hearing it." The lights flickered as Helen tidied her sewing notions. "He's going to love it, don't you think?"

Joseph would have loved it, if he'd ever seen it. The funnel descended over the Quabbin Reservoir, it slammed through the towns of Petersham, Barre, and Jefferson before it ripped through the northern part of the city. Maggie and Helen made it to the bottom of the cellar stairs as the deadliest tornado in Worcester history pulled into town.

While Helen and her parents took shelter in the basement, they listened to the storm devastate their neighborhood. With her eyes closed tight, Helen heard upstairs windows popping; the wind like a chorus sang through the house and down the stairs they huddled under. She heard the sound of a train running through her backyard, but she was not dreaming of Joseph's return on the Number 25 bound for Worcester Station. She prayed with all her might that this raucous intruder would whisk right by her new home, leaving the charming disguise laid out over her parents' garage untouched.

When at last the deafening noise subsided, Helen wrestled with the bulkhead door handle. Even with Father's efforts to pull her back downstairs, she broke free. Standing amid tree branches, pelting rain, and storm winds, Helen stared at the place where her new home once sat.

Gone was the gabled ornamentation that briefly graced the roofline. The cedar trellis supported by pillars outlining the entrance to the enchanted cottage vanished, along with the wisteria that slip-covered the trellis with foliage. The wooden bench was missing, and no longer did twin stone planters flank the doorway. There was no doorway. Her curtains, with their names as unique as pets', were nowhere to be found. There were no windows. There was no cottage.

Father managed to pull Helen back inside. Stunned as she was, she'd lost the will to fight him. She landed at the bottom of the stairs in her mother's arms. Father battled the bulkhead door down and latched it.

"Well, I win," he said. "That's the end of that frivolity. Count your blessings it wasn't *our* house. Or that you weren't still in the garage wasting time and money on foolish notions."

"Oh, dearie, I'm so terribly sorry," Maggie said. Helen wasn't sure if her mother was apologizing for the harshness of the tornado or the cruelty of her father. Together she and her mother wept until the wind was the purr of a kitten, the rain a quiet mist.

Hours after they'd ventured up the cellar stairs, Mother tearful, Father cursing under his breath, her parents began taking stock of the first- and second-floor damage. Helen stood frozen in the tumbledown kitchen, staring out the window, mesmerized by the rain and the ruins in her backyard, oblivious to the pots and pans knocked off their hooks, scattered all over the floor. With the afternoon's clatter silenced, the unnatural quiet played on her nerves so that, by the time the phone rang, Helen nearly jumped out of her skin. She prayed it would be Joseph; he would be there for her, to comfort her through her loss.

"Please let it be him," Helen chanted as she sidestepped broken glass and shards of her mother's prized mirror strewn all over the Oriental runner in the hallway. The sound of Joseph saying her name was the answer to her prayer.

"Oh, Helen, I died a thousand deaths waiting to hear your voice. Are you and your folks all right? I'm in the middle of the Korean War, and oh, darling, don't doubt me when I tell you never in my whole life have I been so scared."

"How did you hear?"

"Carl Ballantine—you know that fella I told you about from the paper, who came over here same time as me—well, he made his regular call to his girl, who lives over on Burncoat Street, and geez, I couldn't believe it when he told me. They say all of Worcester is in shambles."

"We're okay, but our home—"

"Well, you answered the phone, so things can't be as bad as the news coming out of Great Brook Valley. When I heard that whole neighborhood was leveled, dozens of people killed, I imagined all sorts of things about you and yours."

Helen couldn't concentrate on other neighborhoods or the poor unfortunates who'd stood in the path of the storm. She was in a state of shock over losing her cottage. Her speech slowed as she stared at the fleur-de-lis wallpaper, a light rectangle marking the place where the antique mirror was once suspended. All that was left on the wall was her parents' wedding photo, hanging askew from one nail.

She couldn't stop thinking about all she had done to make their place a home. "I refurbished the garage as a surprise for you. Mother will testify, it truly was lovely. We would have been so happy there."

Helen leaned down to pick up a jagged windowpane blown out of the transom above the front door. Looking through the shard, her tears obscuring the view, Helen tried to convince herself that everything was exactly as it had been the last time she'd received a call from her husband.

Days later, when the warmth of a summer sun made her perspire in her sloppy joe sweater, Helen scoured her yard in hopes of finding something, anything from her treasured cottage. Clinging to the dwarf maple at the far end of the property, a tree that sustained nothing more than a ding to its trunk, she found a single swatch of Paradise Garden Sage.

"Sorry about your garage apartment, Miss McIntyre. You sure done a great job fixin' it up." Murray Gilpin handed Helen a letter from Joseph, postmarked the day after the storm.

"I'm Mrs. Tobin now," she said, taking her letter, nodding her thank-you. She couldn't muster another word for how choked up she was.

With no debris-free place to sit in her yard, she walked over to the stone wall that separated the McIntyres' property from their neighbors'. *Unfair* was the word on her lips when she saw their house missing nothing more than a row of roof tiles and a single window. Dismissing her jealousy, she read the letter in her hands.

June 10, 1953
My Dearest Helen,

I know you're blue about the cottage, but when you finish reading this letter, I want you to close your eyes and imagine what our dream home will look like. As pretty as I'm sure you made that bit of paradise in your backyard. I want you to envision a place you and I will build together. I know you're sad about losing everything— all your pretty pillows and your dandy curtains—I'll bet it was the finest home in all of Worcester County. But Helen, I want you to remember that what filled that cottage were only things. What you've got to hold on to is me and I to you. Forever—no matter what kind of wind blows, we'll have each other. Heck, once I get that job at the paper, I'll buy you a whole store full of needles and thread.

The sun came out to lay its rays on the remaining leaves of the beech tree, shimmering in the side yard. With it shining on her face, Helen felt her weathered heart warm. Joseph was right. They had each other. He was getting out of the Air Force, coming home to her for good. It didn't matter where they lived or worked, or how many or few material goods they possessed.

Helen got up from the stone wall and folded her letter, placing it and the square of fabric inside the envelope. Walking through the rubble toward the house, she said a prayer of thanksgiving that all of his letters to her were safely tucked in the drawer of her desk in her childhood bedroom. The storm hadn't taken everything from her. Although she would've liked to say the twister hadn't taken a thing, even in her lighter mood Helen wouldn't go that far.

8

⊰❀⊱

I shouldn't have been surprised that my mother saved her precious words for my brother, a man eleven years older than me who breezed in and out of our lives like the dashing foreign war correspondent in *Love Is a Many-Splendored Thing* played by William Holden, the actor he'd been named for. Holden got his ability to freely come and go from our father.

Cell phone to cell phone, Candy informed me I was in for a surprise when I got back to the hospital. "I didn't really break my promise not to leave her, because Holden got in early. Laurie, she's awake and talking. Not making a lot of sense, but still."

As I walked down the corridor toward my mother's hospital room, I worried he'd disapprove of me for going home to change my clothes and comfort my children. Holden never failed to mention that he found family life a nuisance, my suburban life a bore. He got the judging gene from our mother.

I saw him before he caught sight of me. Frozen upright in the chair I'd left vacant, his body framed by her bedside curtain, striped, faded, and worn. Nothing about the curtain reminded me of the gossamer ones she'd hung over the back windows at Sea Escape to veil herself from the unwelcome strangers who, as she saw it, polluted her beach when the weather warmed. Even in a hospital room, her privacy was still being shielded by fabric.

I thought about my mother's talent for making curtains, the time she spent when Holden and I were children pinning seams, stitching valances, pressing hems. I marveled at what she was capable of making, while he remained stingy with praise, no matter how beautiful each pair turned out.

By the time I was Claire's age, my father was spending three quarters of each year working for the Associated Press in Vietnam. Typical stints lasted two years, but my mother sang his praises like a hymn because he'd arranged to spend two or three months at a time at home with us.

"It won't be much longer, our unusual way of life," she said, regret flitting in and out of her eyes. "One day soon, we'll all be together, a real family—"

She always bustled about the house right before my father was due in, making Sea Escape a showplace. One spring, Holden reluctantly agreed to help her hang a new pair of draperies in the dining room. On a bold floral background, proud schooners sailed inside hazy ovals; spaced a few inches apart, dozens glided all over the cloth. I kept trying to come up with the total number of boats. He distracted me with his sighing and whining.

"Why do you have to change something every time he comes home?" he asked. "There's nothing wrong with that old pair." Holden had no trouble finding fault with the chore even as he easily held up his end of the rod. Our mother took her time snapping each side into its designated bracket. Her attention to detail couldn't be rushed.

"Yeah, I feel bad for the pretty ones you put away," I said, losing count for the third time.

"Why would you want to look at the same old curtains all the time?" she asked. "Enough grumbling, we have a lot to do to make things nice for your father. Holden, if you haven't anything nice to say, don't say anything at all. Set a good example for your sister."

Sitting opposite her in the ICU, the bedside curtain drawn halfway around her space, Holden wasn't complaining. He wasn't looking at her either.

Candy never could have prepared me for finding my mother sitting in a geriatric chair, her body listing to one side, a sheet partially covering her flaccid legs. I don't know what upset me more, the fact that she wore an adult diaper or that Holden made no move to right her.

After covering her, I straightened my mother up by wedging a pillow between her side and the arm of the chair. I gave her what must've looked like the queen's kiss, after realizing she couldn't have felt the light one I'd planted on her droopy right cheek. She didn't acknowledge the repositioning or my presence.

"Glad you could make it," Holden said. "I was telling Helen, I'm dying for a sandwich. I haven't eaten anything since I left O'Hare. I didn't dare leave her alone, but now that you're here . . ."

I didn't know if it was a dig about going to Magnolia to check on the kids or if Candy let it slip that I'd left my mother alone with Henry at Sea Escape. When I'd called Holden from the ER to ask him to come home, I hadn't filled him in on the events leading up to her stroke. I felt bad about my part in it. I couldn't take it if he gave me one of his lectures.

"You got here sooner than I expected," I said. The fact that Holden's last visit was almost two years ago made my comment come off sarcastic.

"Good tailwind," he said, sounding like that was a bad thing.

A woman wearing a hairnet and surgical gloves pushed her way into the room and deposited my mother's dinner on the tray table with a clang.

"You must be hungry, Mother." I lifted the metal lid to find a hockey-puck piece of beef, a shriveled baked potato, and some grayish string beans. The only thing on the tray she could likely swallow was the Jell-O still jiggling in its cup.

My mother shook her head as I started peeling off plastic wrap. With her strong hand, she pointed to Holden and then the tray.

One word came out as if it had three syllables. "Y-o-u."

Holden moved quickly to vacate his seat, getting as far away from the food and our mother as was possible. Less than an hour before, I'd been looking forward to having her to myself, reading another of my father's letters. When Candy told me Holden was there and my mother talking, I did my best to let go of my disappointment over missing the opportunity to read to her. I started to wonder if I would even need the letters. After all, it didn't really matter who drew her back to me—my father or Holden. But I'd been in the same room with my brother for only five minutes, and already I wished that he would leave.

I hated the coat of jealousy I wore over my mother's connection to my brother, especially since all he ever did was ignore her. He made no move to touch her, and he didn't bother to ask me any questions about her medical condition either. Conspicuously, his arrival was an exercise in obligation. His close shave, clean shirt, and fresh breath reminded me that Holden was still very good at taking care of Holden.

"Oh, no. I can't eat your dinner, Helen."

"Go ahead," I said. "She can't swallow regular food yet."

My mother kept her eyes fixed on Holden backing away from her. Her brow crinkled and one side of her mouth turned down, making her look frightening and frightened all at once.

"You're okay. No one's going anywhere," I said, arranging her utensils.

Holden lowered his voice. "Oh, I took care of that DNR order while I was waiting for you."

"I thought we might talk about that first. I didn't ask you to come here so you could waltz in and take over."

"The doctor came in, said you put it off because you wanted my input. I read the thing. It was standard stuff, so I signed it."

"I'm not sure it's the right thing to do," I whispered.

Holden took a deep breath and let me have it as if he'd been waiting for the chance. "You begged me to drop everything and come here, and now you object to my involvement? Look, you know as well as I do what she wants. She's said it a million times. She wouldn't want to live like this."

"Last night she was unconscious. Today she's up in a chair, moving her stroke-affected side. And she's talking. She's going to get better."

"Are you kidding me? Look at her."

"Oh-god. Oh-god," my mother said. She reached her hand out to grab my sleeve. Her eyes weren't tracking very well, but her poor vision didn't mean she couldn't hear us acting like brats. It wasn't until she finally paid attention to me that I realized Holden and I had slipped back into our old roles. Two kids arguing like we were in competition for the front seat of the station wagon or the last slice of pie. Disagreements my mother did not tolerate then and apparently would not now.

"I'm sorry, Mother. Everything's fine. We're worried about you, that's all. Do you think you can give this a try?" I held the cup of Jell-O low in front of her so she could get a better look at what I had to offer. She shoved my hand away, and the container went flying, hitting the wall. A Pollock-like fractal took shape before our eyes. She shook her head again and closed her eyes.

Dutifully, I took the napkin off the tray and bent down to clean up the mess.

Holden made no attempt to help me. He put two fingers between his shirt collar and his neck, pulling the fabric away from his skin as if he couldn't stand how hot things were getting in that small room.

I stood there, strawberry mush all over the flimsy napkin and my hand. The paper tray liner the only place I could think of to wipe my fingers.

My desire to turn and run up the nearest flight of stairs to the nursery or down to my car so I could drive to Anaskaket Beach was overpowering. I ignored Holden and squatted in front of my mother. Using the pillow at her side, I straightened her up again.

"I'll be right back. I'm going to ask the nurse to order another tray and get something to clean that up with. Sit and talk to her," I said to Holden. "She understands what's going on."

When I glanced behind me, I saw my mother staring blankly at him. He massaged his left arm and tossed me a look. "Don't be gone for long," he called.

Out the exit door, up six flights to the nursery. It wasn't until I saw the ID swipe by the door that I remembered I didn't have my badge. An intern whose name I couldn't remember recognized me and held the door open so I could slip inside. I nodded my thank-you, afraid if I spoke I'd cry. I went straight for the viewing window.

It was second shift, so there were only a few babies clustered in the center of the nursery. The ones left behind were usually later-borns whose mothers knew enough to steal sleep while they had the chance. Baby Boy Murphy was howling. His little fists had worked free from his jersey mitts and were punching the air. Baby Boy O'Donnell started wriggling his legs, the cacophony beginning to rouse him; his bassinet was the boxer's closest neighbor. Then I saw her. The only one dressed in pink slept undisturbed by the boys in the room.

I'd run away from my mother and brother, ashamed I hadn't followed her wishes, needing to take refuge in a place I'd come to love. And there I was standing in front of glass, reading the name of a ghost. Baby Girl Rutland. I looked to my left and then to my right, willing the hall to be empty. What would he be doing in Boston? Would I even recognize him after all these years, if the little girl in the nursery turned out to be his?

Not scheduled to work and not wearing clean scrubs, I hadn't intended to enter the nursery. Before I'd thought it through, I was in there reaching for her chart, reading the baby's parents' names: Kelly and Tim. No relation. Just a name. Merely a co-incidence.

"Hi, Laura, sorry to hear about your mother."

I hadn't noticed our nursing assistant, Ginny, stocking the back shelves with cases of formula and water. I should've known the children would never be left unattended.

"Didn't you get the nursing supervisor's message?" she asked. "She covered your shift."

"I just popped up to make sure you're all set. I should really get back."

It took the entire walk back to the ICU for me to collect my breath. Grabbing a handful of paper towels to legitimize my departure, I made my way into my mother's room. She was staring out the window. Holden's eyes were fixed on the door, clearly waiting on me. I wish I felt more flattered.

Men in my mother's life made a habit of leaving. Holden was no exception. Four hours after he got there, he was ready to take off. Early on, after our argument over the do not resuscitate order and my brief disappearance, he actually pretended to be interested in how business was going for Christian. He asked me to remind him again what grades Henry and Claire were in. Soon polite conversation descended into silence and the hospital room became airless; our mother was the only family member with an excuse for not talking.

Holden checked his BlackBerry as many times as an obsessive-compulsive does an iron or a coffeepot, and placed not one but three calls to his wife. Only then did I put it together. He was orchestrating an exit strategy.

I'd met Edwina only twice. Once at the elaborate wedding my mother bowed out of at the last minute. The other time, a year later on a visit Christian and I made to Chicago for a getaway weekend aimed at forging a relationship with the new couple. She had a habit of flashing her left hand, covered in pavé diamonds and finished with a French manicure, while her right clasped her husband's hand. I could see she was afraid to let go. Holden was a flight risk.

He'd roamed through Europe for three years after high school, then stopped back at Sea Escape to collect his things. A few weeks after our father died, Holden declared that he would start Princeton in the fall, and after that he planned to go to law school. I never thought he'd marry. I knew he didn't want kids. He'd said so hundreds of times, starting as far back as when Candy and I used to follow him and his cute friends around Anaskaket.

Edwina was a cool combination of chic and sweet, and I could see why he'd been attracted to her. What I couldn't figure out was why Holden didn't like me. I couldn't remember any huge falling-out, no major disagreements. No minor ones either, since my mother didn't take to us airing our feelings. Holden simply had a talent for making it clear, I was a pest. So it was a relief, really, when he launched into his *new developments in a big case, I have to get back to Chicago* excuse.

"You remember how it is, Helen, a man's a slave to the job. Laura here seems to have everything under control. Looks like you're in good hands."

I turned away when he stumbled over telling our mother he had to go, almost missing his self-serving compliment. I suppose the more capable he portrayed me, the easier it was to justify abandoning us again. Mother was uncharacteristically weepy when he said his final good-bye, her comportment babyish and embarrassing to witness. That didn't change anything for Holden, except perhaps to move him closer to the door. With her good hand, my mother reached out to him. I brushed my tears away in time to see him attempt an awkward hug. Still, there was no promise to call. No immediate plans to come back.

In truth, I didn't mind that he left or that my mother's mixed-up emotions, the by-product of her stroke, left her worn-out enough to doze. Watching Holden's commanding shape get smaller and smaller as he made his way out of the ICU and into the elevator, I waited until I was sure my mother had drifted off. When it was safe, I pulled the letter Henry stole from Sea Escape from my bag.

9

My father was right to trust in the beauty and sway of language. I could tell with every whispered word, my mother could hear him speaking. Her tense facial muscles relaxed, her suffering eased as I read.

Helen, I've fallen in love with a country. It's true, I'm torn between living in our Sea Escape and here in Saigon. Both are extraordinary in their beauty, but it's lovely here in such a different way. The city, with her wide boulevards, French buildings, and exotic landscapes. Vietnam has all the elements of intrigue, it's a page one story, and everything I write about feels important.

You'll have to trust me that our situation won't be like this forever. Not the war. Not our family life. Sometimes I'm gripped by fear, wondering how our future will unfold. But for tonight, I'll picture us putting the children to bed in the beautiful rooms touched by your hands, and then being alone to share the love we have for each other. I'll imagine us puttering around in that garden you want so desperately, the sun setting on our picturesque landscape.

Yes, tonight let's visualize only happiness ahead; believe me when I say the lure that is Vietnam can't break us as long as our hearts remain entwined.

When I was a girl, my father's excuses for leaving—providing for his family and changing the world—were as easy to believe in as his adventure stories. He loved the colorful surroundings he wrote about and his familiar home too. What I couldn't comprehend now, as I sat by her bedside for the second night in a row, watching her sleep, was why my mother put up with that kind of marriage. My father's travels took him all over the world to exotic and stimulating cities while she, competent woman that she was, was left to try to express her love for him in fabric.

My mother never told us that he was on his way back to Sea Escape. She wasn't effusive even when she'd been happy. Her hands always did most of her talking. Whenever she'd whip up a new tablecloth from her basket of remnant cloth and place a small vase of wildflowers in the center of our kitchen table, Holden and I would guess he was getting closer. Maybe that was his plane flying over our house, tipping its wing, waving at me from the sky.

The last time I remember him coming home, they shared their usual first meal together. Like always, it was adults only and consisted of a great steak and baked potatoes with all the fixings. I was bathed and ready for bed before he arrived. Holden went off with his friends. Before my parents ate, I was invited into the living room and offered a fancy glass that held ginger ale and a single maraschino cherry. My mother indulged in a cocktail before dinner. As far as I knew, she never drank when my father wasn't home. For the hour or so I was included, the three of us were happy. Daddy brought home new stories. When I was dismissed with the bribe of an extra episode of *The Brady Bunch,* my parents snuggled on the couch by candlelight. The hi-fi softly played the Jack d'Johns, and he whispered things that made her cry. I knew about that part only because, during commercials, I'd creep down the stairs to peek at them through the bars. Mostly to make sure he was still there.

As a child, I envied their romance. Years later it hurt me to think of it. By my thirty-third birthday, I'd given up hope of finding a man who could live up to my father. One who was strong enough to rip me from my mother's life. Someone I could relinquish my own life to. Because who would take care of her if I moved away? Like a human salve, I was the one to soothe the aches and pains brought on by what she had left. Letters and loneliness. I told myself I couldn't leave, even if she didn't appreciate me being there for her. Someone needed to make sure she was okay. No way was Holden that person. And we both knew I owed her at least that much.

No wonder the man who freed me from Sea Escape had no desire to take me from her.

Single, living at home, and working in Boston, I took care of other people's babies. Under the guise of attending a nursing conference, I decided to break free from the chokehold my mother's depression had on me to spend three luxurious days in New York City. On the first day, I attended a couple of seminars, and once my obligation was fulfilled, I sneaked away to spend a quiet afternoon in the Metropolitan Museum of Art. After wandering around for two hours, I took a seat on a leather bench in one of the second-floor galleries. Rubbing a blistered foot, I chastised myself for not wearing more comfortable shoes.

He was tall and had an athletic build. I found myself drawn in by his sketching in a plain composition notebook; he didn't seem the artsy type. He stood back from a painting of a villa every few seconds, flourishing his pencil across the page. I wasn't mesmerized by the swirls of oil on canvas. I didn't set my eyes on what he was drawing. I stared at his shoulder muscles as they rhythmically tightened and relaxed under his cotton shirt, guiding the smaller muscles of his arm and hand.

"Like what you're looking at?" His eyes were dark yet kind.

His was a face that spent time outdoors. Flustered, I wondered why someone so easy on the eye had to wreck his image by being so conceited. Then I realized he was talking about the painting.

"It's called *A Spanish Garden* by Martín Rico y Ortega," he said.

I smiled at him, doing my best to stifle a laugh. "The flowers around the fountain are what capture your attention," I said. "He was right to name it that."

"I'm trying to copy it for a garden I'm designing."

He sat down next to me and showed me his sketched interpretation. He told me he was in town to teach a master class in oceanside landscape design at his alma mater, City College, and to visit his parents in East Harlem. Ten minutes into small talk, we were amazed to find out we both lived south of Boston. Christian Martinez lived one town over from Anaskaket. Given what he did for a living, his town was aptly named Magnolia, like the tough but elegant trees I'd always loved.

On our first date, without hesitation, he gave me a wide-open view of his world. He introduced me to his priorities. When he asked me if I wanted a cup of the finest coffee in New York, I said yes, and within minutes I was getting into a cab heading across town with a charming stranger.

The name of his family's bakery, El Pan Nuestro de Cada Día, translated to "Our Daily Bread." His mother and father welcomed me as they did every good customer, by offering me a cup of café con leche and the specialty of the day, puff pastry called sopaipilla.

"Sit right there, friend of Christian's," his mother said. Ria Martinez was a round woman of at least sixty. Her lined face appeared older, but the way she bustled around the bakery, cleaning tables and refilling coffee mugs, bespoke youthful energy.

To a bread lover, the panadería was bliss. Loaves with angled-cut tops and plump rolls sprinkled with herbs filled one glass case. The other case was brimming with desserts that could have been showcased back at the museum. The kitchen, where Christian's father, Joaquin, performed his magic, was visible to everyone who sat at a front table in their homey shop.

"Where's Luce, Madre? I thought she was working today." Christian patted an ancient man on the shoulder and kissed a younger woman's cheek as he questioned his mother, who delivered sandwiches to the father-daughter pair.

"Lucia is packing. She got a phone call this morning from that crazy friend of hers, and the next thing I know, off she goes. This time Lourdes." Christian's mother tsked like mine did when I didn't clean up the kitchen to her specifications or forgot to put out the trash before leaving for a shift in the nursery. Which meant Lucia had to be her daughter.

A bigger burst of energy blew into the bakery from a doorway out back. A woman with long, dark hair, twirling in circles between tables, announced her plans.

"I leave for France tonight at eight. Who would like to drive me?" She leaned down and kissed Christian on the head.

"Sorry, I'm hoping to have a date." Christian gestured to me by way of introduction. His sister pulled me in for a hug. Her mother sighed and put her back to work.

"Lucia, make yourself useful. Your brother's young lady isn't interested in your gypsy ways." From behind the counter, Ria brandished a serrated knife and tapped a large cutting board. Her daughter went behind the glass cases, trying to get her mother to dance with her. Ria huffed and headed into the kitchen.

"Don't worry, Madre," she called after her. "No matter how upset you get with me, I'll still pray to Our Lady for you."

Christian's sister didn't let her mother's disapproval affect her. Part of me envied her carefree spirit. Though my first impression of her was more heavily weighted toward thinking she was irresponsible.

"Who will help Madre and Papa while you're gone?" Christian asked. "You know I'm flying back to Boston on Friday. I've got to supervise three jobs this Saturday."

"I've already called Isabella. She is happy to take the extra shifts, she'll work for me. I'll only be gone a week. No worries," she said.

Not one member of the Martinez family had any worries, or so it seemed to me. They laid their feelings out like loaves of bread left to cool on a wire rack. Right there for others to take or leave, the choice was theirs. The family air was clear, like the aroma of sugar sweet and herbs fresh.

Christian's world was filled with faith, hope, and love. His family was everything that mine was not, and it allowed me to set my reticence aside enough to believe he would keep the people he loved close. He would never leave me.

"Whatcha reading there?" The booming voice that belonged to Molly, my mother's night-shift nurse, put an end to me comparing marriages, and it woke my mother. Trying not to draw attention to the letter, I slipped it back into the nightstand drawer. Molly's brusque and controlling bedside manner intimidated me in the beginning, but she'd proven to be one of the few people I could trust.

"Sorry to wake you, Helen, but it's time for some exercise," she said.

As soon as my mother noticed the walker Molly had parked in front of her and the transfer belt coming off her waist, she shook her head and pointed again and again with her good hand to her bed. My mother never did like to exercise. I walked Anaskaket Beach or along Magnolia Harbor most days, rain or shine. No matter how many times I'd invited her to join me, she rarely agreed, making up one creative excuse after another to avoid moving around. Convincing her to get up and go would be even harder without packed sand, low tide, and sandpipers to tempt her.

I watched how quickly my mother became discouraged as she worked now to move her arms and legs. Even the simple range of motion exercises being applied to her right side—with Molly doing most of the work—tired her. Seeing my proud mother's embarrassment on display was even more disheartening. She didn't have the energy to shoo me from my ringside seat, but Molly did.

"Why don't you let Helen and me finish this up? I can get her back to bed, and you really should go home and get some shut-eye anyway."

If Molly said it was safe for me to go home and that she'd call me should my mother take a turn for the worse, I believed, no matter who else showed up, she'd keep her promise.

About an hour after I'd returned home from the hospital, Christian found me in Henry's bed, holding him, stroking his hair. I'd checked on Claire first, pleased to see her sleeping soundly, hugging her doll. But when I'd peeked into Henry's room, he was far from calm and peaceful. His eyes were open yet vacant. He was sitting up, holding something imaginary in his hands, one foot jerking in spasm.

"You're okay. Mommy's here," I said, hushing him back to sleep. Lying bone-tired in his bed, it took a good ten minutes for my presence to settle him. It took no time at all for him to fill the ache in me. The entire time I soothed him, I tried to remember the last time my mother held me like her child. Christian's shadow appeared in the doorway. Reaching out for my hand, he guided me to our bed.

I had enough energy to take my clothes off, none to put a nightgown on. I burrowed under our comforter wearing only my bra and panties. Christian put our laundry away drawer by drawer. When he'd finished, he brought me a long flannel, the one I wore when I had a cold or the flu. He helped me pull it down over my weary body.

"He had a really bad day," Christian said. "Miss Ackart said he pushed someone down at recess and that the other boy did nothing to provoke the attack."

"Is he okay? The boy, I mean." I'd meant Henry until I realized how unkind that would sound, even to Christian.

"He's fine, but she said she had to tell us because they don't tolerate bullying at Lynch."

"Henry's not a bully. He's a bit of a bear at times, but he wouldn't hurt anyone on purpose. Why didn't she call me?"

"I called her. To tell her about your mother. I thought she should know that Henry was alone with her when it happened and that he's having a hard time."

"I meant to write her a note before I left for the hospital. I guess I'm more scattered than usual." My embarrassment over what Miss Ackart might think of me was muddled up with annoyance with Christian for so effortlessly taking over my responsibilities.

"I don't want you worrying about things here. You've got enough to deal with," he said. "What do you think about asking my sister to come spend a few days?"

"That's not necessary. Candy said she'll help out with rides and meals. And if I get the doctor to place my mother at Paxton Rehab Center, my commute will be down to nothing by the end of the week."

"Henry needs more attention than you can give him right now. I'd gladly take the time off, but if I don't line up jobs for the spring, we'll be in real financial trouble. I know my sister's, as you say, *out there,* but she has a good heart and the kids love her."

All Christian had been doing since my mother got sick was to present me with kind gestures and tender words. But with each piece of advice he offered, with every new situation he efficiently managed, I felt more inadequate. Maybe my mother accepted her bicontinental marriage because she liked not having to play interference with my father, the fine points of her mothering remaining free from scrutiny.

"Fine, let her come," I said, curling into a ball, shutting him out by closing my eyes. The last thing I had the energy to do was argue.

"Great, she's already agreed," he said. "Her flight gets in tomorrow, first thing."

10

❧

April 1956

Helen put her hands over her ears to drown out two-year-old Holden clacking and stacking his wooden blocks at her feet and Joseph pecking away at his typewriter opposite her sewing machine. It was a wonder a person could think straight with all this noise. She reviewed the window measurements one more time, knowing she couldn't afford to make a mistake cutting the fabric. If she did, that would be the end of this pet project. Her husband was none too pleased with her latest undertaking, fearing it would take her away from minding Holden. Joseph needed to work. It hadn't helped her cause that she'd been careless, leaving the receipt from The Needle Nook out on the kitchen table for him to see. She should have been more discreet.

"Helen!" Joseph shouted to get her attention. "If you're not going to put him down for a nap, will you please take him for a walk or at least give him a puzzle or something? How am I supposed to write with all this racket?"

Barely looking up, Joseph continued typing. Helen put down her sewing and turned toward Holden, who'd stopped building his tower, his little hand frozen to a block. His lower lip beginning to quiver.

"Don't cry, sweetie. You're a good boy." Helen scooped Holden onto her lap, tickling his tummy. She knew just how to turn the child's serious mood around.

"Geez, Helen, I'm sorry to be such a cad." Joseph got out of his seat and came to the pair. He reached out to pat Holden's back, but the boy flinched from his touch. "You know I'm a wreck about getting this letter right. If I get the job, I'll be picking up such valuable experience, and I'll get excellent references out of it. You know I feel terrible I haven't got much to offer you in the line of a home. I'm so tired of worrying about money. Tell me you understand." Seeing him standing there with a contrite look on his face, Helen could tell Joseph was sincere. She knew he was as concerned about their predicament as she.

"You're right, I should have put him down by now. We wouldn't want a late nap to interfere with bedtime. I can sew when Holden's fast asleep. If that won't bother you." She guided Holden's head to her chest. If Helen stayed seated there, rocking the boy ever so slightly, he would relax and drift off to sleep.

Two weeks to the day Joseph posted his letter of application, he was offered the job. And one week later he boarded the SS *Constitution* to go cover the thing. Though he was a wonderful writer, Helen still couldn't believe he'd been chosen from the more than four hundred reporters who'd applied to cover Grace Kelly and Prince Rainier's nuptials. She didn't share her hunch that it happened because Joseph had served in Korea with a family friend of Judybird Balaban, one of Grace's bridesmaids. While Joseph said he wasn't much interested in this kind of news reporting, they both knew full well he could make a pretty good name for himself by covering the wedding for the *Boston Daily Gazette.*

So there Helen was, weeks later, once again solely responsible for placing a sleepy Holden on his tummy in his crib. Shoving a chubby thumb into his mouth, he brought his blanket up to his face. She pulled down the Roman shades, complimenting herself on her latest creation. They'd turned out even better than she'd envisioned. The naturally woven fabric settled smoothly, evenly, and gracefully into soft folds when the curtains were raised. Yet one, two, three they lay perfectly flat when lowered to meet the sills of the rounded window bay that jutted out of this corner of their apartment. The addition of the muslin lining had been a brilliant idea, better than those old Venetian blinds that hung there for the last two years. Safer too. Helen never liked those strings hanging down near Holden's crib. No one could blame her for seeing a potential calamity in the simplest of things. The new shades surely did the trick, keeping out the lingering spring light so she could get Holden down early. Looking after a two-year-old was exhausting enough, but today her mind hadn't been on it.

Helen turned on the television and grabbed her wedding quilt off the back of the sofa. Curled up, she waited. In moments, she'd get her first glimpse of the star-studded event that took place more than a week ago. Joseph's chance of a lifetime was being dubbed "the wedding of the century." Helen knew shedding happy tears at a wedding was all well and good, but hers didn't drop and plop because she wished the couple well—though she did. She wasn't sad because she wasn't likely to catch sight of Joseph, or because he wasn't home to watch with her. Helen was blue because she sat on a tattered couch in her attic apartment on Proctor Street, missing Mary Pat.

If things were different, Mary Pat would be sitting here right now, clutching a stack of *Photoplay* and *Movie Mirror* magazines, along with her dream of becoming an actress. Helen could almost hear her friend begging her to tell her again what Joseph had seen in that courtyard.

"I'll bet the champagne was really flowing. Did Hitchcock really eat

a plate full of foie gras? Boy, I would've died to see Ava Gardner and Cary Grant in the flesh."

With her singsong voice and contagious laugh, Mary Pat would recite lines from her favorite movies starring the soon-to-be princess, Grace Patricia, Her Serene Highness of Monaco. The minute *The Country Girl* arrived in theaters in '54, she'd dragged Helen to see it, then convinced her to see it two more times. In this very room, Mary Pat had watched Grace Kelly accept the Academy Award for her performance. If anyone had seen her jumping up and down that night, they would've thought it was Mary Pat who'd won the Oscar.

Watching the princess kneel down at the altar of Saint Nicholas Cathedral, holding her pearl-encrusted prayer book, a delicate collection of lilies of the valley on top, Helen remembered the one Mary Pat had given her on her wedding day.

"Carry mine now, then save it for when I marry Warren," she'd said. "It will be your *something borrowed.*" Mary Pat winked at Helen, since she still wasn't engaged to her beau, Joseph's friend from the Totem Pole.

Helen sniffed, using a corner of the quilt to dab her tears. A hollow knock on the door startled her. For a split second she expected to open it to see Mary Pat standing there, her repentant smile her only apology for leaving her best friend in the lurch. But Helen should've known her visitor would be her mother. None of her old friends approved of her life on Proctor Street.

Maggie waltzed into the apartment, heading straight for Holden's crib. She dropped a grocery bag on the couch, and then, one by one, she pulled off the fingers of her gloves. With one hand free, she smoothed Holden's flyaway hair and covered him with his cotton blankie.

"Is it my imagination or has he gotten bigger since I was here last week?" It was a shame that Helen's mother was the only other person who stood over Holden's crib marveling at his cherubic beauty.

"He looks longer lying still. I thought you and Father were going to have dinner together for once. You said you couldn't get away to watch the wedding."

"Last-minute business meeting." Her mother always said the words *business* and *meeting* as if they tasted like a spoiled piece of fish. Helen didn't have the heart to probe her mother to confirm her suspicions about what Father might really be doing night after night away from home when surely the racetrack was closed. Truth told, Helen didn't want to know.

"I wasn't going to be the only woman in America watching it alone, so I told him not to worry about me. I would grab a bite with a friend. Which is true." Her mother turned all her attention on Helen. Putting one hand on her shoulder, with the other she brushed Helen's dark curls off her forehead. In minutes, she'd mothered everyone in the room. "I didn't stop to call since it would've made me even later. Come, let's sit. I'll put out a nice spread next commercial break. Oh my, isn't she a picture."

"You didn't tell Father about Joseph covering the wedding, did you?"

"Oh, honey, I did tell him what a terrific opportunity it was for both of you, but you know your father. He said Joseph's place was here in the United States, with his wife and *the child*."

"*The child* he refuses to acknowledge. *The child* he's seen only a handful of times since he was born. At least Joseph is trying to love the little guy. He knows we're doing the right thing." Helen walked over to the rickety rolltop desk by the front door. From it, she took Joseph's most recent letter.

"Here's his latest. Read this part and tell me we'll be okay." Helen rearranged the letter, putting the second page on top, tapping the page. "I can't do much about Father's stubbornness, but please tell me Joseph and Holden and I can be a family."

Maggie took the letter and read.

The whole time I've been here, I've been thinking about Mary Pat. Gee, she sure would've been on my back for getting to come here and sure as heck for all the details, once I got home. You must be missing her something awful.

Things must be a far cry from what you thought they'd be, married to me. After you lost the cottage, I didn't really understand why you were so adamant about us refusing your father's money. It all came clear when he made his stand about Mary Pat and Warren's baby. They weren't the only couple to give in to temptation before the guy got shipped overseas.

Now I understand why you don't want to take a dime, given the way he feels about you and me, and Holden. I agree with you that your father is one tough cookie, but to tell you the truth, Helen, I have a confession to make. As much as I would never turn my back on the boy, I am having a hard time seeing him as my own. You know how much I loved Mary Pat and admired Warren, but it's hard to feel like he's our child when every time I look at him I see her eyes and his nose. It doesn't help that everyone else looks at him as if he's dressed up in a scandal.

I'm afraid I'm not as perfect as you think, darling. Gosh, one minute I was his godfather, the next thing he's my son. You're right when you say there comes a time when you have to talk yourself out of a feeling. How in the name of heaven will I do it, is the question. Is it terrible of me to admit that what I want most is to someday be a father to my own children? I know they'll have a wonderful mother to look after them. In the meantime, with God's help, I'll find a way to love that boy. I'll do anything for you.

As her mother read the letter, Helen's mind wandered to the day she and Mary Pat got the news that Warren had been killed in a training accident outside Lackland Air Force Base, after having been in the service for only two months. Through her wailing and pacing, Helen learned that Mary Pat was carrying her boyfriend's child. She tried to keep her pregnancy a secret from her parents. Only Helen and Maggie knew in the beginning, and they helped her make doctor appointments and post-baby plans. When

Mary Pat's parents confronted her and she refused to go to stay with an elderly aunt in New Orleans, they banned her from their home. With a face swollen from hours of crying, a pregnant Mary Pat showed up at Proctor Street. She stayed with her newlywed friends, Helen and Joseph, until Holden was two weeks old.

The day before she left them, Mary Pat asked Helen to promise she would look after Holden if anything ever happened to her. At the time, Helen chalked the request up to the overwhelming sense of responsibility the new mother was feeling: a girl with no husband, no home, and no family to support her. Helen had no idea that Mary Pat had a plan to sneak into her parents' house the next day and, like the movie star Carole Landis she idolized, swallow a full bottle of her mother's Seconal and lie down to die on the canopy bed in her childhood room. A room covered with movie star posters that Mary Pat and Helen had tacked up one by one. She wouldn't have fallen into her forever sleep on the couch she'd been sleeping on for three months. She wouldn't have wanted Helen or her love child to find her in Holden's new home.

"There's hope written in every line of this letter, Helen," her mother said, as she folded it and placed it back in the envelope. She brushed her fingertips over the upside-down stamps, Joseph's declaration that this was a love letter, and placed it down on the coffee table. She took her daughter's hands in her own.

"It's no secret your father's unfaithful to me in word and deed. No matter what anyone says, a woman knows these things. But your marriage is different."

"Oh, Mother." Helen gave her a hug, then pulled back, searching her mother's face for evidence of sorrow where there was none.

"I've known for a long time. Don't you think for one second that it isn't my choice to stay with him. I want nothing to do with being a woman alone. But you and Joseph, your love is special. Trust me, Helen, he loves you and he's devoted. You're doing the right thing. In time, he'll open his heart more and more to the little prince. You'll see."

How could her father—dishonest and controlling—be enough for her dear, dear mother, when an innocent child hadn't been enough to keep Mary Pat believing life was worth living? Or for Joseph to claim Holden as his own? Helen was perplexed by her mother's ability to see her marriage through rose-colored glasses, especially after reading Joseph's confession.

Helen turned her attention back to the bride and groom walking into the French sunshine, and then under a tent filled with well-wishers. Grace Kelly would certainly never know the hardship of raising a family in a tiny apartment, worrying if she could sew her way to the next rent check.

Helen wondered if the precious baby she'd just learned she carried would be enough to convince Joseph they were a real family, and not merely a good couple taking care of their deceased friends' son. She had to believe their child—one she was sure was a girl—had the power to change everything.

"What would I do without you?" Helen asked her mother, as she made a slow circular motion over her stomach. "I know you'll always love Holden as much as your very own grandchild."

Maggie broke into a smile that radiated enough love to brighten up even the attic apartment on Proctor Street.

11

Lucia Martinez, known to everyone but her mother as Luce, arrived at the hospital the next morning with a carpet bag and
a trunk filled with treasures from all over the world. Hand-carved
saint statues from France, brightly painted jewelry from Spain,
and relics from tiny countries throughout Europe tumbled out the
minute she popped the lid. She claimed to love her riches so much
she had to take them wherever she went, but Luce wasn't really
tied to her things. As soon as someone admired something from
her collection, she gave it away.

"I'm loose with my skirts and blouses but not with my sexual-
ity," she said to my mother's day nurse. Her *loose* remark her way
of clarifying how to pronounce her name. "Though my mother
worries as much about both, I assure you." Luce winked.

I'd heard my husband's younger sister speak her standard line
and shake her noisy gold earrings so many times I could have done
the routine for her.

Luce insisted on taking the first flight from New York to Boston, heading straight to the hospital by cab. She wanted to see my

mother. I wasn't sure I was up to spending a whole day with her, but I had to admit it was good to see her. Rich purple and red energy, part skirt, part personality, followed her as she flitted about the room. Next to Luce, I had to wonder what color my energy was. She kissed my mother on her forehead as easily as I did when I was ten, and she burbled on about how pleased she was to bring all the Martinez love to her bedside.

"Madre and Papa have everyone in El Barrio praying for you. Father Rivas said a Mass for you this morning. You have to hold on to your faith." Luce opened the clenched fist of my mother's right hand, placed simple wooden rosary beads there, and curled my mother's fingers back around them. "You will get well," she said.

"Do you mind staying with her while I meet with the social worker?" I directed the rest of my explanation to my mother. "I'm going to see if I can get you transferred closer to Sea Escape. Okay?"

To my amazement, my mother closed her eyes and dropped her head in an exaggerated nod. She understood.

"We will be fine. Yes?" Luce never took her eyes off my mother. She used one hand to give me a rah-rah type of encouragement; with the other she reached for some face cream and started gently massaging my mother's cheeks and forehead. "Your skin reminds me of mother-of-pearl—strong, resilient, iridescent—we say *nácar* in Spanish. Laura, you go get the job done, and don't let those bossy medical people tell you what to do. Nácar and I will be fine."

The bossy medical people lobbied for my mother's transfer to the rehab unit three floors up. I was aching to get my mother to talk to me, dying to know more about my father, which meant I had a different placement in mind.

"There's this innovative speech program at a facility south of Boston. Right near where I live," I said. "Can we try to get her in there?"

The social worker wasn't opposed to looking for a bed at the small, well-respected facility near Cedar Point. She even said that moving my mother closer to home would mean getting things nearer to normal for me.

It was Dr. Hasani who disagreed with my plan. "That's an immersion program," he said. "The language retraining piece alone will be far too intense for your mother."

"I know she can handle it. She's been making speech gains every day. And she can be even more persistent than I am if you can believe it," I said, trying to be light.

He let loose a sigh so loud the social worker stared him down.

"Can we at least apply?" I asked.

"I'd like to give Laura the benefit of the doubt," she said. "She knows her mother and what she's capable of."

With that endorsement, we moved out of the conference room and into my mother's. I held my breath as I led the way, hoping the doctor wouldn't call my bluff. I willed him not to try too hard to get her to say something.

Luce had taken one of the hospital blankets, paper-thin from overwashing, and wrapped it around my mother's shoulders like a shawl. She lent my mother some dignity by layering one of her own scarves over it.

Bolstered by Luce's energy, I took a seat on the arm of my mother's chair. I would speak for her, but I wanted them to see us as a team. I longed for us to be a team.

"Don't you look wonderful today," the social worker said. "Your color is good. Have you been up to walk yet this morning?"

My mother's hand held fast to the rosary beads Luce had given her. She looked at the social worker and then the doctor standing there, but didn't say a thing.

Dr. Hasani's arms were crossed in front of him. His now familiar gesture said he was annoyed.

Luce got up off my mother's bed, and with hands on her hips, she started stretching side to side like she was exercising. You would've thought she'd been sitting still for hours, not minutes.

"Nácar is doing great. You know what they say about the power of prayer."

Luce made the sign of the cross. "Our Father, who art in heaven, hallowed—"

I thought the doctor was going to hightail it out of there. I didn't much blame him, because I'd been known to become instantly queasy around my mother's religion too. Though that hadn't always been true.

I widened my eyes, pleading with Luce to stop making a fool of herself. Then my mother copied her, bowing her head in prayer.

"Be—thy—na-me." My mother tried to smile, though her charm was as lopsided as her mouth. She finished the prayer, not missing a single phrase.

Then the doctor spoke to her like a real person for the first time since he'd met her. For an instant, I liked him better. "Good work, Mrs. Tobin."

To me he said, "No guarantees, but I'll see if I can pull a few strings and get her into that program."

I stood up and reached my hand out to shake his.

My mother mumbled something resembling the word *yes,* and he looked from her to me. "God help the staff at the rehab center." Flashing his own version of a crooked smile, he shook my hand and left.

Whether intentional or accidental, I was a little jealous that Luce used the rosary to get my mother to speak. I wished I'd thought of it. Still, I was grateful too. With all the questions I had about my family swirling around my head, maybe now my mother would be able to give me some answers. My optimism was short-lived. As the doctor disappeared into the busy hallway, my mother leaned in close to Luce and started chanting the garbled word *doe.* Using her good hand, her dismissive gesture told me she meant for me to *go.*

12

There's an art and a science to dealing with agitated babies in the postpartum nursery. Almost everyone knows the simple fixes: change, feed, swaddle. It's the experts, like me, who know about safe holds, soothing tones, and getting baby connected skin to skin, human being to human being. That's the reason I always made time to dim the overhead lights and get a colicky baby into the quiet corner of the nursery. I'd whisper his or her name in rhythmic chanting. If Baby Boy Tate or Baby Girl Davenport had yet to be named by his or her mother, I'd choose a secret name, one only we would know. Meaningful ones like the French name Cerise, or the Indian name Sachin, or from the Greek, Zoë. I'd study each face, I'd consider ethnicity. Paying attention to the way she cried or the way he moved his arms and legs, I'd watch and listen for the baby's contribution. A baby's name should celebrate the pure life that each is.

Taking that call Saturday morning, talking to my mother's nurse, what I couldn't wrap my mind around was why, when it came to the elderly, the treatment for agitation was to stab a thigh with enough tranquilizer to lay a wild animal down. If it hadn't been for Molly, my mother's leg would've become the ICU's pincushion.

"She's pretty worked up, asking for Henry and Joey," Molly said. "If you're heading in, that would be great, I can manage till then. Or I can give her something to calm her. I thought I'd run it by you first."

I'd had one sip of coffee, yet my heart was running a marathon. Christian, Luce, and the kids were all staring at me, waiting for clues about what was going on.

"If she's calm now, I'd rather you wait. I'm on my way." I hung up, nodding to Christian, letting him know my mother was okay. Luce slapped a hand to her chest and let out an audible sigh; everything about her presence was big.

"Henry, hit the bathroom, it's a long drive," I said. "You're coming with me." I would stop at nothing to get my mother to open up to me, and taking Henry along was a decision I made in that instant. If she was asking for him, then she'd have a visit with him.

"Did I tell you Nácar tried to tell me something about Joey yesterday?" Luce asked. "And Sea Escape. She mentioned the house a number of times, and *wind* or *window,* but that's all I could understand."

I don't know why when Luce nicknamed my mother Nácar it endeared her to me, because when my mother called my son Joey, it drove me out of my mind.

"What about me? I'm coming too," Claire said. She ran around the breakfast bar, locking her hands around my leg, her fingernails digging into my thigh.

"I don't think that's a good idea," Christian said. I couldn't tell whether he was talking about Claire or Henry. Claire screamed *"No"* so loud Henry took it as his cue to go get his things. I knew he was operating under the notion that he was coming. He just kept moving forward, hoping for the best.

"You can either stay here and help me bake something yummy or go to work with Daddy," Luce said. "What'll it be, Chiquita?" She pulled a screeching Claire off me and gestured for me to get going. I couldn't stand the fact that my daughter's award-winning meltdown didn't place her higher on my list of needy family members warranting some attention.

Claire's Martinez genes led her to choose making cookies over spending time with her father. Like her grandfather Joaquin, she took every opportunity to bury her hands deep in dough. She was covered in flour and pulling chocolate chips out of the fridge before I said my good-byes. I could tell she was annoyed with me, but she wasn't old enough to latch on to the unfairness of me taking her brother, leaving her behind. Christian was the one who looked the most dejected.

I rarely made split-second decisions, and I thought I'd probably regret taking Henry in later, but in that moment I welcomed his company. He sat strapped into the right-hand side of the backseat, looking straight ahead, as if he could face anything because I believed in him.

"What a couple of days, huh? I'm sorry I haven't had a lot of time to talk to you about Nana. I want you to know that nobody thinks what happened was your fault. Not me. Not Nana. You know that, right?"

Henry pulled his feet up under him in a move Claire's kindergarten teacher called crisscross applesauce. His silence was beginning to worry me.

"Is it ever okay to keep a secret?" he asked.

"It depends on what it is. A surprise present is fine. Not telling someone something you think will only hurt her feelings. Those kinds are okay, I guess."

Henry zipped his coat up and down, looking away from me the way he did when he was about to cry.

"Nicholas said you weren't telling the truth." His tone of voice was all-knowing; it made me tighten my grip on the wheel.

"He said Nana was already dead."

"Oh, honey. Is that why you pushed him down at recess? You didn't believe him, did you?"

His black hair fell into his eyes as he nodded, his little cowlick waving like a flag. "For a minute, I did."

"Henry, I always tell you the truth. Nana's very sick, but she's alive. Nicholas is just a little shit."

I glanced in my rearview in time to catch the smile that spread from one ear to the other. Henry held my gaze in the mirror. I went back and forth between looking at him and the road; the heavy traffic afforded me this recklessness.

"You know she isn't really talking the way you and I are. Just a word here and there. But it's a really good sign that she's asking for you."

Henry's smile faded. I knew right then that he'd cry the minute he saw her. My attempt to prepare him wouldn't be good enough.

"Remember the story I told you, about when you were really small and I held you in one of those pouches tied to the front of me? She said it looked like I was carrying a baby kangaroo."

"And you told her that baby kangaroos were called joeys, right?"

"You know the real reason she calls you that is because your middle name is the same as my daddy's first. Nana loved him very much. She loves you like that, Henry. Even if she can't say so."

"I like that story. And I like when she calls me Joey. You shouldn't get so mad at her when she does. It makes her happy."

I had no intention of telling Henry the real story of how my mother arrived at his nickname. It may have made her happy, but it just made me mad.

Christian had driven two-day-old Henry and me direct from the hospital to see my mother. I'd forced my achy body into the back of his Nissan Sentra to be sure I could see my rear-facing newborn. I was so elated by the birth of my healthy boy, with his chubby arms and legs and his angelic features, that I excused my mother for not visiting me in the maternity ward of Boston Memorial. I knew she was an anxious driver once she ventured over Anaskaket town lines. As I recall, she wasn't much for hospitals either.

It became harder to forgive her when Christian and I arrived at Sea Escape and she didn't even peek into Henry's carrier.

"Christian, take the baby please, that contraption's too heavy for Laura," she said, walking ahead of us, fully expecting I would follow her, which I did. And obey her, which I did not. Christian went off to the kitchen. He was starved since he'd skipped breakfast to come get me and we'd left the hospital before lunch. We both figured there'd be something at my mother's to eat.

"Sit down, Laura. You really should have gone straight home to bed. Imagine releasing you from the hospital forty-eight hours after delivery. I was entitled to a week's stay after you were born."

"I'm fine. You sit. I want you to hold Henry Joseph."

"No, no," she said, backing away from me. "You'll learn soon enough, never to wake a sleeping baby."

I ignored her, lifting his curled-up body from the carrier, taking off his blue wool sweater with the little trains chugging across his chest. He never stirred.

"I haven't held a baby in a hundred years."

"I'm only thirty-five, Mother," I said, trying to lighten her mood.

When she saw I wasn't going to take no for an answer, she plopped down in her wing chair and accepted my child in her capable arms. The minute she looked at his face, she took in a sharp breath, and when she exhaled, she whispered only part of his name.

"Joseph."

I let it go.

"You get to know your grandson. I'll go help Christian. Breast feeding has me ravenous."

The tea was steeping, and Christian scouted around for

something to go with it. All he could put his hands on was a box of old biscotti and an unopened container of cashews from the lame basket Holden sent at Easter.

"I would've shopped for her, she only needed to say the word," he whispered. "There's next to nothing to eat in here. No wonder she's so thin."

"She couldn't have mustered the energy to go to Sea and Cheese to get deli meat and a loaf of bread? Why are we entertaining her, anyway? I'm the one who just had a baby. She's sixty-seven, not ninety." I looked out from the kitchen, keeping a protective eye on my son.

"Calm down, cariño." Christian stopped looking through the cabinets. He came and gently wrapped his arms around me from behind. "You can't expect one little baby to undo years of sadness. He can't make everything right."

But that's exactly what I had hoped for. For this baby to make things right.

"Laura, come take him. My arms are getting weak. I don't want to drop Joseph." My mother called me from across the grand room once she noticed Christian and I standing there watching her with him.

I shook myself from Christian's embrace.

"His name is Henry."

"You don't need to raise your voice. I can see it will be painful to call him Joseph. Joey will do just fine," Helen said, gently smoothing down the dark hair that sprouted from the top of my baby's head before handing him back to me.

For the rest of the afternoon, she didn't call him anything. She reverted to her cordial style, the quiet tone of our usual visits, though when I placed a fussy Henry in a baby sling to comfort and sway him, she muttered that I looked like some sort of a kangaroo. I tried not to take it personally, since my mother barely managed to get out a sentence in response to the questions Christian tried using to jump-start a conversation.

I suppose it wasn't fair to say she didn't talk to me on my regular Saturday visits to Sea Escape. Off and on she did. Yet the only substantive things she talked about, over the years, involved people I'd never met and places I'd never been. Mary Pat Finlayson. The Totem Pole. An attic apartment on Proctor Street. She refused to hear anything about my job, as if working part-time taking care of the babies threatened her identity as a stay-at-home mother.

Of course we talked about my father, the things we carried both shared and private treasures. It was hard to say which of my memories—the ferry ride to Nantucket or the trip to the Cape Cod trampolines—were real and which came by way of repeated exposure to old stories and photographs. I didn't need old pictures to remember my favorite times with my father. I had his fairy tales.

The first story I remember him bringing home to me was called *The Story of Tấm and Cám,* a Vietnamese account of Cinderella.

"Once upon a time, in a country with rivers like blue ribbons and mountains like emeralds, lived a girl as gentle as a baby bird. Her name was Tấm," my father said.

I was Claire's age when he began reciting it, and I'd beg him to compare bits and pieces of his tale to my familiar version. The Goddess of Mercy with her green willow branch replaced the Fairy Godmother and her wand. And Tấm's slipper traveled down a flowing river; it wasn't left on a castle stair.

"Close your eyes, little Laura. Do you see what Tấm looks like? She's slight and beautiful like you." My father's voice was soothing and low as he would tell and retell the story. There was no book, there were no illustrations, his vivid language was all I needed to see it. It took him weeks to get to the end of that story, because as I snuggled in his arms, dreams of Vietnamese princesses would claim me. Without my consent, sleep would take me from him.

My father's death put an end to the telling of those stories. My mother wasn't likely to be telling me hers either. Seventy-seven and flattened by a stroke, I'd already begun to miss imagining her in a cocktail dress with a long, knotted strand of pearls dangling from her neck, giggling about boys in a nightclub booth with a girl named Mary Pat.

"Mom!" Henry shouted. "Isn't that where you're supposed to park?"

If Henry hadn't yanked me from my memories, I'd have had to circle the block. I'd brought him to work often enough that he recognized the employee garage in time to save me the trouble.

Pretending I had Candy's confidence, I walked Henry into the ICU knowing full well children were not allowed. I stopped breathing and gripped his hand when I saw my mother's empty bed, thinking, What kind of a mother marches her child right into the middle of a crisis?

"Don't panic." Molly came out of nowhere, carrying an armload of supplies. "Helen is around the corner in the step-down unit. She's doing great. You must be Joey. Your gram's said your name more than once, I can tell you that."

Barely above a whisper, Henry said, "I call her Nana."

"I'm setting a room up for a new admission, due any minute, and then I'm heading over there for the rest of my shift. She's much calmer over there. It's not as noisy." She gave me an elbow nudge and then went right back to business.

My mother was sitting with the head of the bed upright, the bottom slightly bent at the knees. One of Luce's more garish statues of Mary stood watch on the bedside table. A black lace mantilla lay over the ordinary white thermal blanket; it gave my mother a noble look. Her hair was pulled off her face by a single peineta, the Spanish ornamental comb used to hold the mantilla on a head. A hint of blush on her cheeks and the glossy sheen of lipstick gave my mother a healthy glow she hadn't had in years. Only her lopsided face and lethargy gave away the reason she was there.

Henry stared at her. I'd expected him to hesitate, to treat her like one of his father's distant cousins from Puerto Rico. Before I could allay his fears, he ignored the side rails and the mantilla draped over her legs and crawled in from the bottom of the bed, scrunching the bedclothes up as he went. Even as I moved to take him off the bed, I realized his hug had the right touch. He was the best medicine, so I let her drink him in.

Guilt surrounded me like one of Luce's scarves when I realized I hadn't hugged my mother since days before I'd found her lying on the floor. Our pre-stroke hugs weren't worth counting either, given the lack of genuine feeling she put into them. Henry's cheek rested on my mother's left one, as if he instinctively knew she would feel him there. Her right side motionless, she moved her left hand onto his back. She closed her eyes, and still the tears fell down.

Memories of my mother crying could be counted on one hand and therefore stood out in my mind. She favored sitting in her living room chair for hours without moving. She'd stare out to sea as if she were waiting for her captain to return home. Sea Escape didn't have a widow's walk.

Watching Henry hug her and seeing her accept it was ironic. I'd been forever heartbroken over her never fully embracing me.

Christian startled me in that hospital room by using both hands to massage my neck and shoulders. "How are you holding up?" he asked, kissing my hair.

I pointed to Henry sitting next to my mother engaged in an animated one-way conversation.

"Hi, Dad. I didn't know you were coming."

I put my finger to my lips, not wanting to draw any attention to us. Molly hadn't minded that I broke the no kids allowed rule, but I wasn't so sure the other nurses would be as lenient. Henry took care moving out of the bed the way he'd gone in.

My mother wagged one finger at Henry as she exaggerated a smile. "Strai-ght," she said.

His face broke into a wide grin. "I remember, Nana."

I did my best to smooth out the mantilla for him.

After hugging Henry, Christian expertly lowered the side rail of my mother's bed to give her a kiss on the cheek. He tucked a piece of hair that had escaped the peineta behind her ear. Henry clearly got his unconditional love traits from his father. Christian still had the power to knock me over with his tenderness.

"You gave us quite a fright, Helen. Forgive me for not getting here sooner. You know, kids." He playfully jabbed Henry in the stomach with one finger and turned to me. "I hope you're not angry I came, Laura, but I knew you'd want to stay. Someone needed to take Henry home after their visit."

"I didn't think about that," I said. "I'm glad he came, though."

My mother closed her eyes and nodded.

"Are you happy, Mother?"

She puffed out the word *yes* as if she were blowing up a balloon.

"Helen Tobin, this is a hospital, not a nightclub." Molly came in, bustling about as usual. Luce must have been the one to tell her my mother loved to dance, a long time ago.

"One of you can stay, the rest of ya scoot. How about you?" Molly tapped Henry on the shoulder. His eyes darted over to me, but he didn't move. Molly would be the type to throw him off balance. "I'm kidding, Joey. It's got to be one of the adults." She took my mother's pulse and adjusted her IV. Multitasking was her forte.

Christian stayed only a few more minutes, and then it was time to say good-bye.

When they left, I took a seat on my mother's good side, evening out the wrinkles on her sheets. The fluorescent night-lights cast shadows, making things look garish and insincere. In minutes, with only my mother and me in the picture, the color flickered out of the room. And as I felt the familiar gloom about to overtake us, leaving us with nothing to say, my mother closed her eyes. Tired of losing myself in her diminished presence, I chose to conjure her whole by reading my father's letters. I reached into the drawer of her bedside table and ran my hand over the envelopes, but all I could hear were Henry's words. *Is it ever okay to keep a secret?*

13

⊰3⊱

August 1960

Helen pressed a razor-sharp crease down one leg of Joseph's trousers. This pair was the last of the lot she needed to iron and roll just right. Once tucked into his Pullman, there would be plenty of room left for sweaters. When she thought of Russia, all she could visualize were men dressed in ushanka hats and valenki felt boots. She kept her focus on clothes, refusing to mull over the potential dangers associated with traveling there to cover the spy plane trial, especially since this was the very assignment she'd cajoled him into taking.

As she made a mental list of the things she'd already packed and those things that still needed to go in, she realized how easy it was to corral her thoughts when she was alone in the apartment, touching fabric. Joseph was off to get traveler's checks, and Holden was spending the morning with her mother. Maggie had picked him up early so they could stand in line at Denholm's for one of those advertised superhero costumes: "On sale while supplies last." Helen wasn't much for allowing Holden to watch television, but Joseph had parked him in front of the TV one day when he had an article to finish and she was grocery shopping. Holden had been transfixed by cartoons every since.

Familiar footsteps hit the top landing, silencing the quiet of her morning. She was thankful it was Joseph. At least she could finish his packing before Holden was once again in Joseph's way, running around the cramped apartment with a mock cape pinned to his T-shirt. Helen wanted peace and harmony to be all her husband remembered once he departed for the Soviet Union.

"I took out as much as I dared. I couldn't leave you wanting for cash while I'm gone." Joseph counted out three piles of the checks, then placed some in a hidden compartment in his suitcase, some in the zippered pocket of his leather travel pouch, and some back in his wallet. Helen smiled, pleased to see her husband being practical.

"Mother's hairdresser asked me to make her a new window seat cover and matching pillows. With what I'm charging Jan, above and beyond the fabric, we should be fine until you get back and get paid. Don't you worry about us."

Helen folded the trousers lengthwise and then rolled them tight to minimize wrinkling.

"You sure are going to a lot of trouble to pack me up right. If I didn't know better, I'd think you were trying to get rid of me." Joseph flashed a teasing look as he rummaged through what had been loaded into the Pullman thus far. "Geez, the other reporters are either going to think I've got it made in the shade, married to a swell girl, or watch to see if I walk light in my sneakers. Good thing I'm wearing a wedding ring."

Helen scanned Joseph's face for sarcasm or sincerity, his expressions so easy to read. She chose to see genuineness in his eyes before he began rubbing one lid; a speck of dust perhaps caught there.

"I suppose I'm trying to make it up to you for taking this job," she said. "I know you wanted the Washington assignment. I just couldn't see us snubbing our noses at this opportunity." By opportunity she'd meant money, but she hadn't wanted to bring it up again. Always talking about finances was crass, not to mention exhausting.

"I've got to admit it, I'd have loved to stay and cover Kennedy and Nixon duking it out over the election. But as always, you, my dear, are right. I'd be gone days at a time with that job too, and the money's worlds better covering the Powers trial."

Helen turned off the iron and bent down to unplug it. Joseph lurched forward to stop her from reaching. Once he'd disconnected the plug from the outlet, he placed his hand on Helen's burgeoning stomach. She placed her hand on his.

"Now see, this is what I'm worried about. If anything happens to you or that baby while I'm gone—"

"I'll be fine. I'm almost thirty weeks. The doctor said not to worry. It'll be different this time."

That's what Helen told herself every day since she'd learned she was pregnant for the third time. It's what she needed to believe. Her first child, taken from her four years ago, had been a boy, not the girl she was convinced she carried. Her crampy stomach and blood-soaked underwear told her to get to the hospital, this was an urgent matter. Helen hadn't needed anyone to tell her the child was in peril. She could see from the looks on the nurses' faces when she said she was in labor that there was no way a child born so early could live.

Helen begged the doctor to let her see her baby. He refused, patting her hand, calling her child a fetus, and telling her seeing him would leave a distressing image in her mind. Still, she was haunted by the boy. Not because she'd seen him but because she hadn't insisted the doctor let her. Without ever holding their son, Helen and Joseph claimed their boy with a name. One carefully chosen weeks before, honoring Saint Paul, the patron saint of writers.

Two years later, Helen was with child again. Her second pregnancy ended one day after she'd realized she hadn't gotten her period on schedule. She wouldn't have known so soon if she weren't practicing the rhythm method. Other Catholic women measured and recorded their temperatures in order to avoid adding another child to the family table. Helen knew her rhythm as well as she knew the daily weather forecast, all because needing to be pregnant and wanting to be sure Holden was dressed properly to go out to play were her early morning priorities. There had been no time to celebrate or be hopeful about expecting her second. There was, however, plenty of time to feel overwhelming sadness when the telltale blood dripped from her as she prepared Holden's dinner that evening. Her body telling her that yet another child would not have a life, and this child wouldn't even have a name.

Helen understood Joseph's concerns about leaving now for Russia, especially with her nearing the end of her confinement. But they needed to be practical.

"It's a safe time for you to travel. I'm well on my way," she said. "And we don't have much choice, really. There's hardly room enough here for the three of us, never mind adding another child."

"You've got to promise me you'll take it easy. No stretching and absolutely no carrying heavy things up those stairs. When I think of you here alone, that's when I start lambasting myself for needing to take any assignment away from you and our baby."

And Holden, Helen thought. Don't forget Holden.

"I've got a strong boy ready to lend a hand. Try not to worry."

"I do worry, Helen. I can't think of anything I want more than for us to have our own child."

And for us to be able to move out of this hovel, Helen thought.

"Then go over there and write the best stories you can. I just know our sacrifice will be rewarded. When you get back, the *Gazette* will have no choice but to offer their best stringer a permanent position. You'll only be gone a few weeks, and home in plenty of time before the baby comes."

Joseph put up his left hand to meet her right, his way of inviting her to dance. Placing his other hand low on her back, they started waltzing to his humming of their song. She let him lead her around the only clear path in the apartment. With her eyes closed, Helen dared dream of carrying a child of his to full term.

Yet once again, she was without Joseph when contractions began. Two weeks after he went overseas, while reading Holden a bedtime story from his favorite Uncle Wiggly book, Helen went into labor. Nestled in the crook of her arm, she let her smart first-grader take over sounding out words when she felt the muscles pulled tight like a belt, grabbing hold of her stomach and squeezing until she winced. She knew from the extent of the grip it was real labor, not those practice contractions her mother told her to expect. It was the real thing, and again it was happening too soon.

It wasn't Joseph's fault she was alone and afraid. Helen blamed herself. She'd thought it reasonable for him to make the trip, to take the assignment. She'd been the one to invite risk into their family.

When the next contraction came, quicker and stronger than the last, Helen knew she couldn't wait for her mother to make it from Fiske to Proctor. Making the sign of the cross, she held out hope there was still reason to hurry. Grateful she didn't need to gather much more than a light sweater for Holden and some books to keep him occupied until her mother could meet them at Saint Catherine's, Helen made her first call to Yellow Cab, the second to her mother.

Doubled over, holding Holden's hand, she made her way down the four flights of stairs and into the summer evening. On the ten-minute cab ride, Helen tried hard not to think about her two previous miscarriages, pregnancies that lasted four months and one month, respectively. She feared if she did, she'd be complicit in yet another child being lost to her.

With no time for medicine to induce sleep, Helen was awake during delivery. She watched the expectant looks on the nurses' faces vanish, and she was fully aware when the doctor finally told her why her child never cried.

Helen didn't cry either. She propped herself up despite the afterpain, demanding she be allowed to hold her son. Joseph Robert Tobin, Jr. She threatened to get up off the table and follow whoever took him from the delivery room. Helen vowed to crawl down one corridor after another until they let her have him.

"This is not a good idea, Mrs. Tobin," the doctor repeated. "You will never get his face out of your mind."

"That's exactly what I'm hoping for," Helen said. "I need to hold my son."

The delivery room nurse, without saying a word, disregarded the doctor's objection and wrapped Helen's still child in a blue blanket, placing the tiny bundle in her waiting arms. Helen held her newborn like any new mother would, gently, for fear of harming her delicate creation. She took in every inch of his face, and then she opened the blanket to gaze at the rest of him. Her Joey was perfect in every outward way. His small body warm, though the thin blue line outlining his bow-shaped lips reminded her that, exactly like her other children, he had never taken a breath. And exactly like the others, the reason for his death, she would never know.

Twelve hours after she'd arrived at Saint Catherine's, Helen heard the mews and wails of tiny babies. She thought it cruel to have been admitted to the unit where happy mothers and fathers oohed and aahed over their bundles of hope. Helen looked down at her rounded stomach, which repulsed her, propelling her eyes toward the hospital window. There was no use watching, waiting for it to move, or caressing it like she had yesterday. She wouldn't feel a miniature foot poke her hand or see her baby stretch his growing body as he made himself more comfortable.

Her little one wasn't safe within her or swaddled in a bassinet parked in the brightly colored nursery with all the other babies. He wasn't wearing a blue cap to keep his perfect head warm. Her baby was in a dark, cold place somewhere in the bowels of the hospital basement. A place she'd never really thought about until last night, when her tiny baby slipped from her into the grim-looking doctor's hands and she heard him whisper the word *morgue*.

Now, lying in a hospital bed for the third time postpartum, she realized the doctor had been right. Helen did have an imprint of her child's face in her mind. The image dissolved with the arrival of her mother. Maggie came into her room bearing gifts.

"Did you get any rest at all last night, dearie?" Her mother put her purse and shopping bag on the chair next to Helen's bed. She placed a vase filled with calla lilies and her prize dahlias accented with dusty miller on the bedside table.

Maggie kissed Helen's cheek. She sat down on the bed and held her daughter's chin with one hand. She asked her straight out. "How much does it hurt, Helen?" Her mother wasn't talking about the soreness commonplace following a birth; Joey had been too small to tear her skin. Her mother wasn't asking about Helen's cramps, the ones responsible for shrinking her womb down to size so that she might try once more to bear a child for her husband. In truth, a child for her. There was no need for Helen to answer. She allowed herself to weep in her mother's arms.

A candy striper all of fifteen interrupted them, completely missing the heavy emotion that filled the room like the bounty of flowers she carried.

"Mrs. Tobin? These are for you." The girl stole a glance at Helen's abdomen. "You must have delivered your baby yesterday to be getting such beautiful bouquets this early in the morning. So what did you have, a boy or a girl?"

Through her tears, Helen said, "A boy. Joey."

"Look at those big ole happy tears."

Maggie launched off the bed. "Get out, you stupid ninny. Leave the flowers and keep to yourself."

The candy striper, still oblivious, put the flowers down next to Maggie's and in a huff marched out of the room to her waiting cart.

Maggie went on to share news as if the mishap had never occurred, much the way the nurses had been treating Helen since she'd arrived in the room late last night. As if not talking about it somehow eased the pain.

"These must be from Joseph. He called this morning to give me his flight details. He's flying out of Moscow this afternoon. Boy, did he go on a tirade about these rooms not having phones. He's desperate to talk to you." Maggie slipped the card from the envelope and reached it out to her daughter. Helen looked at the words, "All my love always, Joseph," written by another person's hand. She made no move to take it.

Maggie shoved the card into the arrangement, then stooped to pull the most beautiful baby blanket from the Denholm's bag. Helen had finished sewing the satin edging on it last week. Her mother laid it out over her daughter's lap.

"I don't want it. Put it away, please." Helen pushed the luxurious blanket off her legs.

Maggie persisted, knowing the comfort Helen took in the things she created with her keen eye and skillful hands. "Reminders are a good thing, honey. Look at the care you took sewing on all these rosettes. Trust me, it will console you."

Helen relented, letting her mother tuck the blanket around her empty womb.

"How's Holden?" she asked. "What did he say when you told him?"

"Before you get upset with me, the dear boy was exhausted this morning. He wouldn't eat and he kept on asking when he could see you. I didn't have the heart to send him to school."

"He's still at your house? It's bad enough you brought him to sleep there when I specifically said to bring him to the Tobins'. Tell me you didn't leave Holden with Father."

Maggie turned away from Helen and rearranged the already perfect flowers. "I thought it was a big step toward mending fences when he volunteered to mind him. He feels genuinely awful about—"

Helen could see through her mother's nervous gesture of attending to the arrangements. She wouldn't look her in the eye. "What is it you're not telling me? Please."

"I was on the phone with Joseph, writing down his flight details, and before I knew it, I heard your father telling Holden to get down to the business of breakfast. 'God doesn't like naughty boys,' he said." Maggie's delicate face was pinched and pained. "Holden asked him if his brother had been a naughty boy and that's why God had taken him."

Helen pushed her achy body up in bed. "And you left Holden with that awful man?"

"Your father told him that God took the baby because he was sick, not because anyone had done anything wrong. He was tender with him, Helen. Truly."

"A man like Father doesn't know a blessed thing about tenderness or about my God. And he doesn't get to decide anything about my life. Not who I marry. Not where I live. And certainly not how to explain the inexplicable to my six-year-old. Joey was my baby. I carried and delivered him. I held him in my arms."

Maggie ripped a tissue from the box on Helen's table; she dabbed and dabbed under her dark eyes, all while nodding her head.

Helen pulled the baby blanket up to her face. Placing a satin corner to her cheek, she stroked it. "I'm begging you to go home, Mother. Stay with Holden until Joseph gets back. And starting now, I don't want a single person to talk to me about my baby. For ten minutes, he was all mine. I will not share him with anyone. Joey belongs to me."

Maggie gathered her purse, kissed her daughter's forehead, and did as Helen had requested.

14

L uce had taken to getting Henry and Claire off to school, and
today she agreed to grocery-shop. I'd given her a list of per-
ishable and pantry staples, ordinary things, though I don't know
why I bothered. Last week she'd taken this job off my to-do list
and came home with twice the number of necessary bags, each
one containing something the kids wouldn't eat, like pomegran-
ates and partridge, chickpeas and garbanzo beans. I took her
up on her offer because her cheery smile made it impossible for
me to say no, and I needed to stop at Sea Escape. Rehab rules
didn't allow its residents to stay in johnnies all day. I needed
to pick up some clothes for my mother and another letter if I
could find one.

To call Sea Escape a bungalow was to betray its size. My parents' American dream, with its wide, overhanging eaves, wraparound porch, and breezeway connecting garage to house, was two
stories of beauty and heartache. Perhaps because it was a house
with a name, it had a personality, all entitled and sophisticated,
as if it considered itself a resort sitting on a cliff commanding the

tide. Name or no name, majestic view or no view, this house was not home to me anymore, though it most certainly still was to my mother.

I hadn't been there since the day she was taken from the bottom of those stairs, placed on a stretcher, and whisked off to Memorial. That was two weeks ago, and evidence of her demise—the one shoe askew on the third stair—was still sitting there. My fingers burned with guilt each time I collected a pearl. The strand's remains were scattered all over the rug.

Looking around the house, I realized there was more to do than I'd originally thought. I should check the furnace for fuel oil and fill it if need be. Clean out the fridge of leftovers gone bad, though there never was much food. As I walked through the house, these and other mundane tasks came to me, one right after the other. My distracted mind told me to write them down, otherwise I'd forget.

I opened and closed each kitchen drawer, not able to find a single thing to write on. The hunt for a blank sheet of paper reminded me just how spare my mother's world had become.

In the last kitchen drawer, under the phone book, I found a French country appointment book with an attached pen. A notepad graced the inside cover. Leafing through the date book, the only things written in it were doctors' appointments and visits from me and the kids.

Never was it sadder to me that her countertops were bare. They didn't hold stacks of bills to be paid; she took care of each one as it arrived in the mail. There were no magazines she hoped to get to or books she ought to return to the library. These reading materials didn't rate compared to the letters. She merely existed there, shuffling around three rooms out of ten. Her kitchen, where she cobbled together her meals. The grand room, where she'd spend her days mesmerized by waves crashing and couples kissing. And her bedroom, where she slept or didn't.

Though her public rooms were graceful, original dark oak

paneled walls, hardwood floors, leaded glass windows with draperies swept up in gathers, tied back to the wall they billowed, it was the private rooms that held her genius. Yet I couldn't remember the last time there were guests to enjoy the beautiful bedrooms she'd taken such care to decorate throughout my childhood. Back then, she sang moody ballads but wasn't sad. She hummed but was not unfocused. She planned and measured and sewed, all while she patiently gave me all the time I needed for my job. My mother let me have a hand in each room's naming.

The room that most befit the expectation of being part of our beachy home was Summer Breeze, a bright room at the back of the house, with its ocean view and indigo and yellow bedspread with matching curtains. Whitewashed beadboard walls and my mother's ability to blend checks and stripes and florals without being overbearing gave the room its get-away-from-it-all persona. The best thing about the room was the rolled-arm couch that looked down on the dunes.

Then there was Saigon, with its cloth-covered headboard, a mural of three cranes flying over a waterfall, a mix of creamy beige and green. All the furniture in that room was Asian inspired. My favorite touch was the cherry blossom shoji screen my mother let Candy and me play Barbies behind while she came and went from her sewing room. That was the last room she decorated, and she was uncharacteristically serious as she crafted it. I still wonder if she thought a touch of Vietnam in Anaskaket would be enough to bring my father home for good.

Holden's bedroom was at the front of the house. Perhaps his room without a view was why he grew up cranky. His sleigh bed, heavy yet attractive, prefigured he would sail right out of Sea Escape the first chance he got. I wondered if my mother ever regretted her design choice.

I walked past my first bedroom, a place I dared not remember, a place I cared not visit. Like my father's office.

The only time I saw my mother open up my father's office was to dust it. Though how was I to know how often she went in there when I wasn't around? I hadn't set foot in my father's office for a very long time, a room virtually untouched since he'd left us. It hurt too much to go there. I imagined her ocean-gazing from the leather chair where he wrote his stories, touching his pens, feeling the heft of his paperweight. There was nothing to obstruct her view of Anaskaket, this being the only room in the house without her signature curtains. Though he admired her creativity, my father never wanted fabric hanging there, being in favor of hoarding daylight and moon glow. *Light is my inspiration,* I could remember him saying.

Color was my mother's muse. The fondness my father had for his office, my mother felt for her sewing room. As sure as I was that she visited my father's office when I wasn't there, I knew she hadn't set foot in her sewing room for years. It had been such a happy place when I was a girl, her deluxe sewing machine always buzzing and zigzagging. She had boxes of loose buttons and bric-a-brac and rolls of fabrics of all textures lining the walls. It was the only room in the house she didn't fuss over. In there, disarray was acceptable; it fed her creativity. With her material and notions out in the open, she told me she could see all kinds of possibilities. I wondered what the disarray of my house said about me.

Walking through the house without my mother's reminiscing to distract me, I had a chance to do my own. Sea Escape lulled me into seeing only her beauty. Yet when I got to the threshold of my mother's bedroom, she could no longer hide her wounded side. This room without a name was aloof, like the figures on its toile-covered walls. Once a room with sharp black and white accents, time stole the light, giving it to darkness. The white turned beige gave the place a despairing tone, like the woman who spent her days there. The only color in the room came from my parents' wedding quilt. Green and pink peeked out from under the covers half pulled down. The remote to the TV lay on the mattress in the depression her body had made. The drapes were drawn, trying their best to keep out the sunlight that attempted to push its way in where the panels met. I threw them open in an effort to stop the room from pulling me away from thinking better of Sea Escape.

Ignoring the bed, I went straight for my mother's closet. I was there to gather her clothes; other distractions must wait. I collected a few pairs of slacks and some sweaters, realizing I'd need to go shopping for her, since these clothes wouldn't lend themselves to physical therapy. With only underwear left to pack, I moved to her bureau and saw a medicine bottle sitting lonely on its top. Before I picked it up, I made out the word *Paxil*.

I read the original date of the prescription. It was the second bottle my mother had filled. Fumbling, I opened it, counting out pills. I couldn't believe she'd started on antidepressant medication back before Christmas and never told me.

I absentmindedly placed her clothes in the small overnight bag I'd found at the back of her closet and zipped it shut. Then, remembering the underwear, I returned to the bureau to find that my mother had left me another stunner. This one had my name on it.

There in her top drawer was a large envelope labeled "For Laura." I dumped the contents on the bureau. The first thing out was one of my father's letters. This time there was no doubt; my mother had left me an invitation to read.

November 28, 1963
My dearest Helen,

Congratulations on finding our new home! You did it, and no one can take it from you now. I can't wait to see your vision of our Sea Escape.

And to think you made it happen without any help from your father. Good for you, Helen. You know I'll never be able to forgive him for what he did to your mother. For the record, that's one thing you don't have to worry about with me. I could never bamboozle you. You've worked too hard on my behalf for me to dare try to pull one over on you. Seriously, it isn't very hard for me to stay faithful to you; I realize how lucky I am. You sure got a rough deal in the father department, but I hope you feel you more than made up for it with your choice of a husband.

One dream down and one to go. You didn't need me to make things happen with the bank. But don't you forget you need me to realize your most important heart's desire. I'll be back in a few months, and we can take care of that. I'll be home at last in your arms, on that stretch of coastline.

I read the letter a second time to be sure I was reading it right. My grandfather cheated on my grandmother? No wonder my mother, with her stone-carved values, spoke nothing of him to this day. Few memories of my grandparents were solid; their visits had been infrequent before my father died, almost nonexistent after he did. I always felt bad about the way my mother ignored Grandpa Lee when they came. Nana Maggie hugged me a lot, begging me to stay and keep her company since it was getting harder for her to move around. All I wanted to do was go outside, to run away from the bitterness that hung between my mother and her father. I hated watching his feeble attempts to get her attention. I never imagined I would someday know exactly how he must've felt.

Did Nana know he'd betrayed her, and if she did, why did she stay? What was with the women in my family and their marriages? Suddenly I felt guilty for all the times I got mad at Christian for being too helpful. He was only forever coming to my rescue because I was comfortable with him taking charge.

I turned my attention back to the contents of the envelope, wondering why my mother had left me these things. I picked up the loose key, turning it over in my hand. It meant nothing to me, but I couldn't say the same for the old-fashioned savings account passbook. It having spent one whole day tucked into the back pocket of my jean shorts when I was seventeen.

I didn't plan to steal the passbook. No, my first idea was much more heartless. I came home from lifeguarding to find my mother sitting in the grand room staring out the window, exactly where she was every afternoon, especially that summer.

"Hi, Mother," I said, catching the screen door before it slammed against the casing. I hated seeing her jump whenever I entered a room. I wrapped my towel tightly around my waist, pulling my sweatshirt down to secure it. No need to worry about how I looked; she never lifted her eyes from her letters anyway. I wasn't halfway to the stairs when she noticed me.

"Did you wipe your feet?" she asked. "I don't have the energy to sweep. It's so humid."

I didn't answer right away. I hadn't expected her to acknowledge me with more than a nod or a sigh.

"Aren't you hot?" she asked, looking me up and down.

"I had to bring a kid in who drifted out too far. He was too tired to swim to shore on his own. Water's cold."

The more I talked the guiltier I felt. And I hadn't stolen anything yet. I was covered in sweat, but I couldn't take off my sweatshirt. She'd notice my swimsuit. She'd see that I was dry.

"Need anything?" she asked, as she put her letter on the table next to her chair. "As much as I hate to, I've got to head in town. Errands."

I couldn't think of anything I needed more than for her to go. "No, I'm good. I've got to hurry. I'm meeting Candy and some friends back at the beach." I ran up the stairs without giving her a sideways glance. Once inside my room, I leaned against the door and closed my eyes. She never paid any attention to me. Why did she have to today?

I was showered and dressed in a T-shirt and shorts when I heard her car start. Drawing back the curtains to peek out my window, I saw her pull out of the driveway slowly, carefully.

The door to her room was open, her bed was made, everything just so. Walking toward her bureau, opening the top drawer, I felt as if someone else's feet and hands were moving me to do it. I kept telling myself to hurry; Candy needed the money by tomorrow.

The easy part of my plan was lifting the lid of the heart-shaped box where her pearls lay. I was a teenager, living in the moment, not capable of understanding the full weight of shame I would someday feel for what I was about to do. Still, my hands resisted picking up the strand of silver-white beads. I knew how much my mother treasured this gift from my father. How many times had I watched her stand in front of that mirror clasping them about her delicate neck? She'd lay her hand on them, against her throat, no doubt thinking of the day he gave them to her.

During the brief moment I hesitated, wondering if I could really go through with stealing them, I scanned the rest of her things. That's when I saw the bankbook tucked off to the side of her jewelry box. Slipping it from its plastic sleeve, I found three names listed inside: Lee J. McIntyre, Helen E. Tobin, Laura M. Tobin. I was surprised to see my name under my grandfather's, under my mother's, typewritten on a separate line. But the real shock was the amount of money, all alone on one line: one hundred thousand dollars.

I wouldn't need to steal her pearls after all. It was way more than I needed. I thought, Why shouldn't I take it? According to the bank, it was partially mine. Sick of thinking about what I was doing, I ran my hand over the pearls and put the lid back on the box. I slid the passbook into the back pocket of my shorts, thinking I could take some money and then put it back. I walked backward out of the bedroom, leaving her things almost exactly as she'd left them. Confident now that she would never have to know.

All these years later, I was staring at that same bankbook. The amount—on that single typewritten line—remained unchanged from the day I'd stolen it from her bureau, thinking a fraction of it could solve my problems. And once again, I was going through her things. Only this time she'd given me permission.

Thanks to my mother, in one hand I held a letter revealing my grandfather's infidelity and in the other a random key and a passbook. I knew what I was keeping from her, but now I needed to find out what else she hadn't told me.

15

※3℮※

November 1963

Helen parked her Fairlane out back so Mr. Kemp of Mechanics Bank and Trust wouldn't hold her clunker car against her ability to keep up with payments. While she touched up her lipstick in the rearview mirror, Helen practiced three different arguments for why she should be able to sign the loan agreement without Joseph present. Getting out of the car, she aligned her skirt and her military-inspired jacket, with its padded shoulders and epaulets. Only this morning, after Holden marched off to school, did she have time to finish sewing on the double rows of brass buttons and the half belt in back.

Helen had antiwar sentiments, especially with everything Joseph told her about what was going on from his vantage point in Saigon. Letter after letter, he told her not to believe what the government chose to tell the American people about the conflict, that things were worse than they were saying. Yet she had no intention of speaking out in Mr. Kemp's company. His son was serving.

Instead, Helen would use her appearance to play to his weakness. She'd decided to do whatever she had to, to get him to give her the loan for the magnificent piece of land she'd found in Anaskaket. There was no time to waste; other couples were interested in the acreage. Helen needed to make this happen. If she spent one more month in that dreadful apartment, she feared she'd go mad. It was high time she had a home of her own. A real home, not a rented pad over an increasingly cantankerous landlady's apartment.

"Tell the boy to stop running. Must you use that blasted sewing machine all hours of the day and night? The noise is driving me batty." Mrs. Booth had nothing but complaints for Helen these days. Each morning, she'd poke her head out her door to reprimand Helen for one thing or another.

Helen wouldn't miss Mrs. Booth one bit, though with Anaskaket a three-hour drive away, she would certainly miss her mother. Their frequent visits were sustenance to her now that Joseph was in Southeast Asia, having signed on for a reporting stint of at least six months.

Helen took solace in the vision she had of a beautiful new home built high on a cliff at the end of Cedar Point Drive. The mental picture calmed her nerves. She would rather have Joseph employed by a local newspaper and an infant cradled in her arms—cramped apartment and Mrs. Booth notwithstanding— but that was no longer a practical ambition. What they needed now was an ample paycheck and an acceptable place to raise Holden. Once they had their own home, complete with a swank office overlooking the sea, Joseph would have moved up the ranks, eligible for a big job stateside. He could be persuaded to write his stories near her. And maybe she'd dare try again to have his child.

She walked past the flag at half-mast, saying a prayer for the president and all those who mourned him. The image of Mrs.

Kennedy, days ago dressed in that raspberry-colored suit with navy trim and then two days ago all in black, inserted itself into Helen's mind. Now there was a determined woman. Reports were that she made it known to the powers that be exactly how she wanted her husband's visitation and funeral ceremonies to be carried out. From lying in state right where Lincoln had been, to the horse-drawn cortege, to John-John's salute to his father, Jackie was the picture of tenacity and grace, rolled into one.

No need to dwell on that unhappiness. Helen would take a page from Jackie's book and be a young woman who looked to the future. As an upstanding customer of Mechanics Bank and Trust, Helen was convinced she would get her loan.

She entered the bank, making her way to the desk where Mr. Kemp was attending to a mountain of loan applications. Hunched over his papers, his face a sickly shade the color of peas, he looked like Father did the day she and Joseph announced their plans. Joseph would take the Associated Press job as a foreign correspondent while she would begin the hunt for their ideal home.

Three months ago, Maggie had the Game of Life set up on her dining room table. She and Holden were filling their miniature autos with pink and blue pegs representing husbands and wives, daughters and sons. Father sat in his chair, reading the paper.

"This is my big break," Joseph said. "It's my chance to set Helen and Holden up right. My girl here has been as patient as a fellow could want. It's time for us to say bye-bye to Proctor Street."

Helen rested a hand on Joseph's arm, her cue telling him not to bring up the subject of money in front of her father. Her mother was aware that for the last few months they'd been looking at land on which to build their dream home. Back then, it had been just that, a dream. Now, with Joseph's predictable salary—though it came with a different kind of price tag—finally they could entertain buying a house, making the wish a reality.

Holding a pink peg in midair, Maggie looked from her

daughter to her son-in-law, then back again, trying to gauge their true feelings about the overseas assignment. Helen would not say how she felt. If they couldn't have more children, then at least she deserved a proper home.

"How long will you be gone?" Maggie asked. "Is it d-a-n-g-e-r-o-u-s?"

"D-a-n-g-e-r-o-u-s spells dangerous," Holden said.

"You're a wonderful speller," Helen said, giving a look first to Joseph and then to her mother. "Maybe we can talk about this after dinner."

"Why don't you go play?" Joseph said to Holden.

"I *am* playing."

"Not much more *to* discuss," Helen's father said. "He's not going to change his mind and stay right here in Worcester. Where he belongs. Taking on a responsible job." Father never looked up from his paper.

"Responsible? You think soldiers want to go there?" Joseph asked, standing up, pacing the dining room. "They'll be brainwashed to believe they should. They don't see it as old men devising plans for young men to fight. I'll tell you, no journalist believes this will come to good end. I'm a reporter. I've got an obligation to set the record straight."

Helen dragged Holden from his game, plastic car in hand. "I think Nana has some yummy cheese and crackers we can put out to tide us over until the roast is done." She ended the discussion by casting a stern look at her father.

Helen was determined to brighten her life, to lift the shadow that had crept over her family as they lived day in, day out in that horrid apartment. Her hope—in what a new house could do for them—rested with the bank manager who sat in front of her now looking a little too much like her father.

"Good morning. Shall I take a seat, or are you ready for me?" Helen asked.

Mr. Kemp looked up, flustered by the sudden company.

Walking toward her, he opened the wooden fence gate that separated his work area from the lobby of the bank.

"Right this way, Mrs. Tobin. Have a seat. Give me a minute to set things aside, and then I can concentrate solely on you." Mr. Kemp tidied his piles. As he did so, Helen could no longer compare him to Father. His piles did not inspire confidence, especially as he stacked them this way and that, with no method to his madness. Father hadn't amassed his assets by being blasé.

"How is Theodore?" Helen asked. "Have you heard from him lately?"

Mr. Kemp stopped in the middle of clearing his desk, a melancholy look coming over his face. "Last letter was over a month ago. Said he's managing all right. Misses his girl and his mother. He's sure proud to serve his country, don't you know."

Helen brushed imaginary lint off her right shoulder and down her arm in an effort to draw his attention to her military support via her fashion statement. "I imagine his next letter will arrive any day now. My husband says the boys write often, it's the mail system that gets hung up, is all."

"Good to know." Mr. Kemp pulled a folder from his mess and placed it on the desktop. "You'll be happy to know, I've spent a significant amount of time considering your request for a loan. You're a fine customer of the bank."

Helen clutched her purse in front of her. Sitting tall, she tried to hide her childish enthusiasm. Every night before sleep, she'd come to linger on visions of the breathtaking landscape, imagining the house she'd have built. Each room's design came to her in vivid detail.

"Unfortunately, there are a number of problems with your application. First and foremost, we can't consider your husband's income if he isn't available to be a signer on the loan. I see you presently have a consistent income, but I'm afraid it isn't nearly enough for the amount you'd like to finance. And of course, you may not always wish to work as your family grows, don't you know."

Mr. Kemp kept looking down at the paperwork, doing his best to avoid her hard stare.

Helen's mind raced, sorting through all of her arguments in favor of the loan. What she wanted to say was mean, how she wanted to say it cruel. She wanted to tell Mr. Kemp that the only way her family would grow would be through an immaculate conception. Right now her husband spent half his time in Southeast Asia, it being the most lucrative option they had to sustain their family. And she couldn't manage to hold on to a child of her own.

While Helen deliberated, Mr. Kemp continued to argue against her loan. "We have no idea whether your husband is even in favor of such a large advance."

Helen opened her purse, pulling out Joseph's latest letter. When she closed it, the loud snap echoed off the tiny office walls.

"My husband is one hundred percent in favor of my request for this financing." She moved to the edge of her seat, holding the letter out to Mr. Kemp.

He put his hands out in protest. "No, no."

"Please read it," she said, her hands shaking as she pulled the letter from the envelope, extending it to Mr. Kemp. Her pleading forced him to take it. She had to believe Joseph's words would draw the banker in. Vivid descriptions of the places Mr. Kemp's son walked, the things his boy had seen, would soften his heart. He would be forced to reconsider.

Helen regretted giving him the full letter as soon as tiny wrinkles appeared over the bridge of his nose, and his lips parted and became tense.

"The mere fact that the Associated Press is providing your husband with a furnished apartment, complete with housekeeper, doesn't change the bank's requirements."

"That's not the part I meant for you to read. May I?" Helen didn't much care for the part about the woman named Ta Sang, who made terrific meals using her mother's traditional Vietnamese recipes, either. She didn't like that sometimes the woman sat with Joseph while he ate.

"Right here," she said, finding her place, beginning to read.

You've described the place so well when I close my eyes I can feel that ocean breeze and hear the pounding surf. I agree with you, there is no place any healthier to raise a family. So yes, let's buy the land so we can escape from all of this. We'll spend the rest of our lives soaking up the sunshine. Living in such a beautiful place, as you describe it, will surely help me forget what's happening here. I'll recover from this trip by going to the beach and staying there. I wouldn't want you to live any other way. You deserve all the luxuries in the world.

Mr. Kemp sat upright, placing both hands on the papers in her file. Helen folded the letter and put it back in its envelope, misconstruing his first few words as surrender.

"I'm convinced his wishes are in line with yours. But even if we could send him the papers and he could sign and have them notarized, yours is a high-risk loan that Mechanics Bank and Trust simply cannot make at this time. Forgive me for being frank, Mrs. Tobin, but as your letter so clearly points out, your husband is in a dangerous situation, his future uncertain. As is the future of our country, given the recent death of our president."

He closed the file and stood up. Helen thought she was being dismissed until she saw him reach his hand out.

"Mr. McIntyre. I didn't realize you were joining us." Mr. Kemp's tone took on an insincere joviality.

Helen turned to see Father initiating a handshake.

"What are you doing here?" Now Helen was the perturbed member of the party.

Father nodded his hello. There were no hugs or kisses. There hadn't been an affectionate greeting in years. "Your mother told me about your appointment."

From the breast pocket of his three-piece suit, Father pulled out a savings account passbook stamped with Federal Savings and Loan on the cover. He never took his eyes off the bank manager. Mr. Kemp opened the book, and his eyes grew wide as he took in what had to be a sizable sum in the deposit column.

"Well, it seems this changes a great deal." He wrote down the account number, slid the passbook into the clear plastic envelope, and handed it back to Father, who gestured for Mr. Kemp to give it to Helen.

"I will confirm the sum in the account, complete the necessary paperwork, and give you a call, Mrs. Tobin. If everything is in order, you can expect funds to be available within a week of signing."

Helen wasn't going to give either man the satisfaction of inspecting the balance, one that clearly made her loan possible given Mr. Kemp's earlier declination. She was speechless, partly because these two men knew what was in the passbook while she did not, and partly because she was furious with her father. She stood without saying a word, afraid if she did she would cause a scene. She refused to shake Mr. Kemp's outstretched hand. Helen made her way out of the gated area surrounding his desk. Her father strolled right behind her. Out of the bank manager's line of vision, she turned a menacing look on her father.

"How dare you come in here and interfere with my private business?"

"I think a thank-you is more in order. You're a smart girl. You must realize that thanks to me there's a sizable amount of money available to you. Go ahead, look. Your poor mother isn't thrilled with you moving so far away, still, all I ever do is aim to please you, Helen."

She opened the passbook. Under his name was hers. The balance at the bottom of the page was a hefty sum her father must have thought could brighten her shabby, lonely life with green. But then Lee McIntyre had never really known his daughter.

There wasn't enough money in the entire bank capable of buying her forgiveness for all her father had put her mother through. She couldn't understand how her mother looked the other way while he dishonored her and then risked her security with his addiction to bets and wagers.

Helen put the passbook inside her purse, hating the fact that she felt more secure than she had for a long time. She emphasized her disdain with another loud snap of the clasp. She turned away and left her father standing in the lobby. Outside the doors of the bank, she bumped into a young woman dressed in a tie-dyed shirt. Tab splashed from the bottle the teenager carried.

"Hey, lady, watch where you're going," she said.

"Sorry," Helen replied, taking a step toward her Fairlane, away from the girl. Then a moment later, she stopped and turned back.

"Wait a minute," she said. One right after the other Helen undid the rows of brass buttons she'd taken care to sew on that morning. "Here, have this." Taking it off, she tossed her military jacket at the girl. Walking to her car, she called over her shoulder, "Throw it away for all I care."

16

⁘

The Paxton Rehabilitation Center looked like it had been dropped in the middle of a garden. Christian loved this project he'd won in a bidding war eight years ago. Even his early sketches captured the serenity and confidence he'd hoped to convey to patients and their visitors. The finished project had winding paths wide enough for more than one wheelchair and flowering shrubs for every season. He'd spent hours choosing the right point of visual interest. The property could handle it, so he chose to build the garden around a rose of Sharon hibiscus with its saucer-shaped blooms, pink with dark centers. In the tighter spaces, he'd clustered three or four varieties of hydrangea, his favorite *H. villosa,* a gem with its porcelain blue flowers. His landscaping had the ability to convince a person she wanted to sit and stay awhile; of course, only if she hadn't already taken a peek inside.

There weren't enough pretty flowers in the whole of Massachusetts capable of camouflaging the reality of the place my mother had been transferred to. As I walked through the double doors that divided the lobby from the patient care area, the smell hit me. The place reeked of defeat, it sang of surrender.

Carrying my mother's overnight bag and a plate of cookies, I walked by a woman tied into a geriatric chair, hunched over a baby doll. She rocked her pretend child and murmured sweet nothings. So this was the place that prided itself on being a leader in the field of rehabilitation.

I stopped at the desk to introduce myself and to drop off the plate of cookies Luce had made the night before with the kids. I'd walked into a full-blown kitchen disaster, after spending almost two hours fighting commuter traffic to get from Boston to Magnolia. I'd foolishly expected to come home after a long day of getting my mother ready for her transfer to rehab to find clean children and a simple meal waiting for me.

"I thought it would help to get off on the right foot at the center," Luce said. "Get the nurses to like Nácar and her family right away. Yes?"

I didn't disagree that the gesture was a thoughtful one; it was the dough I had to pick out of Claire's hair while she screamed at me and Henry's complaint of a stomachache from eating too many biscochitos instead of dinner that turned Luce's act of kindness into a source of aggravation.

The unit secretary accepted the cookies, marveling at their shape and aroma. She placed them on the desk, and the woman next to her got up to point me in the direction of my mother's room.

"Hi, I'm Maeve, your mother's case manager. She arrived an hour ago. She's in the private room at the end there, next to our activity lounge." She pointed a few doors down. "I'll send her nurse in to say hello in a few minutes. Jenny's finishing up some morning care with another resident."

If my mother's new home hadn't been in plain view, I got the sense that Maeve would've walked me there. Her welcome was my first personal contact at the center, and I thought maybe I could like the place.

Alone, I navigated the hallway. A perky physical therapist

guided an old man toward the activity room. Mumbling to himself, he gripped his walker, stopping as I came in step with him. My presence distracted him from remembering how to advance his feet. A woman in a wheelchair used her left hand to propel herself forward, her one-sided efforts kept her going in circles. The place was full of people traveling somewhere and nowhere all at once.

In her room, my mother was sitting in the same type of chair as the elderly woman and her baby, a recliner on wheels, her legs were elevated, and she was covered with a bright yellow blanket. Comfort and color and people who introduced themselves almost made up for my mother staring out yet another window.

I didn't want to startle her, so I knocked lightly on the door. She turned her head, and one side of her face offered a weak smile. She lifted the fingers of her hand off the arm of the chair, a gesture that said hello. I felt hope come from her effort.

"Mother, you look fantastic." I parked her suitcase next to the wall and moved toward her. Shrugging one shoulder, she dismissed my praise but held my gaze. I leaned in, about to kiss her on the cheek. A right-sided spasm seized her, so I left my intention hanging in the air between us. She still wasn't ready to embrace me.

"How-Jo-wee?" The one cheek that puffed out as she spoke was less noticeable than it had been.

"Henry's fine," I said.

Her white hair, its usual perm relaxed, was pulled off her face with Luce's peineta. The rest of my mother's Spanish-inspired hospital room sat in a small box on the floor by the window. Unpacking it gave me something to do while I searched for the right words. Maybe this was my chance to really talk to her. To come out with things I'd never said and wished I had. And I had so many questions. Like what made her agree to take those pills? Why had she left me the envelope? Did she know I'd once stolen the passbook?

Instead, I started in with Mary, the mother of God.

"Do you like this statue?" I pulled the gaudy saint Luce had given her from the box. Someone back at Memorial had wrapped her in casting gauze so she wouldn't break in transit. She looked like a patient from orthopedics. "You won't hurt Luce's feelings if you don't want her out in the open. Nothing brings her down, trust me. Or I could get you one that doesn't look like a drag queen."

"Drab," my mother muttered, closing her eyes; her lips flinched.

"Do you want a drab statue or did you like my poking fun at this one?"

She pointed a finger at the statue.

"You'd like to keep her?" I asked.

She nodded, wanting Luce's Mary to stay. I was elated. I'd known she could understand me back at Boston Memorial, but here she was more engaged, her stilted conversation somehow brighter. In a strange way, we were doing better.

Clomping clogs and a cheery hello made me turn from my mother to see a living doll. She entered the room with a tray containing a paper cup full of pills and a glass of orange juice.

"Laura Tobin, I thought Helen was your mother. How the hell've you been?"

Jenny Landers looked exactly the same as she had in nursing school. The only evidence that she couldn't outrace her age was her wrinkled cleavage poking out of a neon pink V-neck. Back in nursing school, my cattier friends called her Midge behind her back, her red hair the only thing that ruled out a comparison to Barbie. Still her long legs, small waist, and uppity breasts made the association with the icon's best friend a perfect one.

Jenny put her tray down on my mother's over-the-bed table and pulled me into a firm hold. Her tight squeeze nearly knocked the wind out of me.

"Hello again, Mrs. Tobin. Laura and I were in the same graduating class. It's been years. What have you been up to?"

"I work part-time in the postpartum nursery at Memorial. I'm married, two kids. You?"

"Let's see. I've been married for a total of twenty years—to three different guys—but I'm single now. Helen, you don't know anyone you could fix me up with, do ya?" Jenny laughed and winked at my mother as she pulled the pill container and juice from her tray.

"Okay, let's see if I can remember what we have for you this morning." Jenny pointed to each pill with her acrylic index finger, painted to match her sweater. "The little green one's your happy pill. This white one, your blood thinner. This long one's just a multivite."

"She can't swallow pills whole like that," I said. "Can you crush them?"

Jenny was as flashy as the Mary statue I'd taken from the box. Like the saint, her appearance didn't inspire a whole lot of confidence. I dug through my memories of her, trying to conjure up what kind of a student she'd been. My recollection was that she was smarter than most of us gave her credit for, but I couldn't believe she was about to give a mouthful of pills to a woman who had trouble swallowing. I wanted a normal nurse with observable clinical skills, dressed in plain old scrubs. I wanted Molly.

"Good to know," Jenny said. "Do you like applesauce, Helen? I can put them in a bit of that if you like." She didn't wait for my mother to respond. Everything went back on the tray, and she turned to me, lowering her voice.

"I shoulda read her discharge papers from Memorial before pouring her meds. Don't you worry, I would've checked her gag reflex before I gave them to her. Oh, and we're having a team meeting about Helen in an hour. Nursing, speech, physical and occupational therapy, the whole crew. You can come. We're big on family-centered care."

Jenny filled me in on where to find the conference room. She was gone only a couple of minutes. When she returned with the crushed pills, I volunteered to feed them to my mother, not sure I could trust my old classmate. And knowing I had all the time in the world, I welcomed having something to do.

I spooned tiny bits of multicolored flecks mixed with applesauce into my mother's mouth. She took forever to maneuver each mouthful to the back of her throat and finally to swallow. It reminded me of feeding Henry and Claire when they were learning to eat solid food. I couldn't imagine how my mother would find the strength to learn to walk and talk.

"I found the bottle of pills you left on your bureau. I'm happy you decided to do that. Before all this, were you starting to feel better?"

My mother gulped her last bite; seconds later she said *yes*. Every action she took was discrete; each task took enormous energy to complete.

"I found the envelope too. The one in your drawer with Daddy's letter in it. Boy, do I wish you could tell me about that."

She started shaking her head with more effort than she'd used for any of her other movements combined.

"I didn't mean to upset you. The envelope had my name on it, that's the only reason I went through your things." As soon as I said it, I realized I was lying to her. I had a history of going through her things. And I hadn't hesitated to scan the letter she'd left in her wing chair on her birthday before Claire stopped me. I hadn't really struggled with whether or not to read the two letters bedside either, reciting them to her only after she'd fallen asleep. Seeing her strong reaction, even about something I didn't understand, made me feel awful for rifling through her stuff.

"Half-it." My mother worked harder to say those two words than she had to take her meds.

"Have it? You want me to have the letter?"

She shook her head and started slapping her good hand on the arm of her chair. "Re——"

"Do you want me to have something else? The key. The money?"

She nodded and exhaled the word *yes*. It came out louder and more forceful than I thought could possibly emerge from such a broken body.

"That money's yours, I don't want it. Anyway, Christian and I are doing fine."

All her agitation was coming off her left side. One leg swinging, she reached out to grab my sweater. Her desire to say so much when she was capable of expressing so little hurt me.

"We'll talk about that later. Right now, we need to concentrate on getting you home."

In a snap she calmed, as if my line about going home had finally jumped from one sick synapse to another. Seeing her settle, imagining Sea Escape as her safe place, I thought, That's it! She'd left me the letter as a reminder not to take her away from home, not to take her home away from her. With her dark eyes pinned on me, I wondered if she was trying to send me her message telepathically. Nothing came out.

Only moments before, she'd let me feed her applesauce laced with antidepressants and blood thinners; maybe she'd let me give this to her. There was plenty of money in that one account to arrange for the home care she'd need after rehab, never mind what other funds she had stashed away. With home as the goal—and her less depressed—we were in a better position than ever to find our way back to each other.

She let her head fall back against the chair's attached plastic pillow, making no attempt to keep the tears from streaming. With her left hand, she made a weak attempt to point from her head to her feet, tacking on a frown.

"I know your body isn't cooperating, yet, but you haven't even started rehab. You've got to promise me you'll work the hardest at speech. There's so much we need to talk about. And physical therapy too. I know it sounds tiring, but all the hard work will be worth it. You'll be out of here in no time, and with all that money, we'll be able to pay for the extra help you'll need."

"No fa—tha—mon—" she said.

"I don't understand. Try it slower."

She didn't answer me with a nod, or a gesture, or a word. Her repertoire and her body exhausted; the simple conversation had worn her out.

"It's okay. We don't have to talk about it now. You rest."

Her breathing slowed, her grip on the chair went lax. She'd fallen asleep.

I rearranged the blanket over her legs, tucking it in at her sides. "Promise you'll try to get well. If it helps, think about Henry," I whispered. "Or you could do it for me."

Reaching into the drawer of her bedside table, this time bypassing the letters, I pulled out a piece of Paxton Rehabilitation Center stationery. Like Christian would, I began to make a list. I would do everything I could to get her back to Sea Escape. I'd find a way to bring my mother home.

17

My father's letters were enchanted, his loving words capable of working their way into my mother's addled brain, drawing her to his light. She was getting better. Everything about the letters gave me confidence. Driving home from the rehab center over coast roads, blessedly without traffic, all I could think about was throwing on a nightgown, reading to the kids, and curling up with Christian to tell him my plan to get her home. I was certain, once back there, protected by the windbreaks offered by the dunes, my mother would feel alive again. She'd be happy, and maybe that would give me the courage to try once more to tell her why the seascape soothed to me. Any reservations I still had didn't matter.

I opened our back door to find everyone doing something. Henry was lying on his stomach on the rag rug leafing through a *Better Homes and Gardens* magazine. He'd ripped out pictures for what looked like a homework collage. The subscription had been a Christmas present from my mother to Christian and me. Back then, I thought it must be a subtle message to keep a better home, since mine was more shabby than chic. It couldn't have been for Christian; she knew firsthand the gift he had for creating gardens.

Claire sat in an armchair, the one I'd fought to slipcover two months ago. She was wrapping a scarf around her doll, no doubt given to her by Luce the magician, a woman who had a remarkable talent for producing one colorful handkerchief after another out of nowhere, each with a new purpose. With the children occupied, Luce was ironing. She'd set up in front of the ceiling-to-floor windows at the back of the room. A sedate-for-her skirt draped the ironing board; a white peasant blouse hung from one of the window casings, already crisply pressed.

"How's Nana?" Henry asked as he popped up to welcome me with a hug.

Claire looked over at me but didn't stop readjusting her doll's outfit. Luce parked the iron upright and joined in the embrace. The three of us stood in a circle behind Claire's chair.

"So Nácar is settled? Do you like where they moved her?" Luce went back to her skirt, continuing to chat.

"She lucked out and got a private room. I went to nursing school with the woman taking care of her, which may or may not be good. We'll see."

Henry returned to his magazine clippings. He collected the pages, leaving scraps of paper crumpled on the rug. "Will Nana ever sew again?"

I sat on the arm of Claire's chair. "Oh, honey, Nana hasn't sewn anything in years. What she's really going to need to work on now is walking. And talking."

"Nana can't talk?" Claire asked. No matter how focused she was on something, my daughter always managed to tune in to the conversation, whether I wanted her to or not. Looking at her, lost in combing Josefina's hair, I realized I hadn't spent any time trying to explain what was going on to her.

"She can too talk, stupid. It's just hard for her to remember the words." Henry shook his head and sighed at Claire.

"Little man, I understand you're upset about your nana," Luce said. "No need to take it out on Claire. Why don't you take a break upstairs?"

Henry tossed the magazine on the antique trunk that doubled as a coffee table and reached for the book he'd tucked under the couch cushion. I didn't need to see the cover to know which one it was. He muttered something to Claire as he took the stairs.

"Come back here and say you're sorry to your sister." I hated when either of them took a parting stab at the other's feelings. I'd been home five minutes, and already things were going south. At that point I noticed evidence of a recipe search spread out all over the family room floor. While I'd been gone, Luce must have dug up every cookbook I'd ever accumulated. Apparently she'd found what she'd been looking for, because the smell of something baked with cinnamon and apples wafted through the house.

"Henry will be fine," she said, lifting the skirt from the ironing board. "I've told him when he gets overwhelmed with sadness to go to his rocker. Christian says it soothes him, and I find he comes back calm and composed. No need to force him to apologize."

Luce clipped the skirt, a midlength floral, mostly a mix of shades of brown, onto a hanger.

I leaned down over Claire, trying to hide how annoyed I was with Luce. I couldn't believe she was telling me how to discipline my own children. With one hand, I smoothed Claire's black hair off her face and kissed the top of her head. I was sad that she hadn't run to greet me but thankful she was content to play, not cling.

"Now, do you think this will fit?" Luce asked.

"Looks like it. Why don't you go try it on? I can take it from here. Where are you going?" I asked.

My crooked pose hurt my back, so I got up and took off my parka, hanging it on the hook by the door. Luce took the hanging blouse down, matching it up with the skirt. When my hands were free, she handed both off to me.

"For you," she said.

Puzzled, I took them from her. She winked and went back to the iron, checking its heat, wrapping its cord. "My sister, you have a date with a very handsome man. Christian is meeting you at the Old Mill. He has been home from work already. Showered and changed. He's doing a quick estimate for a potential client and he'll meet you at the restaurant. Seven sharp. Get, get. You don't want to keep such a man waiting."

"Wow, that's so nice of you, but I'm exhausted. And I shouldn't leave the kids again." I pointed to Claire, hanging the clothes back up. "Thanks, though. Maybe another time."

"You have to go, Mommy. Auntie Luce said it's kids' night. We're having dessert for dinner, and she's going to show us how to make bisutería. I'm going to make you a bracelet."

Henry came running downstairs in a huff, getting right in his sister's space to reprimand her. He stomped one foot.

"You weren't supposed to tell her!" Now it was my son's turn to demonstrate his uncanny ability to know exactly what everyone was saying no matter what part of the house he was in.

"Your mother and Nácar will still appreciate your creations. No worries. Each piece of jewelry is unique."

"Never mind, I should stay home tonight. Auntie Luce can show me too."

Henry said he didn't mind if I went out. And in a first for Claire, she said she would be fine staying up late with Luce. So I put on the outfit that would clearly have looked better on my sister-in-law and drove to meet my husband at our favorite restaurant, leaving his sister to make another mess with my children.

The Old Mill Restaurant dated back to the 1800s, when, as a working sawmill, it provided most of the nonfishing jobs for Anaskaket residents. It was the site of our first date near my home, the one we'd planned after spending three days together in his New York neighborhood. We marked every special occasion there, anniversaries, birthdays. We chose it for most ordinary nights out, too. We never tired of its rustic charm and the soothing lullaby the waterfall sang while we dined on fine food and homemade desserts.

As I pulled into the pebbled drive, I perked up. Maybe the water waltzing over the milldam and a hearty meal of pork chops glazed with an apple bourbon sauce were exactly what I needed to take my mind off my mother. I made a mental note to thank Luce for pushing me out, and for filling my nostrils with the smell of her baked apple concoction. The aroma memory had effectively done away with my usual dithering over what to order.

I parked next to Christian's truck, pleased he was already inside. I wouldn't have to feel either lonely or overeager, staring at the door, willing him to arrive. After handing my trench off to the coat check girl, I straightened my borrowed outfit. Running my fingers through my hair, I walked into the dining room.

Christian was schmoozing his way to a better table, one far away from a bustling family of six. A true evening out for him— and for me, though I wouldn't have fought for it—involved candles, cut flowers, and wine in real glasses. No children. Ours or anyone else's.

Seeing me, he used my welcome as a way to maneuver us to the new table, overlooking the mill falls; he wouldn't have wanted to offend the other customers. As a local business owner, he knew he couldn't afford to tick people off. Anaskaket was the epitome of a small town.

"You look beautiful. Though I have the distinct impression your stylist is my sister." Christian's accent was softer and more refined than Luce's or his parents'. It was as delicate as the kiss he left lingering on my lips. His hand placed firmly on my back radiated heat through my flimsy blouse. Maybe I didn't need to eat.

"She foisted it on me, but once I tried it on, I kind of liked it." Self-consciously, I took my seat and smoothed out the flared skirt, suddenly feeling like an impostor in costume. Thankful for the long tablecloth, I placed my napkin in my lap, hiding the busy pattern of the fabric. A fabric my mother would have had a name for.

"You look perfect in whatever you wear. Or don't wear," he whispered.

Christian was a master of seduction. Walking us ever so slowly toward bed, he'd start wooing me right in the restaurant by ordering my favorite wine, complimenting me on my hair, even with its uncooperative curl defying the bobby pin I'd used to keep it off my forehead. Usually when we'd go out to dinner, we'd save catching up on the details of home stuff and kid talk until after we'd made love. These nights were ours alone. Yet on this date, orchestrated by his meddlesome yet well-meaning sister, he knew enough to start with the obvious.

"How was your mother when you left?" He browsed the menu, though we both had the pages memorized.

"In some ways, the same. In others, she seems a lot better. It's funny how her feistiness shines through even though she can't say much. It used to drive me crazy, but now it's kind of endearing."

I closed the menu. Browsing it made me doubt my resolve to order the pork.

"It looks like she's got a long haul ahead, but at least she's closer to home." As the wine steward deposited our caddy and began to open a bottle of Pinot, our waitress came. The woman had served us many times before. Her easy, no-rush manner garnered healthy tips.

Without skipping a beat, Christian sampled the wine and ordered our meals.

"The lady will have the sole with cranberries. I'll have the salmon. And two house salads, please."

He closed the menus, and she took off. There was no time for me to object to his meal choice for me, especially since the sole was what I always ordered when I couldn't make up my mind.

Annoyed with him for taking over, I hid my irritation behind my glass. He could have asked me if that was what I wanted. Sipping my wine, I found the confidence I'd had driving home from the rehab center. "Speaking of home. I'm going to do what I can to get her there." As soon as I said it out loud, it sounded ridiculous.

"Ours or hers?" Christian leaned in, his knit brow registering concern.

"Sea Escape. She has plenty of money for home care. I haven't had the chance to tell you. This morning, I found a passbook savings with a hundred thousand dollars in it. And I found out she's been taking antidepressants since Christmas. When I went to get her clothes, the bottle was right out in the open."

"Isn't Helen a cagey one?" He swirled his wine, taking his time to put the glass to his lips. The way his mouth turned up, I knew the wine was fine. Christian was gearing up to disagree with me.

"Let's be realistic," he said. "No amount of money will be enough. The home care will be you, you, and more you. Luce has to go home eventually, and then you'll have Henry and Claire to worry about. You'll be over there every minute, and when you aren't, you'll be worried she's fallen down or become confused, forgetting to shut off the stove or something. And how will you go back to work?"

I wanted to go back to work. I missed the babies. But the way he said it made me resent him for suggesting it. I had no idea how I would manage everything, but I wished he believed that I should try, that maybe I could work it all out.

"I'm not saying she's going to get there overnight, she's only starting rehab. She's more likely to get confused in the hospital than she is in her own home. And I've got to tell you, they say she's doing great."

How easy it was to embellish the encouraging words her nurses dished out or her speech therapist tossed around. Workaday phrases they used to get my mother to try harder. I refused to believe that Christian was right. I wouldn't give up on her.

The candle flickered, the water spilled over the mill falls. So tired of reading people's body language, I looked away from my husband and let the cool taste of the wine invade my senses. One more glass and I could blame the Pinot for my numbness.

18

August 1967

Helen had almost given up hope of having a child of her own—Joseph's child—yet here she was with a toddler, beyond blessed, rocking in a chair, hemming a pair of organdy sheers that would filter the light coming in the nursery windows.

Her mother had found the Boston rocker at a tag sale and had it refinished for the pair after Helen dared say her news out loud. She'd had an inkling within days of her rendezvous with Joseph in Bangkok but waited until her ordinary clothes literally burst at the seams before telling anyone. She was terrified to murmur the words or to put them in writing. She tried desperately not to think about the child she carried, fearful she'd become attached. Afraid to believe this pregnancy would have an outcome different from the ones that came before.

On a day when Holden would be in school, Helen invited her parents to visit. She planned to tell her mother. Father could listen, but Holden would be safely out of earshot. He would be the last to know about the child. She couldn't take the chance that he would once again become fond of the idea of a sibling.

Helen prepared the delicate green tea she'd purchased while overseas; it had been impossible to enjoy it upon her return. With her morning sickness now well under control, she looked forward to sharing the special brew reminiscent of anise and vanilla with her mother. The coffee table set in the grand room looked wonderful. Her mother deserved a pleasant afternoon, given she rarely experienced a lovely day now that Father's gambling debacles were out in the open. He'd recently pushed his luck on a thoroughbred named, ironically, Foolish Pleasure.

"Did I tell you Mrs. Booth passed?" her mother asked as she settled on the sofa, running her hand over the gorgeous fabric. "The calling hours were yesterday; hardly anyone went. I wonder who'll buy the house on Proctor."

While her mother filled her in on the goings-on in Worcester, Helen fought the images showing up in her mind, the memories of that tiny place she'd lived in, so dreary, so filled with unpleasant memories. Father sat off on his own, peering through the windows toward the sea. Though she knew he'd never say so, even he couldn't deny the brilliance of her decision to build Sea Escape in this wonderland. The outdoor space, steps from the dunes, had spectacular views of the expansive beach. The only thing that could heighten the beauty of the property would be a garden, lush and lively. She imagined beach roses and daylilies all around the grounds, adding the perfect color to her scene.

Helen hadn't invited her parents to Sea Escape to revisit her lonely life on Proctor Street, so as nonchalantly as one woman commenting on another's new draperies or the freshness of the scones, she changed the subject with her news.

"I'm five months along," she said.

Maggie clasped a hand over her mouth and then guided her daughter to the comfortable couch, insisting she stop pouring the tea and sit down. Right past her father, Helen walked. He glanced at her stomach, as if checking to see if she were telling a tale.

"Good luck with that," he murmured.

"I didn't dare hope that was the reason for your fullness," Maggie said, ignoring her husband. "When are you due?"

It was true, Helen was pregnant, but for how much longer she could not say. Even as the weeks marched on, she refused to accept the tiniest booties or the simplest maternity dress from her mother. She'd insisted there be no baby shower, no talk of names. No discussion of due dates, birth weights, or baby fates.

Month after month went by with Helen running her home and parenting Holden as if nothing had changed, or were about to. This time Joseph made it home with two months to spare, the crushed-shell driveway announcing his arrival. Helen stood in the vestibule, smoothing out the black tunic and slacks she wore, waiting for him inside the home that had become her refuge. Her dark getup minimized her size, drawing less attention to her condition, its color a companion to her mood.

Joseph acted surprised to find his wife standing there. Helen had wondered how uncomfortable this reunion would be. Now she would find out.

"Wow! There you are. Pregnant. And as beautiful as ever."

Helen could see he'd changed since the last time she'd seen him. The skin around his mouth was less taut, the hair at his temples thinned and salted. Worry had taken up residence on her once carefree husband's face. Another woman might never see these subtle differences in her man's look. Living day-to-day with him would keep her oblivious.

"I've made a meal if you're interested in eating before you lie down." Helen reached out to take his shoulder bag. "You must be exhausted."

"I couldn't sleep now. I just want to look at you. And I want to talk." Joseph dropped the bag on the floor, inching his way toward Helen. When he stood directly in front of her and she remained statue-still, he dared glide his hand over her abdomen. No matter how hard she resisted, her tense muscles relaxed in response to his caress. With her on the verge of surrender, he pulled her into his arms.

"We can get through this," he said. "It'll all work out. Oh, Helen, I don't want to lose—"

Helen pulled her head from his shoulder. Backing away from him, she would not speak of it. "I don't want to talk about— For Holden's sake, let's not discuss it. For the next few weeks, I think it's best to pretend that everything's fine," she said. "Let's just see how things go."

During the last weeks of her pregnancy, Joseph gave Helen the gifts of cooperation and teamwork. He marched to her drum, in step with every request. Helen knew Joseph. He figured, under the circumstances, it was best to give his wife whatever she asked for.

Holden and Joseph were playing baseball on Anaskaket Beach when Helen went into labor. They were engaged in their nightly ritual, and she watched them trying to have fun. There were compliments for good pitches and applause for first-rate hits, all-around good spirits capable of convincing Helen there was hope they could be close. She went through the motions preparing to leave for the hospital. Placing a call to one of Holden's friends, requesting an impromptu sleepover, putting a few of his things in an overnight bag. She'd learned there was no need to rush.

Much of her labor was a blur, though she did recall wedging her body into the passenger seat of their car while Joseph, hurrying to put her suitcase in the trunk, tripped over the Boston rocker waiting expectantly in the corner of the garage.

The last thing Helen remembered before being wheeled out of her hospital room on a stretcher was her baby kicking between contractions. She allowed herself one caress, one final prayer that he or she would breathe. The orderly whisked her by Joseph, but she wouldn't look at him, afraid to catch even a trace of doubt on his face. She knew that he'd already given up on her ability to deliver a healthy child.

All Helen could hear was Joseph begging to be included. "Please let me come in." But the doctor adamantly said no. Husbands were not allowed in the delivery room. They left him standing outside the double doors.

Even as Helen breathed deep, sweet ether, the mask held to her face by a nurse, she didn't believe she'd leave the room any different than she'd come into it. Alone.

When she woke from her brief sleep to the lullaby of a baby whimpering, the first thing Helen noticed was a room filled with smiles.

"Say hello to Baby Girl Tobin," the doctor said.

In an anesthesia haze, Helen thought she must be dreaming. Her desire to hold a living, breathing baby of her own was so intense, she imagined she'd willed a child into the room. Then her miracle was near, her face round and pink, her legs wriggling.

"My Laura," Helen said, stretching out her arms to receive her healthy daughter.

Only after she'd listened to the whispers of her daughter's night breathing for a week in the hospital and was wheeled out of it cradling her baby, did Helen really believe she had another child to raise.

Once back at Sea Escape, as Laura slept in the bassinet, Helen eased her achy body down in her favorite wing chair, the one covered in a tapestry of seashells, conch and nautilus. She gave Joseph the nod. He knew then it was time to get the rocker from the garage and bring it to the spare room that would serve as Laura's nursery. A room Helen had been in no hurry to design and decorate because of her fears, and still felt in no rush to spruce up. Laura Madeline Tobin's room decor would be painstakingly chosen. This baby was here to stay.

Though predictably Helen's husband was not.

One month later, Joseph went back to Vietnam for another stint of reporting; except this time the melancholy that usually lingered, sometimes for days after he'd left, didn't present itself. Helen was consumed by all things Laura. Working whenever she could stay awake—and Holden would keep an eye on his sister—she'd taken two months to complete the rose petal stencils that tiptoed around the center of Laura's room.

Sitting there now, watching her two-year-old play at her feet, Helen was particularly proud of the ruffled bed skirt she'd made, the ball fringe barely touching the scatter rug laid out in front of the crib. Helen put aside her stitching to soak in every inch of little Laura playing with the Vietnamese doll Joseph had brought her on his last visit home. Her tiny fingers worked to fasten the delicate frog closures on the traditional ao dai coat it wore over long satin pants. Laura persisted in trying to dress the rigid doll nailed to its circular base. Helen had given up attempting to wrestle the inappropriate gift away from her. She'd tried to tell Joseph that the child was too young to be fiddling with the fancy collectible. How could he not know what little girls could do? Their little girl should be playing with the cloth-covered baby doll Helen bought her, the one that looked like her. Laura's dark hair, what little there was of it, swayed to the rhythm of the ocean breeze coming in the open window, her eyes the color of sea glass focused intently on dressing her make-believe little one.

Laura got up off the carpet, having grown tired of manipulating the doll's complicated outfit, and brought it to Helen to dress. "Mommy do."

Helen brushed wisps of hair off Laura's forehead. "Why don't we give Mai Mai a rest and you and I will go for our walk? We'll see if Holden wants to join us."

Laura wrapped her arms around Helen's neck, giving her one of those delicious hugs. Helen pulled her onto her lap, feeling her life complete. Laura squirmed free and started twirling around the room in a circle, calling out. "My beach, my beach." The front of her simple gingham dress with its hand-sewn appliqués of cherries appeared and disappeared as she spun.

"No, *my* beach." Helen teased her sweet girl, catching her dizzy little one before she landed in a heap on the rug.

"Hoden?"

"Holden?" Helen echoed Laura, who was still unable to pronounce her brother's name. As she tidied her sewing and placed the half-dressed doll on the toy shelf under the window, she registered a strange quiet within the house. Where was Holden? She didn't hear him downstairs reenacting battles with his collection of army men. She hadn't noticed him walking past Laura's room on the way to his own. She didn't hear anything but a distant dog barking and families flocking to the beach on this glorious day. Her mother's instinct told her either Holden was up to something or something was wrong. He'd better not have left the house again without telling her. She scooped Laura up and took the stairs as quickly as was safe for her to, holding her squirmy toddler. There in the living room he sat, surrounded by Helen's keepsake box and piles of Joseph's letters.

"What are you doing? No one gave you permission to read my mail, young man."

Helen plopped Laura on the couch and bent down to snatch the letter Holden was engrossed in. She spoke so loudly Laura began to cry, though she'd only meant to startle Holden into dropping the letter. Crawling out of her reach, he scrambled to his feet and backed away from her.

Laura wriggled off the couch and went to her brother. Helen thought it uncanny that a child so young could sense her brother needed comforting. "Hoden," she said, this time with her arms reaching toward him, gesturing for him to pick her up.

"Take her outside to play," Helen said. "And do not let her out of your sight. Do you understand?"

"Come on, Laura. Let's get out of here." Holden hoisted his little sister onto his hip and took off through the screen door. It was clear he'd made no attempt to stop the thing from slamming shut. From the glass-backed room, Helen could see him taking the boardwalk toward the beach, Laura's little head bobbing up and down as he ran.

"Stay in the dunes!" Helen shouted through the open window.

Shame on him. At his age, he knew right from wrong. She made the sign of the cross, praying Holden hadn't read the letter Joseph wrote years ago confessing his inner struggle to love Holden after the deaths of Mary Pat and Warren. Parents Holden knew nothing about. Hand across the letter against her chest, Helen finally breathed when she checked the postmark and realized this wasn't that one.

In fact the one he'd been reading was tame in comparison to others in the same batch. Though Helen hoped Holden hadn't read Joseph's pleas, pressing his case for accepting a White House job, asking her to consider selling Sea Escape to relocate, even if he had, why should she feel guilty? She could say without hesitation that she'd kept up her end of their marital bargain, taking care of home and family. As she saw it, Joseph hadn't suffered one bit. Prestigious job, a decent wage, his own housekeeper.

Enough. There was no point in rehashing the painful times of her marriage. Helen finally had her girl and her seaside home; she certainly wasn't going to shake everything up to start all over again on Joseph's terms. She was determined to keep adult matters from her children. From the looks of it, so far she'd succeeded, though some of Joseph's telltale letters lay dangerously near the one Holden had been reading. She would never forget certain of those postmarks.

Holden needn't know certain things, especially related to his parentage. He'd been scarred enough by baby Joey's death, his questions about the boy rejuvenated during her pregnancy with Laura. Now that his sister was here, Holden rarely mentioned the brother he'd never met but longed to know.

Helen placed the letter back in its envelope, tucking it into the stack tied with a purple grosgrain ribbon. Rearranging the letters by year in her keepsake box, she thought perhaps now was the time to place them under lock and key. Making a mental note to buy a lockbox, one only she would have access to, she'd visit the hardware store at the same time she took care of other errands. She'd been meaning to stop off at the bank to add Laura's name to the infamous savings account passbook. The legacy wouldn't be tainted to her daughter.

Then, as if someone pushed her from behind, the sound of an angry dog mingling with Holden's cries for help made Helen drop the handful of letters.

"Get away from her. Let go. Mom!"

Helen skidded on the letters now scattered all over the floor. Out on the wraparound porch overlooking the beach, she shielded her eyes from the sun. Mahogany blond hair flashed in between dancing dune grass. Heads—one boy, one dog—jerked this way and that. Helen couldn't tell where her boy began and the dog ended. Not a single hair of Laura's could be seen from Helen's vantage point. Where was her daughter?

Helen shouted her name like a wish or a song or a prayer. And she ran. The faster she tried to move, the more time slowed. Though it could only have been a matter of seconds between the time Helen left the deck and when she landed in the dunes. She was conscious of a young man in a bathing suit trying to wrestle Holden free from the death grip the dog had on his arm. The man bellowed at the dog, telling it to *let go*! "Bad dog, bad dog," he yelled at the thing as he finally unclenched its teeth and dragged it farther and farther from them, snapping a leash on its collar. Helen was hunting for Laura.

Pushing back beach grass, frantically searching for any sign of her daughter, only once did Helen dare look down over the bluff toward the beach.

"Where is she?"

The hem of a cherry-covered dress pulled Helen back to the

dunes. Laura was lying a few feet behind Holden, almost completely obscured by sea oats. Her small hands were fastened tight to her ears. Helen dropped to her knees and pulled her daughter to a standing position. She ran her hands over each arm, then each leg. In search of bite marks, Helen found relief; her daughter's fair skin was intact.

Holden began to rock, holding his ravaged arm, blood splatter all over his shirt. He sniveled and gulped air as he chanted. "You love her more than me."

Helen refused to believe she was torn between her children. When she couldn't see Laura, there had been only one choice for her. To find her daughter. She wouldn't deny the fine, strong thread that bound her to her daughter, yet it took only one instinctive move, a single reaction on Helen's part, for Holden to suppose his mother played favorites.

In between Holden's sobs, Helen tried to reassure him. "I love you both the same. I couldn't see her. That's all."

Holden recoiled from Helen as she tried to get a better look at his arm. Laura buried her head in her mother's shoulder, comforted by the hand pressed firm against her back. Helen kept telling herself he was just shaken by the calamity. Once his arm was dressed, his pain under control, he would see she'd done no wrong. She would make it up to him. And things would go back to the way they'd been. The three of them living happily by the seashore.

19

The pitch-black room and the depth of my sleep allowed me to resist getting up, even as I registered the low tangle of voices coming from downstairs. Not fully conscious, I went back and forth between going deeper and getting out of bed to find out why my children were up so early and what they were fighting over.

A quick glance at my alarm clock through bleary eyes ripped the cobwebs from my mind. It was eight-thirty. I'd overslept. Henry and Claire would be late for school. I grabbed the cardigan I'd thrown over my bedside chair the night before. Wrapping it tight over my pajama top, I made it halfway down the stairs to the family room when I saw a fort made out of sheets. Draped over kitchen chairs and end tables, its peaks were created by an assortment of broom handles. Books and dolls and plates with half-eaten waffles swimming in syrup were strewn from one end of the room to the other. Even for me it was a mess.

"You have to go to school. Because Auntie said so." Henry's voice was loud and clear once I'd made it to the first floor.

"You're not the boss of me. I don't have to go if you don't."

Claire's shouting stopped abruptly. I knew by the time I rounded the corner, she'd be in tears. Her ability to start an argument off strong was a testament to her persistence, her meltdowns proof of her age.

"What's going on? Where's your father?" Startled by my voice, Claire turned and ran to me, wrapping her string-bean arms about my waist. Henry didn't know which way to turn.

"He had to go to work early. Auntie's in charge," he said, looking down the hall, willing her to come to his rescue.

"Oh, Laura, go back to bed." Luce came out of the downstairs bathroom looking fresh and clean, a throwback to 1950s domestic life. Her casual blouse and tapered slacks the perfect mix of bohemian style and old-world charm. I wondered why she always bothered to look so put together when she wasn't going anywhere. She tsked at Henry and Claire for rousing me, the way I'd seen her mother do at least a hundred times since I'd known her.

"Quick, quick, put on your boots," Luce said to Claire as she gathered coats from the hall closet. "You will have a turn another day. Let's not be late for school."

"I'll wait here for you, Auntie Luce," Henry said. Triumphant, he backed away from me, retreating through the flap of his home-made tent.

I looked from where he'd been to Luce.

"Do you mind filling me in on what's going on?" I asked my sister-in-law.

In a surprising move, Claire followed Luce's simple command to put on her boots. Her tongue moved in and out of her mouth as she struggled to tie up her laces. She would never ask for help, determined to successfully complete her newly acquired skill no matter how long it took or how frustrated she got.

"I am treating Henry to a special day in Boston. There is a new exhibit at the Museum of Fine Arts." Luce raised her voice in the direction of Henry's tent. "What's it called?"

Henry's head popped out of the tent enough for me to know

he'd been listening the whole time, hoping Luce's plan would fly. I never agreed to let him skip school, no matter how many times he'd begged me, and he knew it.

"One Thousand Years of Textiles."

"I didn't think you'd object. Our outing is educational, of course. And it will give us time to enjoy each other's company. He's been through a lot."

I felt backed into a corner. How could I, of all people, refuse someone a day off? Or Henry time with the aunt I knew he adored. The one thing Luce never made a mess of was the way she treated the people she loved. She was open, warm, and honest. Things I wasn't feeling at that moment. Still, it was impossible for me to say no, feeling as guilty as I did. When had Henry become interested in art?

"Would you mind cleaning up the place before you go?" I asked. "I'll go throw on a pair of jeans and drive Claire."

With her boots done up, I took Claire's parka from Luce, offering to help her with it, but she shrugged me away. "Help Henry and Aunt Luce, okay? I'll be right back."

Taking the stairs in twos, I hurried, hoping to avoid being caught in the bus line. Dropping Claire off by the front door positioned me better for a nonclingy getaway, and with the clothes I was pulling on—a worn pair of jeans and a threadbare Henley—I didn't want to get out of the car to walk her inside.

Rebelting my pilly sweater, I heard Claire shriek. "Now there's syrup all over my boots!"

I closed my eyes, wondering how in the world I would get through the day when any energy I might have had was already spent. It wasn't even nine in the morning. I couldn't imagine what Luce had been thinking when she said they could eat that breakfast in the family room. For grandparents and people without kids, being in charge was all about the fun. It never came down to being practical or realistic. It never involved just saying no.

To Claire's singsong crying I heard Luce's calming lyrics,

"no worries." Like an instrument added in for good measure, the phone rang. Immediately my fears about getting *the call* resurfaced.

"Hey, I didn't expect you to be there," Christian said. "I'm heading out of the office to go check on a contractor. I was going to leave you a message."

"Can you make it quick? I have to drive Claire to school."

"Why didn't she make the bus? What's up with Henry? Isn't he going too?"

"It's a long story having to do with forts and your sister and now apparently syrup. You don't want to know."

With the phone lodged between my ear and shoulder, I pulled on a pair of mismatched ankle socks and shoved my feet into my Crocs.

"Joe LaBritton called last night. He said you were looking for him to give you an estimate on building a handicapped ramp at Sea Escape? I thought we agreed getting your mother back there wasn't a good idea."

"Where was I when he called?" I hadn't remembered a phone call or that I'd agreed to anything.

"You fell asleep in Claire's bed. You're not still thinking your mother can live there alone, are you?"

"I'd like to know what I'm up against, that's all. She's getting better, Christian. It's just an estimate."

"As it is you're exhausted going back and forth to Paxton. Luce is looking after Henry and Claire, and you haven't picked up a shift in almost a month. I don't know how you think you'll be able to do all of this."

"I'll call in for a shift after we hang up if that's what you're concerned about."

I stepped into the bathroom to run a comb through my bed hair. Like the famous mirror on the wall, it spoke to me. This time it told me to save us both the trouble.

"I don't want you doing things to Sea Escape and then being

disappointed, that's all. And you don't have to work this week. We'll be okay if you need more time. It's just—I know how much the babies soothe you."

"Mommy!" Claire called up the stairs. "Henry won't take the tent down."

"I have to go. Luce is watching the kids, and like you said, there's a lot to do." He said all he was doing was looking out for me, only somehow it didn't feel that way.

As if the morning had started off all sweetness and light, Claire sang "The Wheels on the Bus" ten times on the ride from our house to Lynch Elementary. I'd had my fill of buses after she'd missed hers and then sang about one until I got a headache. Turning onto Collin Street, I sighed. I hadn't arrived before the line of them. I would have to walk Claire inside.

"Miss Relihan says mommies get to stay anytime they want. She's reading us *Betsy's Little Star* today. Can you? Please?" Claire clutched her backpack to her chest, making no move to unbuckle her seat belt as the car came to a stop in the parking lot.

I looked into the rearview mirror as much to see if there was anything I could do about my hair as I did to gauge how hard it would be to get my daughter to class.

"I can't today, honey. I have to go see Nana." I got out and opened her door, praying she would oblige without a scene. It was too good to be true. She took my hand and led the way, past the walkers and the stream of kids coming off the buses. I planned to leave once I saw to it she was safely headed inside. Then I could duck out before anyone saw me.

Once Claire saw Sarah, she dropped my hand and took her new best friend's. Off they skipped to the kindergarten wing. She didn't cling, or screech, or turn to wave. Claire didn't shine a spotlight on my inadequacies as a mother. Henry's teacher, Miss Ackart, did.

Holding a stack of books and wearing a sweater covered in apples and chalkboards, she looked around me, dramatically taking note that

my son wasn't there. "Is Henry ill today, Mrs. Martinez?" I felt like
a kid being called on in class for an answer she knew I didn't have.

"He's on a field trip with his aunt, who's visiting." I tried to
sound positive and confident in my decision to let him skip.

She clenched her teeth in a way that told me I'd made a bad
one. "Oh, dear. He really can't afford to be absent. I wish you'd
consulted me beforehand."

"There's a lot going on in our family. I think this is where Henry
needs to be. I'm sure missing a few papers won't be a big deal."

Miss Ackart placed one hand on my elbow, guiding me out of
the main flow of hallway traffic. She lowered her voice. "Actually,
I need to talk to you about Henry. There are some issues we really
need to discuss. I've got to dash now, and I've got another conference this afternoon. Let's meet tomorrow before school. Say eight-
fifteen, in my classroom?"

She left me no room to object, so I nodded my head, trying to
take in what she meant by *issues*. I stood there, once again backed
into a corner. This time, Candy pulled me out.

"Hey, Laurie," she called from the end of the long corridor. "I
could've driven the kids. Why didn't you call me?"

Candy was the second picture of domesticity I'd faced that
morning. Dressed in a stylish pair of jeans, a cable-knit sweater,
and down vest, she was holding a Tupperware container filled
with sprinkly cupcakes. I wasn't imagining my own lack of flair
for fashion. She came right out with it.

"You look terrible. What's wrong?"

"Thanks," I said, my eyes filling with tears. I wasn't getting
emotional in public because my best friend didn't like my outfit.
I was losing it because she'd asked me such a silly question. What
wasn't wrong?

"I'm sorry, that was a lousy thing to say. Let me drop these off
at the bake sale, and then we'll go grab a cup of coffee."

Christian was right, I couldn't juggle anything. My friend's
cupcakes and the mention of the bake sale were the triggers that

reminded me I'd signed up to bring in brownies. I pointed to her container. "I completely forgot."

"You're fine. I called Joanie last week and had her take your name off the list. I knew it was the last thing on your mind right now."

"So you assumed I'd forget?"

"No, I thought—"

"Never mind. Look I've got to go. I need to shower before I go over to see my mother."

I didn't wait for her to finish. I darted in between tall children and small children, all grounded by heavy backpacks and light moods, doing my best to make it to the door without crying.

Back at home, my personal Mary Poppins hadn't put the family room back in tip-top shape as I'd asked her to. Claire's boots were oozing syrup on a carelessly folded mound of paper towels I had to hope was Henry's doing. In the time it took me to drop Claire at school, get chastised by Henry's teacher, be insulted by my best friend, and then drive back home, Luce had had plenty of time to take the tent and all its architecture—along with the toys and plates of food—and make them disappear. Instead, in true Martinez style, she cleared the air before tackling her next adventure by laying out pastry. I must have just missed them. The welcome smell of coffee brewing, accented by a plate covered with a chilled sprig of grapes and a piece of warmed pan dulce placed next to a "sorry" note from Henry, was their collective act of contrition.

Neither Henry's apology for waking me and fighting with his sister nor the cinnamon bread had the power to cheer me. Christian and Candy would forgive me, chalking my separate snits up to my stress level. Luce, Henry, and even Claire already had. The kids were resilient, and Luce never registered an emotion below high spirits. No worries there. Of all the conflict I'd participated in before the clock struck ten, it was Henry's teacher who had me most on edge.

Imagining the next day's meeting, I knew what she'd say.

I'd sit at her round table, perched on a chair that would have my knees in my throat, and she'd cross her hands and give me one of those looks. She'd tell me Henry needed more of me, even though there was less and less of me to go around.

The longer I thought about how inopportune her concerns were with everything else I had to deal with, the more certain I was that I could take care of Henry without her help. I pulled apart my piece of pan dulce and swigged the coffee I'd poured, nearly scorching the roof of my mouth. I'd call the school and leave a message for Miss Ackart, canceling the meeting I didn't have time for. First I needed to check in with my mother's day nurse, to pass along a message that once again I was running late, and to see what kind of night she'd had.

Maeve, my mother's case manager, answered in her chipper voice. She apologized twice for putting me on hold while she paged my mother's nurse, who wasn't answering.

"Jenny's probably in a room with the music going. Mr. Fricka loves it when she plays his German folk tunes. Let me see if I can find her."

I remembered the day I'd tried playing big band music to my mother in an effort to remind her of happier times. Bing Crosby singing Gershwin brought on hiccuping sobs. She scratched me by accident when she pointed toward the CD player's stop button. So much for that bright idea.

"No, don't bother her," I said. "You haven't heard about any change in my mother's condition, have you?"

"No, Laura. No change," Maeve said. "She refused speech this morning, but the physical therapist was able to convince her to go to the gym."

I thanked her for the update, thinking if I hurried, I could get there for the end of her session, to see how she was really doing.

When I walked into the physical therapy department, the mishaps of my morning disappeared in the way I'd wished

Henry's tent had, and I was no longer ready to take my mother to task for skipping her session with speech. A woman in a wheelchair lifted hand weights. An old man lay on a bench doing leg exercises at the command of a boy in his twenties. But the star of the Paxton Rehab physical therapy department, otherwise known as the gym, was my mother.

Wearing her new tracksuit, she was taking halting steps without the assistance of a physical therapist. Her elegant hands clasped tight to the handles, her rounded shoulders hunched over her walker. I covered my mouth to hold back my impulse to shout *congratulations*. When Henry took his first steps, I'd cheered him on so enthusiastically that I made him lose his balance, and his diapered bottom hit the rug. Instead I stood there, watching my mother right herself each time she wobbled. Half the muscles in her face twisted and flinched the same way Claire's had earlier that morning as she fought to lace her boots.

Ten miraculous steps and she was back in her wheelchair. My mother seemed almost as proud of her talent for walking as she had been when she and my father were dancing to Glenn Miller. Though when she saw me, her muscles lost their rigor. Her lovely face, young for her age, was capable of displaying only half her emotions. Still, she was beautiful when she smiled.

"You're walking. That's fantastic."

She cringed and moaned as she picked up one leg at a time and placed each on the wheelchair's footrests. Finally, when she dropped her hands in her lap, her upper arm muscles went slack. I wondered how they'd been able to hold her up in the first place.

"She'll be tired now," the therapist said, her toothy grin declaring my mother's vanishing enthusiasm to be fatigue.

"I think we should celebrate." Really reaching, I was willing to do whatever I could to see my mother's smile return. I didn't care if it was lopsided, crooked, or upside down, it reminded me of life before my father died, when my mother's happy look was a constant in our relationship.

"Do you feel up to going to the staff cafeteria for a cup of tea or something?" I asked.

"Shot," my mother said. "Ort."

"Short? You think you can go for a short time?"

My mother nodded. Even as I wheeled her there, I knew it was probably too much for her. "Let's pick out something sinful and take it back to your room. They won't have anything as good as the panadería, but it's hard to mess up a muffin."

The day had brightened significantly since my morning madness. I was standing tall as I wheeled my mother back onto the unit, past the woman and her baby doll. Through the hallway we strolled and rolled; slow walkers and harried staffers couldn't stand in our way.

Maeve stood up from her post. "There's a team meeting to discuss your mother's progress—it's routine. Can you join us in twenty minutes?" she said.

There was nothing routine about my mother's progress, I wanted to say. She was walking. And it was getting easier to understand her with every day.

Like a kid eager to show off a good report card, I headed down the hall to the conference room to revel in my mother's latest accomplishment.

The physical therapist was there; her fabulous grin was not. Jenny was there, wearing an olive green turtleneck that accentuated her large bust, casting shadows on the rest of the dour faces. My mother's team, the staff responsible for her rehab, looked all around the room. No one looked at me. Except for Maeve.

"Come in." She tapped the back of an empty chair right next to her. "We've started reviewing your mother's—" Maeve paused briefly, searching for a word like my mother would. "Situation," she said. Gone was her welcoming tone. Absent was her can-do attitude. Unlike my mother, she chose that word precisely to set the tone for the rest of the meeting.

Jenny reviewed the meds my mother was taking, crushed pills that still took her an eternity to swallow, though she said it more delicately than that. She reported that my mother's food intake remained inadequate given her need for high calories. Rehab was hard work, she said. I wanted to tell them my mother had just polished off half of a blueberry muffin, but I worried someone would launch into a lecture on empty calories.

The speech therapist was a sour woman with such flat emotions I wondered if she were the right person to treat stroke patients. She dragged the meeting further into hopeless land with her report. "Your mother is still only able to speak in halting one- to four-word phrases. I'm limited in how long I can work with her, because once she decides we're done, we're done. And that's when she actually agrees to a session. But my biggest challenge in working with her is that she's so often confused."

"My mother isn't confused. She's as sharp as a tack."

The speech therapist closed her folder. "The last two times I worked with her, she kept repeating the words *Vietnam, operation, baby,* and *curtains.*"

Maeve didn't move a muscle until the speech therapist finished bringing me down. "We're afraid your mother is approaching a plateau in her recovery." She opened her folder and pulled out two nursing home brochures. "I've made some phone calls to these superb facilities, and each of them would love for you to drop by to take a tour."

In a state of disbelief, I took the expensive foldouts and glanced at them. They must have commissioned a landscape designer like Christian and gone further to hire a first-class photographer and some marketing genius. The trio made these places look like time-shares in Florida, not warehouses where impatient people deposited slow-walking, nontalking women.

"Wait a minute. I disagree with you about her speech. The words might not be there in sentences, but she's very clear about what she wants and needs. I'll bet she's just trying to tell you about my father. He worked in Vietnam. And she used to sew. I'll talk to her about working harder, not skipping sessions."

Maeve pointed to the brochures I'd let drop on the table.

"These facilities have all the same services your mother is receiving here. She will continue to get physical, occupational, and speech therapies."

"Why can't she stay here and continue with the people she already knows? The ones who already know her?"

Maeve repeated her foolish mantra. "We're afraid your mother is approaching a plateau."

"Wait a minute," I interrupted again. "A plateau isn't something you think you're approaching. I don't think you can say she's at one until she stops making progress for a period of time. She took ten steps with her walker today. Tell her," I said to the physical therapist. "It's premature to move her to a nursing home."

"The powers that be don't feel your mother is up to the rigors of our costly—aggressive—program of rehabilitation." Maeve tapped the brochures and avoided eye contact. "I assure you, these facilities are more than adequate to meet her specific needs."

There it was. Savvy Maeve didn't think I would notice her slipping the green into our conversation. "Look, I get it. It's a money thing, right? Who are these powers that be?"

Jenny reached a hand across to me. I shied away from her. Maeve remained unflappable. Nothing rattled her. Hers was a gatekeeper's job. She doled out beds based on a person's ability to be the poster child for one of those showy brochures. And, of course, for the diversity of a resident's stock portfolio. It was easy to guess which category the old woman rocking the baby fit into. Maeve didn't care about my mother, or me.

"Tell the truth. Either she's not getting better fast enough or you don't believe she'll ever make enough progress to warrant one of your expensive beds. Don't pretend there's some man behind the curtain making the decision."

"We see this all the time. As a nurse, I'm sure you realize your mother may very well be at her potential. As a daughter, it must be very difficult."

All of Maeve's earlier pleasantries had been bait to set the trap in case she needed a meeting like this one. The nicer she was, the more she thought I'd like her. She'd pegged me as the pushover I so often was, and when she needed to move my mother along, she expected me to cave under her strength.

"Someone speak up," I said, looking away from Maeve. As soon as I raised my voice, I realized if I lost control, she'd have more leverage. Maeve could pounce on my emotional attachment to my mother, though I could've told her that was undergoing its own kind of rehab. Rational played better with her type. Pleasant yet persistent people got what they wanted.

"She walked today. How is that a plateau?"

I picked up the brochures and calmly placed them back in front of her. I folded my trembling hands and rested them on the table. Throwing my shoulders back, I got up in one smooth motion, leaving my chair midway between the wall and the table.

"My mother is not to be transferred without my consent. I want all of your reports in writing." I looked at each person sitting there trying to seal my mother's fate, taking my time to make eye contact with every single staff member. "Maeve, let me know what I need to do to appeal your decision. Consider this official notice that I have a grievance. I'll be in my mother's room if you need me."

20

Lynch Elementary School without students was a forlorn and shabby place. Colored-paper masterpieces hanging from hall walls were merely gobs of glue and wads of tape without small hands framing their edges, the missing smiles that should be arced above the creations the real artwork. The stillness of the music room was stifling without cymbals crashing and recorders piping. Industrial-strength cleaner coated the floors and lined my nostrils. The chairs in each empty classroom surrendered, legs raised, held hostage by desks.

"Come in. Sorry, I'm running a bit late." Miss Ackart bustled past me, her arms full of books and papers. Since I'd forgotten to cancel the meeting, I was happy to discover that even she could be tardy. I pulled a chair down from a child's desk and was about to sit. She tapped the back of one next to her desk as she tidied the things on a shelf in her closet.

"Right here. The children's chairs are dreadful on the back and knees." Miss Ackart took the chair I'd put on the floor and placed it back up on the desk where it came from. She was the type who lived the saying "a place for everything and everything in its place."

She started in on her concerns even before I was seated. "Henry is stealing." Making no move to conceal her strict timetable, she checked her watch and then pulled her glasses with strings from their case. I wouldn't have minded being the one to hang them about her neck. If I were a teacher I would've at least allotted a couple of minutes to tell a mother what I liked about her child before charging him with a grown-up's crime.

"I found a box of chalk and my scissors in his desk, and Eileen Iverson's sweater in his cubby. When I tried to reprimand him for taking things that didn't belong to him, he had great difficulty regulating his emotions."

I hadn't spoken since I'd left the house, so my words came out all croaky and broken. "I—don't know—why he'd want your things, but we're friends with the Iversons. Eileen probably lost the sweater and Henry found it. Maybe he just forgot to give it back to her." I fiddled with an apple-shaped bowl of paper clips sitting near the edge of her desk.

"He's fixated on this book he refuses to put away. Something to do with sewing. Perhaps he took it from you."

The paper clips escaped from the apple, splaying all over Miss Ackart's desk. She puckered her lips, as if to say, *See what happens when you don't keep your hands to yourself.* Together we gathered them up.

"He got it through your school book club. It was a gift for my mother. He was going to give it to her the day she had the stroke. Henry's really upset about what's happened to her."

"Yes, I realize things are chaotic at home, but I think there's more going on here. You recall the incident a few weeks back? Since then he refuses to do a thing at recess. He won't play with any of the other boys."

"Miss Ackart, it was the day after my mother got sick. And Nicholas said some pretty mean things to Henry about me and my mother. I talked to Henry. He won't do it again."

"I take my responsibility as his teacher seriously, and I'll be honest, his issues appeared long before his family problems. And then there's the lying. Quite frankly, I'm worried."

"Worried about Henry?" The smooth lilt that was Christian's voice filled the doorway. I turned to see him glide through the classroom in a few confident strides. I must have given him a puzzled look. "Luce," he said.

"Mr. Martinez." Miss Ackart stood up, extending her hand. She hadn't bothered to shake mine when we'd met in the hallway. Christian returned the favor as he squeezed behind me, planting his long body against the radiator, pushing aside a fern. A plant Miss Ackart did not put back in its place.

"Sorry I'm late. I hate to have you repeat everything." He looked at me and then Henry's teacher, trying to gauge the seriousness of our discussion.

"Your wife and I were talking about some of the challenges facing your little gem," she said.

Suddenly, with Christian's arrival, Henry was a prized child. Why hadn't I warranted hearing about the crown jewel of her classroom?

"I make it a point to meet routinely with parents, especially once I become aware of disturbances on the home front. It's critical we stay in touch to ensure that Henry gets all the support he needs."

"I'm confused," I said. "A minute ago you made him sound pathological, telling me he's stealing and lying. Now you're concerned about how sad he is over my mother?"

Miss Ackart pulled a used tissue from the sleeve of her sweater and dabbed her nose. She cast a commiserating look in Christian's direction, as if to say, *Poor man, you have to deal with both Henry and his mother.*

"Parents often overreact to those words. I invited you to come in because I feel it's my duty to keep you abreast of his difficulties here. Henry has been asked repeatedly to bring notes home to you. He says he's given them to you, but then I find them at the bottom of his backpack. Two days ago, he told Nicholas that you took him to see a dead man, and yesterday Missy Anderson said he told her that your mother is teaching him to make curtains. It isn't my intention to alarm you. This type of hyperbole is quite common at his age, especially given the stress he's under. I thought you would want to know."

Christian looked at me. He squinted the way he does when he's thinking hard. He didn't know what to say about Miss Ackart's mixed bag of accusations or Henry's exaggerations. It was my fault for bringing Henry in a second time to see my mother before she was transferred to rehab. It seemed like a good idea at the time; it had gone so well the first time. I remembered exactly where he was when my mother's nurse, Molly, drew the bedside curtain before they wheeled the expired patient by, but astute Henry hadn't missed it. I explained things the best I could, and since then he'd stopped asking me about it. I decided bringing it up would do more harm than good. As for the notes, I was to blame for that too; I hadn't been checking his backpack. Weighed down by all I had to do, I'd left that after-school routine to Luce, which had apparently been a mistake. But what child willingly digs deep into the innards of his bag to pull out a note from his crabby teacher?

It was Henry's wishful thinking about my mother teaching him her magic with fabric that I found the saddest of the lot. My sensitive boy was trying with all his might to figure out how to cope with missing his grandmother. I should've been helping him to do it, except that I wasn't much of an expert myself.

"My wife has a lot on her mind," Christian said. "Perhaps you could boil things down to what you need us to do. Confront him about lying? You don't suggest we punish him, do you?"

When Christian put his hand on my shoulder in a gesture of support, I wanted to shake it off. His *my wife has a lot on her mind* remark conveyed that somehow everything *was* my fault. Funny how *I* could think so, but I hated it when he did. What I couldn't believe was that he used words from Miss Ackart's dictionary. Why was he asking her for advice? Couldn't either of them chock it up to Henry feeling lost? No one knew better than I did what it would take to make a ten-year-old feel better. Henry needed his mother in a full and whole way. Yet his need for me and my ability to deliver stood as far apart as Miss Ackart did from compassion.

Even before the office secretary announced the arrival of the buses over the loudspeaker, I decided that, at least for me, the meeting was over. "Why don't you two come up with a list of things you need me to do? I'm going to meet Henry at the bus."

I made it out to the lobby before the hall was streaming with children. A palette of colored coats, in pairs and in clutches, like fish they swam to their respective classrooms. I imagined Christian thanking Miss Ackart for bringing the matter to our attention. I didn't want to give her the satisfaction, but in a small way I was grateful that she'd hit me over the head with my priorities.

"Hi, Mommy," Claire said. Arm in arm with Sarah, she breezed by me, blowing me an air kiss. She'd been the one I thought would have the most trouble with our topsy-turvy life after my mother got sick, yet there she was skipping down the hall as if nothing had changed.

"Hi, honey." I gestured to Henry to come over against the wall. I was tempted to give Nicholas a threatening look, but seeing all four feet of him standing there, I remembered that he was a child too. I smoothed down Henry's cowlick and wiped the dot of jelly near his mouth. When he jerked his head from me, I realized I probably shouldn't have done that right there in the hallway where kids like Nicholas could see. It threw me off my game. "Miss Ackart wants you to focus on catching up on what you missed yesterday when you went to Boston."

"She doesn't like me," he said. "I wish I could stay home with you and Auntie Luce." He jerked one shoulder up to keep his backpack in place while he slipped a warm hand in mine. He probably thought his touch could sway me.

"Of course she likes you. You need to be in school, and you need to pay attention. I promise we'll spend some time together after school. Maybe we can walk the beach."

"Anaskaket? Can we go to Sea Escape?" His hand squeezed mine, and a smile replaced his long face.

"We'll see. Right now, you get to class." I bent down to his level, wanting to tell him how much I loved him and that everything was going to be fine.

"Do what Miss Ackart asks you to do, okay? Pay attention." I didn't get to finish sending him off in style. Christian rounded the corner and took over for me.

"Hey, pal, have a great day." He readjusted Henry's backpack to position it squarely on his shoulders, making it easier for him to carry the load. He kissed the top of his head without reservation. "Love you, Henry."

Our son headed toward his classroom. As he got closer to the double doors, he turned and waved. He disappeared when Christian stepped into my line of vision.

"Laura, we need to talk."

21

❧⊰❦⊱

I drove behind Christian to his office after he insisted we debrief the school meeting. What else had Miss Ackart told him after I'd left her classroom? His usual way of navigating our family ship was to be gentle. But I could tell from his expression that he had lots to say. So did I. We couldn't go home, Luce was there, and it was too cold to sit in the parking lot at Lynch.

Coastal Landscapes derived its name as much from its location as from the services Christian offered. I never minded going there. It was a soothing space. The main office walls were lined with a series of remarkable sketches. The focal point, and the largest of the collection, was a garden designed years ago, when I was pregnant with Henry, for an all-too-familiar home in Anaskaket. Wands of beach peas, sweet pepper bush, and Ruby Lace oleander meandered the shoreline, lending the home called Sea Escape all the color it needed, its weathered clapboards providing the contrast. Though my mother wouldn't allow a single lamp to be replaced or couch to be reupholstered inside her fortress, the grounds around Sea Escape were, to her, a blank canvas. She said she'd always dreamed of having a garden, and while Christian sketched and shared his drawings with her, she was connected. For a brief time, because of passionflower and honey locust, she lived looking to the future. The only other time I'd seen her that way was with Henry, right before her stroke. Apparently thanks to a secret, yet regular, dose of Paxil.

"Should I make coffee?" I asked, reaching out to take his coat, hanging his and mine together on the antique coatrack by the door.

He closed his eyes and shook his head as if he were annoyed with me for being nice. I walked away from him, heading into his private space, where I took a seat on the couch that faced his work area. I'd helped him pick it out when we first met. His business was blossoming, and he needed a comfortable area for client meetings. We both fell in love with the fabric, fanlike plumes of fountain grass and foxtail. It complimented his vista, a view of the jetty that divided the Atlantic Ocean from Magnolia Harbor, a beach that went on for miles. I searched it then. Not a single soul braved the March wind.

His drafting table was angled in a way that afforded him the best possible seascape inspiration for his famous coastal designs. Early work was always done from there. Before we married, I'd curl up on the couch with a book on weekends. Furtively I'd watch him as he sketched drawing after drawing on that huge paper, extra rolls of it standing at attention in the corner near the closet. Christian prided himself on being able to offer his clients hand-drawn sketches, showcasing that he was, first and foremost, an artist. Only after several rounds of fine-tuning would he turn to the computer-simulated programs. From multiple points of view, he would unveil the realistic images that completed his vision. Christian's clients knew they were lucky, getting the best of both sides of my talented husband—creative genius and consummate businessman. The final plans, once clients were raving, would be turned over to the landscape contractors he recommended, teams of people who would make his imaginary landscapes into real live gardens.

He followed me into his space, and in one twirl he spun his chair around and mounted it. His cross look made me suddenly feel like I was back in Miss Ackart's classroom and not in the safe place I would come to take a break from the never-ending weekends I'd experienced when I still lived at home with my mother.

"I can't believe what a big deal she's making," I said. "You'd think a teacher would be patient with a sensitive boy. Back when Henry was put in her class, Candy told me we were in for a tough year. I should've pushed to get him moved into the other fifth grade."

Christian's arms were folded over the back of his chair. He didn't move a muscle, he didn't take my side.

"I'm sure Henry will be fine. It's you I'm worried about."

I picked up a couch pillow and clutched it to my chest, squeezing it. I braced myself for the barrage of failings I expected him to unload on me.

"Last night you went on and on about the staff at rehab trying to ship your mother off to a nursing home and how you had to get the house ready. Did you forget to tell me Henry's in trouble at school, or did you think it was unimportant?" He ran his fingers through his silky black hair, something Henry did when he was frustrated too.

"I know you're under a lot of stress, but I don't know why you make things harder. Your mother going back to Sea Escape is a complete mistake."

"This isn't your decision to make. I can make her happy by moving her back there. So it's going to be a little hard. It's the right thing to do."

"You're trying to fix things with her, but this isn't how to do it. At least you could accept the help that's offered to you."

"What, your kind of help? Advice, that's all you ever offer. I can't even let off some steam. You haven't changed one thing about your work schedule to help with the kids since she got sick. Don't go telling me I have Luce, because you're not there to pick cookie dough out of Claire's hair or force Henry to try another bite of her quirky meals."

"My sister put her life on hold for you. I don't see your brother making any of his grand entrances. Maybe you could give Luce a little more direction."

"On hold for me? Or us? You act like taking care of the kids and running the house are my jobs." I kept the conversation on Luce because I wasn't up to thinking about Holden. I hadn't figured out yet why my brother didn't care enough about his mother, or me, to visit, whether I wanted him to or not.

"No, working in the nursery at Memorial is your job. You're the one who doesn't seem to think it's a priority. But someone has to bring home a paycheck. I don't know many fathers as involved as I am, and this is the thanks I get."

"How can you say in one breath that you're worried about me and then in the next bring up work again? You act like I can plot this whole thing out like a garden. Maybe I don't know how to make everything perfect. Maybe I can't make a plan and then hand it off to someone else to do the work. For God's sake, what do you want from me?"

I got up and threw the pillow back on the couch. I walked toward the reception area to grab my coat.

"Where are you going?" he asked.

"I don't know, let's see. I could call in for a shift, pick out a nursing home, or go sit with my mother, who can't or won't talk to me. Then after I square all that away, I can go home to make sure Henry didn't steal anything or lie to his teacher, and then give your sister a list of messes she can clean up. I'm sure I've forgotten something, but *no worries,* someone from the Martinez family will figure it out for me." I kept walking while I lit into him. I pulled my parka from the coatrack with such a jerk, the thing lost its footing. Christian was there to catch it. I didn't bother to try.

He didn't say anything. I don't think he knew what to make of my outburst, and frankly he wasn't the only one. I left him standing in the middle of Coastal Landscapes. On the way to my car, I flipped open my phone and dialed my nursing supervisor. Getting her voice mail, I left a message, telling her I could take the next available shift in the nursery, as early as that night if she needed me. I pulled open the driver's-side door and threw my bag on the seat. Shoving my phone in my parka pocket in case she called me back, I covered my head with my hood and zipped my coat all the way up.

Once, other people—my father, my mother, and Christian—had the power to center me. Walking toward the jetty, I tried not to remember when it was I'd turned to holding on to strangers' newborn babies or walking nearby coastlines for strength. Unlike the ornamental grass that lined the path to the beach, planted near the seashore because of its ability to bend to the constancy of the wind, I felt as if I were about to break.

22

April 1975

Helen placed the empty bobbin that supplied the bottom thread on the winding spindle. She couldn't remember a time when her machine held a black spool. Cornflower blue, goldenrod, and orchid comprised her usual color palette. And though she would occasionally whip up a pantsuit or an autumn cape, she wasn't much interested in cutting patterns for clothing, unless she was making something for Laura. The last garment she'd worked on was months ago, a simple jersey to overlay a pair of store-bought trousers. Marking pleats or stitching darts or inserting zippers provided very little fascination for her. Sewing curtains brought Helen her greatest artistic pleasure.

She liked the new term *window treatments*. Two simple words proclaiming her hobby esteemed. When Holden and Laura were young and money scarce, her curtains were café, tier, and sash. In those days, Helen longed for draperies, festoon and jabot. She told herself those would come later, after Joseph was promoted a time or two and she had more time and cash to dedicate to her craft. And they had.

Now all of Sea Escape's rooms had been transformed into the home away from home she'd hoped would beckon Joseph back from Vietnam for good. The very last room she'd decorated a true testament to her love for him. When Helen's overt gestures didn't do so, and the fall of Da Nang forecast the fall of the rest of the country, she finally came out with it. In a request she'd never made out loud, or by pen on perfumed stationery, not so much as once before, she told Joseph to choose his life at Sea Escape over the one he'd created in Saigon. *Take what you love and bring it here,* she'd written. Helen felt that their peculiar arrangement had reached its conclusion. It was time to be a real family. One that lived together, on the same sand, in the same village, in the same country.

Helen felt detached from her hands, as if they belonged to someone else. She remained awash in disbelief as she pressed the foot pedal, setting the synchronization of her machine's parts in motion. Up and down, in and out, it performed its task and the line of its skirt, chosen to resemble that of her wedding dress, took shape. No matter how hard she tried to concentrate on the garment, she couldn't stop replaying the scene of a week ago, when Joseph's AP colleague Dick Burbank stood in their living room and told her the unfathomable news.

In that moment, and for four whole days afterward, Helen refused to believe that Joseph died when that plane's back door exploded open, expelling more than one hundred and eighty of the three hundred passengers from its cargo hold, sprinkling them on rice paddies not two miles out of the Tan Son Nhut airport. Staff. Volunteers. And children. Helen covered her ears and turned her face to the sea, which was her favorite room's tour de force, praying Mr. Burbank would go away.

Still refusing to accept it, Helen placed a desperate call to her mother, making it clear Father was not to set foot on her property.

She could not handle him amid this news. And she wouldn't say a word to Laura or Holden about this malicious rumor told to her by Joseph's so-called friend. Mr. Burbank, who came with no proof, just a story. These men and their stories.

Laura was ensconced at Candy's house, Helen having finally been successful at encouraging her shy girl to go there directly from school. Holden, not in college and without a job, was wherever Holden went. Maggie was the only person Helen wanted to see or speak to after Mr. Burbank left her standing in the living room by herself. The new aloneness she experienced so very different from the kind she'd grown accustomed to. Helen's day-to-day missing of Joseph did not begin to compare to the things she felt as she tried to lose herself out that picture window. Without realizing it, she'd gone and grown content living at Sea Escape, raising her two children alone. Holden and Laura were enough.

Within hours, her mother arrived. Her father did not. For days, Maggie attended to all the things grief bequeathed. The arrival of food and flowers. The telling and retelling of the horrid details of the tragedy whenever someone new came to pay respects. Not all of the unbelievable particulars of her husband's circumstances were allowed to be shared, per Helen's strict orders. Given Holden's age, it was no longer easy to keep him in the dark; there were things he was privy to. But she'd made him promise to let Laura remember her father fondly; certain things should be kept from lodging in one's mind.

The first tangible thing Helen's mother gave her, besides the hourly hugs that nearly crushed her already broken heart, was Joseph's last letter. It came two days after the news did, four days before the remains did; both arrivals confirming Burbank's claim.

Maggie found Helen sitting on the lone patio chair Holden left on the deck so he'd have a place to smoke the cigarettes Helen banned from the house. As the sun retired, casting yew-shaped shadows on the path leading down to the beach, Helen sat oblivious to both the spring air and the goings-on inside her home.

"Do you want to read it now, dearie, or do you want to wait?"

Maggie wrapped a shawl about her daughter's shoulders and smoothed her windblown hair from her face. With all the energy of a wounded bird, Helen gestured for her mother to read it. She closed her eyes and listened, replacing her mother's voice with Joseph's. She prayed the clarity of his sound, the cadence of his words, wouldn't slip away from her as over the years he had.

March 30, 1975
My dearest Helen,

For years I've struggled with leaving, and just as it became near impossible to get out, I read words from you that changed everything. All my confusion and uncertainty vanished when you came straight out with it, and it meant the world to me.

I read your letter in church, and as I prayed God would show me the way home to you, Sister Maria Loreto pulled up a pew and told me about Operation Babylift. She asked me if I would help her get some of the hundreds of babies and children out of the country. World Airways has agreed to provide the planes, and all kinds of supplies have been donated. There'll be one adult for every ten children; some of the little ones are real sick. I didn't have to think twice. What a way to come back to you, Helen. I knew you'd approve. It's a sign, it is. You put your foot down, insisting it's time for us to be a true and whole family, and while I'm thinking of a way to honor your request, God taps me on the shoulder. I'll be saving these children for you.

When I get home—and it will be for good—I'll give you a very happy life. I thank God that you've forgiven me for all I've put you through.

Remember this: there is no obstacle great enough to keep us apart. I promise you, there won't be any more good-byes. Hold on, my darling, I'm coming home.
All my love always,
Joseph

So there Helen sat at her sewing machine because her husband had done as she'd requested. Her wish had been fulfilled. Joseph home. Forever. She didn't curse as she pulled the fixed patterns from her cutting table, or weep as she loaded her machine with thread for the dress she needed to make—the one she'd had a hand in preordaining. For as sure as this dress would be black, she knew it would be sewn to perfection. She decided right then and there that she would stay up all night sewing her widow's garb, and that it would be the last thing she would ever let her hands create. Her sewing had always been about hope. She'd pinned her dreams to a home of their own, babies of their blood, and a family connected by faith and fidelity, a marriage unlike her parents' in every way. And look how things turned out. Her sewing began with some ordinary cloth and a sewing machine as she embarked on a lifetime of waiting for her perfect life to materialize. Funeral attire would mark the end of it.

As Helen finished rerunning the story of Joseph's exodus from Vietnam through her mind, she closed the final seam. It was then that she saw Laura lying across the threshold of her sewing room, lulled to sleep no doubt by the hum of her machine. She tidied the room, knowing it would be the last time she would spend her days and nights there. Rolls of fabric were returned to the closet, notions put back in their boxes, the cutting table swept of its remnants. She pressed her dress with a warm iron, then slipped it on a cloth-covered hanger. Carrying the garment toward the door, she hung it on the rack stationed in the corner. Helen stepped over Laura's curled-up body. She could not bring herself to pay particular attention to the little girl. Once in the hallway, second thoughts made her stop. She turned back to the sewing room when she realized she would need something to cover her head in church. Helen would complete the thing with a veil.

23

Tears threatened to expose my fragile state. Taking report on the eight babies I would care for on the evening shift, I fought to hold the tears off when first a seasoned nurse barbed me with sarcasm for leaving them short-staffed for a month and then a new mother demanded I stop wasting time sitting in the nurses' station drinking coffee and go get her baby from the nursery. The reason my shift got off to a rocky start had nothing to do with the fact that I hadn't worked in a while and my nursing skills were rusty or that my ability to handle stress was deteriorating further still. It was because I took the shift to get Christian off my back and in doing so I broke my promise to Henry.

He'd been reenergized in the hallway of Lynch Elementary when I'd said we'd go to the beach after school. Instead, I'd walked the freezing shoreline outside Christian's office alone, and when my cell phone startled me, a bird chirping close to my ear, I accepted my nursing supervisor's offer to work without a second thought. It wasn't until I merged onto 93 North that I realized I'd once again let Henry down. I even felt bad that Luce would be the one to see his disappointment when he learned there would be no walk on Magnolia beach or on the stretch of shore that lay outside Sea Escape. His disorganized, promise-breaking mother had gone to work.

Thank goodness for Baby Girl Binh. I was grateful for her company though not for the jaundice that kept her in the nursery while the rest of my charges in ordinary bassinets were wheeled up and down the corridor to spend the evening with their moms and dads. This tiny girl, born at thirty-seven weeks, was in more danger than most. Her risk factors, an incompatibility with her mother's blood plus her skin the color of dandelions, put her under the bili lights and in an incubator. She would be my companion, and not her mother's, for the full shift. I tried to reassure the baby's mother through a thick-walled language barrier. I used simple words to tell her the best I could that her child would be fine in a matter of hours. I wondered if mine would be, as I pierced the tiny foot of the girl I whispered my hush-hush name to, through the holes in the Plexiglas crib. *Lien.*

Lien required periodic blood tests, done so efficiently by me that my little friend did nothing more than turn toward the source of the irritation. Like a movie star settling in for an overdue nap, Lien wore the protective eye pads that kept the light from damaging her delicate retinas. The only other thing her miniature body wore was a security sensor strapped to her ankle like a fashion statement. She shook her foot for freedom from the thing aimed at keeping her connected to her mother. It was a requirement every baby wore to guard against being separated from her family. An alarm meant to alert staff if any baby wearing one was removed from the unit. Though the postpartum nursery could proudly say no baby had ever been taken, who wouldn't be tempted to claim a baby as lovely as Lien for their treasure? She tried to escape my grasp as I held on to her heel in an effort to collect blood for a sample, a semi-regular progress report of her body's ability to accept light and destroy bad blood.

Never before had I cared for a Vietnamese baby girl. Our unit certainly boasted the demographic, but I could only recall bringing one boy to his mother. I'd been saving her name for as long as I'd been christening babies. It reminded me of my father and a story I cherished still. Lien and the lotus flower.

On a walk I remember in vivid detail—one not embellished by anyone else—his big hand in mine, we made our way down Anaskaket Beach. My father was home for Holden's graduation from high school. By then I must have been eight, and on walks with my mother I was allowed to run free to skip stones or collect shells. On that walk, I didn't dare let go of my father, and I couldn't stop looking at his windblown hair and reassuring smile for fear he would disappear as suddenly as he'd arrived. I remember thinking he was very good at coming and going. What hadn't changed about him was that once again he held me captive with a fairy tale, my father, who told stories for a living. I longed to hear his new one of a faraway girl, small with dark hair and big eyes like mine.

"Lien lived in Vietnam, the country I live in when I'm not here," my father said. He slowed his pace so my short legs could keep up with his long ones. I was glad he wasn't good at walking with children. That meant he saved his walks for me.

"She lived along the River of Perfumes. It was a beautiful, peaceful place with flowers of every color, everywhere she looked. Lien was a good girl; she always did what her mother and father told her to do."

We both glanced back at my mother sitting on the seawall. In a lime green paisley shirt and matching pedal pushers, she readjusted her kerchief to keep the wind from ruining her hairdo, the one she'd made a big deal about getting before my father came home. Before I turned back to where we were going instead of where we had been, she became wistful. I wondered if she was mad at me. Even at eight, I felt guilty for taking him away from her, when all she ever seemed to want was for him to be home, paying attention to her.

"One day her father told Lien that they would have to leave

their beloved home, and that she must be brave whenever the time came," my father went on. "Lien was sad so she went down to the river to take one last look at the place. Worried she would forget the beauty of her home, she plucked a lotus seed from a bloom more beautiful than even Lien's mother, and as she did, a stork flying overhead dropped a plume at her feet. She tucked these remembrances into her pocket and went home. In the middle of the night, her father woke her and said they must leave the house quickly and quietly. With her mother's hand in hers, Lien obeyed. Her father told her to hurry; she didn't have time to gather her silk robe or pearl combs."

"She still had the seed and the feather, right, Daddy?"

I was rewarded with a bigger smile. My father rubbed the top of my head, a gesture that told me he thought I was smart. He didn't think Holden was very smart for deciding not to go to college.

"Yes, Laura, she kept them close wherever she and her mother went. She held them especially tight when they traveled in the dark of night, for Lien was very scared."

"Didn't her daddy come?"

"He tried to follow them, but they weren't the only ones fleeing to safety, and they became separated. Lien and her mother were taken in by relatives in a neighboring village. She treasured the seed and the plume until one day, long after they'd left their home, her mother found them. In her anger and sadness, she told Lien they were foolish keepsakes of a place they could never return to, reminders of people they would never see again. She threw them into the nearby marsh. Lien wept as she watched the seed sink and the plume float away. Months went by, and still mourning the loss of her keepsakes, Lien walked down to the marsh. She longed for the things that reminded her of her father, her home, and her friends. Rounding the corner, she saw a giant lotus flower with its thick stem emerging from the muck. It was strikingly simple with pointed petals, graceful and perfect in its beauty. Like you, Laura."

"I'm not a flower, Daddy," I said with a giggle.

"You are to me, my little lotus flower."

"So did she show her mother? Did her daddy come home?"

"Lien begged her mother to come see the miracle flower. When her mother saw it growing clean and pure in the mud, she bowed before it. And as she did, Lien's father came walking toward them. He said, 'Love gives life. Only love can mend the heart.'"

"And they lived happily ever after, right? I love that story. Do we have lotus flowers in Anaskaket?" I asked.

"No, but if you're a good girl, I might bring you one from Vietnam the next time I come home." I must have pasted on a worried expression, because he playfully hoisted me over his shoulder. "But I'm not going away for a while. I'm staying right here with you. Have you been eating all those shells and rocks you've been collecting? I can hardly lift you." I giggled again as he made a show of how hard it was to hold me. I squirmed until he placed me back down on the packed sand.

When my father told me he was staying, I believed him. And only then did I feel I could let go of his hand. I'd been dying to pick up the scallop shells I'd walked past the entire time he told me his story.

My father's image vanished when the baby I called Lien cried, pulling me back to the present. At thirty-six hours old, she had the strength to make enough noise to let me know she needed to get back to her mother.

I caressed her fuzzy black hair and whispered, "Thank you." It took a newborn baby to tell me it was time for me to speak up too.

24

More tired than a person should be, I bypassed the kitchen when I got in last night because I didn't have the energy to leaf through the mail or check to see if anyone ran the dishwasher. I flicked off the light left on for me and made my way upstairs in the dark. After peeking into Henry's room, then Claire's, with heavy breathing all around, I closed their doors and went on to complete the rest of my bedtime ritual. Within minutes I slipped into bed. Christian mumbled a sleepy "I'm sorry," spooned me, and in seconds his own breathing became deep and regular.

Up before everyone else, pumped to take charge of my life, I saw it. Like a sign, the single fragrant lily stood erect in a bud vase. It took center stage on the clean counter in the kitchen. It was the closest thing to a lotus flower this side of Asia, and absolutely uncanny that Christian would choose this particular blossom for his apology.

As I admired the flower, the sound of music came down the back stairs. I thought I'd have more time to rehearse the lines I wanted to deliver, first to Christian and then to Luce. Henry and Claire marched into the kitchen dressed and ready for school in clean jeans and sweaters, their singsong voices making me smile. Each in a good mood, I was relieved that Henry wasn't mad at me for skipping out on our beach walk. A walk I was determined we would take after school today. Luce's suitcase bumped down step after step, while Christian's boots added in the bass. Strong as he was, he struggled to carry her trunk of treasures.

"Kids, remember you can choose your own cereal, but leave the milk to me," Christian said. "Mom doesn't need any messes to clean up this morning. Luce, drop your bag right there. I'll load everything in the truck." He leaned her trunk on the back of the couch and jerked his head sideways, telling me to come closer.

"It was her idea," he whispered. "I didn't say a word. I'll drive her to the airport and then we'll talk. You're right, I should be helping more. And I will the minute I get back. I took the day off."

"You don't need to. I know exactly what has to be done now." I kissed him. "Thanks for the lily, it's beautiful. Where did you find one out of season?"

"I wanted to get you something special. You're not still angry?"

"No. I know I should apologize for yelling at you, but to tell you the truth, it felt good."

"Maybe you should do it more often. You look even prettier than usual this morning. It's all that fire in your cheeks. You might be more Martinez than you think." Anchoring Luce's treasure chest with one hand, with the other he touched my hair. His caress was so welcome I leaned my head into it. I got self-conscious when I realized that I'd pulled back the piece of hair that always hangs in my eyes with one of Claire's pink plastic barrettes. Hardly alluring.

"You're beautiful, cariño."

Christian, once again tuned in to me, knew exactly what I was thinking.

"I need milk," Claire shouted from the kitchen.

Christian playfully rolled his eyes. "I guess we won't have to worry about her holding her feelings in, yes?"

"I'll do it," I said, returning his smile. "I need to talk to Luce anyway."

The rest of breakfast went off without a hitch. Christian volunteered to walk the kids to the bus stop. After wiping tears and reassuring them that Auntie Luce would be back in no time, I waved them off and closed the back door.

In the kitchen, Luce was unloading the dishwasher. Once again overdressed for the occasion, she could have been in a high school musical the way her skirt sashayed while she completed the ordinary chore.

"How did you know I was going to ask you to leave?" I asked, as I poured two cups of coffee and brought them to the counter.

Luce joined me there. "It was time. You are stronger and no longer need my help. Please know I am willing to come back any time you need me, my sister. That's what families do." Luce didn't sit down, she just stopped moving. Something she rarely did.

"Excuse me, I'll be right back," she said.

Without putting a coat on over her sheer blouse, Luce went out to Christian's truck. I leaned my stool back so I could look out the window, wondering with mixed feelings if she could be changing her mind.

She came back into the kitchen, rubbing her arms up and down. "My goodness, the temperature has dropped again. Will spring ever come?" she asked.

I didn't remind her this was New England and only the middle of March. She walked straight for me, and as she neared me everything about her frenetic pace slowed. Her hands, strong and as beautiful as her brother's, reached for my head. She unsnapped the childish barrette in my hair, laying it down on the counter.

From her pocket she pulled an oval mother-of-pearl hair clip. She gently gathered enough of my hair to fill it and clasped it shut.

"You know I call your mother Nácar. Mother-of-pearl." Luce pulled me into an embrace. "You are the pearl, Laura," she whispered. She kissed one cheek and then the other. "Now enjoy some peace and quiet. I'm off to New York and back to the panadería where I belong."

Luce and Christian weren't gone ten minutes when I got up the nerve to call my brother. Holden and I hadn't spoken since I'd called to tell him our mother had been moved to the rehab center. He hadn't phoned me once since she got sick, and I didn't expect he would.

I told his receptionist it was an emergency. I knew if I asked her to give Holden a message, I'd be waiting until Magnolia Harbor froze over for him to call me back. Even using the word *emergency* didn't guarantee he'd pick up when I was the caller. There was no point in trying him at either of his homes. He rarely went to one, and I didn't have the phone number for the other. He kept a town house in downtown Chicago, where he stayed on weeknights. And if I called him at home in Winnetka, I'd probably get stuck listening to Edwina make excuses for him. I assumed that Holden's wife—like my mother and I—remained an afterthought to him. I bet he didn't spend any time with her either.

When he answered, he didn't even say hello. "Is she—?"

"Mother's fine," I said. "The rehab center wants to transfer her to a nursing home. I need you to help me insist she stay there until she's well enough to come home."

"Home. Are you insane? You can't deal with her in your house, not unless she's a hell of a lot better than when I saw her. They're the experts. If they think she needs to go to a nursing home, what do you want me to do about it?"

Leave it to Holden to forget I was a nurse. For the courage to be bold, I leaned in to the lily and took a long whiff of its perfume. "You haven't seen her in over a month. She's better, only not quite ready to go back to Sea Escape."

"Now I know you're crazy. She can't go back there. Look, I'm prepping a big case for trial in two weeks. I don't have time to entertain your outlandish daydream." Holden sighed at me, and I knew he was rolling his eyes. Eyes that didn't know whether they were blue, or green, or brown; they were fickle. It was his mood that was consistent.

"You're so naïve," he said. "I can't come there and hold your hand every time something goes wrong."

"They're pushing her out because of money. I want her to stay there on her insurance until she can take better care of herself. All you have to do is come here and fight the transfer."

"This is a ridiculous waste of time."

"There's money. I found a bankbook. A nursing home will eat up thousands of dollars a month, and we might not see a penny from the house."

"Well, well, maybe you aren't as self-sacrificing as you lead everyone to believe. It would be a shame to see Helen lose that museum to the bank. Let me put some things in order. I'll call you with my flight number."

"You'll have to take a cab or rent a car, I've got a lot to do. I'll leave the side door open. You can stay in the room over the garage. Unless you want to stay at Mother's."

"I thought Christian's nutcase of a sister was staying with you."

I ran my hand over the hair clip she'd given me. "Luce was a wonderful help, but she left this morning to go back to work."

"She serves fancy doughnuts in a bakery, that's hardly what I'd call a job. How the hell that family makes a living is beyond me. Speaking of money, leave it to sly Helen, hiding some. How much are we talking about?"

I pulled the bankbook from the drawer by the phone where we kept our bills. As I took it from its plastic protector, the key I'd found along with it fell out, making a clatter as it hit the counter. I stopped the racket with my hand, then opened the passbook and looked at the figure, a number that must have grown substantially since that first deposit had been made. "I'll give you the details when you get here," I said. "I have to go see Mother."

Without waiting for a response, I slipped the key into my pocket and hung up on my brother.

25

August 1982

Helen sat in her wing chair, mesmerized by the sun inching toward the horizon, the letter she'd chosen to read today resting in her lap. Back when Holden lived at home, he'd christened her favorite vantage point for watching morning come and daylight go her "control station." According to him, it was the place from which she was forever telling him what to do, while she did nothing but read letters and gaze at the beach. She didn't suppose he knew or cared that she'd overheard his sarcastic refrain, the one he cavalierly offered to his friends or his sister, always behind her back. Helen didn't know how many more summer sunsets there would be, but she knew she should stop hoping Holden would come home, if only for a weekend, to see one. Strangled by the rigors of law school was his usual excuse, yet this was the first summer he hadn't bothered to offer her one.

The hazy day gave way to a red sunset. Called the sailor's

delight, it predicted that tomorrow was likely to be fair weather. As beautiful as this evening was, Helen was simply eager for the day to come to a close. This date on the calendar, no matter the weather, was gloomy every year. She'd never stopped missing her baby dear.

Like a bright searchlight, a sun pillar rose from the wavy water. Vertical and horizontal beams of light formed a cross in the evening sky and reflected back on the sea. Only a handful of people littered the beach. One couple hand in hand reminded her of her younger self walking the beach with Joseph. She hoped the lovers knew how lucky they were to be on the same sand. Seagulls beckoned fellow seagulls, heralding the places where abandoned food lay waiting to be claimed. One young mother held a beach towel on her lap as she waited for her daughter—a dancing shadow—to finish playing in the surf. Something Helen had done countless times for Laura.

Three loud knocks and the squeal of the porch door with its see-through fly screen announced Candy's arrival. Equal parts grateful she didn't have to get up and annoyed the girl never hesitated to march right in, Helen wondered if Candy's parents had ever taught her to wait for someone to answer the door before barging inside.

"Hey, Mrs. Tobin. Is Laurie upstairs?" She was halfway up the winding staircase by the time Helen cobbled together an answer.

"I believe so. I haven't seen much of her since the two of you got back from Boston." She kept her eyes on Joseph's words; like a hypnotist, he lulled her, slowing the rhythm of her heart.

October 20, 1960

My dearest Helen,

It's been two months since we lost him. Every day I wonder what he looked like. Would I have seen myself in him? I sure wish you'd talk to me about our son. I guess I should've thanked you for insisting they release his body to us so we could have a Christian burial for Joseph Jr. I did find it a comfort to visit him at the cemetery while I was home, though it was disturbing to see his name—my name—on stone.

Helen hadn't gone with Joseph that day. Even now, all these years later, she couldn't bring herself to visit the gravesite. Headstones listing names, scorched grass sprinkled with dying roses, the cemetery did not soothe. Retreating into letters did. Remembering a face did.

Lost as she was in her daydreams, it took several seconds for Helen to register Candy's repetitive screams to *come quick.* Her joints ached as she made her way up the stairs and down the hall. By the time Helen reached Laura's bedroom, both girls were quiet. The amount of blood in Laura's bed accentuated the lack of color in her face and the receding white of the bath-size towels Candy was shoving between her daughter's legs. Laura lay there without moving; she said nothing. It was as if, even with her eyes open, she wasn't really in the room.

"Hold these, come on." Candy was yelling at Helen again, imploring her to do something while she dug beneath piles of magazines scattered on the bedside table, trying to locate Laura's Princess telephone.

The next person Candy shouted at was the 911 operator. "Hurry up, she's bleeding real bad—down there—no, it's not her period—yeah, pregnant." While answering questions Helen couldn't hear being asked, Candy, with the phone lodged between her ear and shoulder, kept putting pressure on the towels. Helen stood there. Her daughter's best friend directed a sorry expression in her direction, as if to say how awful she felt that this was the way Helen should learn the news.

Yet Helen knew her daughter was no longer pregnant. The amount of blood streaking across Laura's rumpled bedclothes told her that. Though she and her daughter had become distant over Laura's summer vacation, a period of three months during which she'd apparently committed at least one mortal sin, Helen was no stranger to miscarriage.

She showed no surprise. She wasn't angry or afraid. Those emotions were deep, overpowering, beyond her normal range. Helen was confused. Looking at Laura lying there with beads of sweat on her forehead, her breathing shallow, her body still, Helen didn't see her daughter. She saw herself. The paleness of the face, the vacant eyes, the wavy hair untamed. Helen's cloudy thinking had her standing outside herself, watching as she miscarried her children. First Paul. Then her nameless child. And finally her dear boy. Twenty-two years ago today, she'd been in the exact same position as her daughter. Curled into a ball, losing her Joey. Standing there, it occurred to Helen, though only briefly, that, thanks to Laura, she had moved on to losing grandchildren.

Candy's shrill shouting hadn't snapped Helen out of her trance. The piercing wail of the ambulance that arrived to whisk her daughter to safety didn't do it either. The truth took longer to seep into Helen's consciousness than the time it took for life to ooze from Laura's body. When reality hit, Helen was sitting in the family waiting room of Boston Memorial Hospital, bombarded with noise. On her right was a family prone to fits of laughter. As if this were a place where humor was welcome. They gabbed as they drank cup after cup of bitter coffee, leaving their refuse all over the tables and on the floor. Raining down from the television that was bolted to the ceiling came the canned chuckles of an out-of-view sitcom audience. And to her left, Helen was inundated with incessant chatter from the girl who quite possibly saved her daughter's life. She wanted to order the girl with dried blood all over her dungaree shorts and peasant top to shush, but she didn't. Helen had no right to ask anything of Candy, since she hadn't had the wherewithal to do one single thing to stop another of her children from being taken from her. Her clothes were perfectly clean.

Laura was being treated in the emergency room by the resident on call, a Dr. Michael Sterling. The fact that it was taking so long to hear news of Laura's condition was not a good sign. The one glimpse Helen had of the doctor told her he was far too young and alarmingly attractive to be attending to the female problems of any teenage patient, never mind her daughter. He couldn't possibly have enough experience. It was then that Helen realized he wasn't the first inexperienced male—with or without her consent—to explore her daughter's body.

Helen stood and walked away from Candy. She knew the girl would follow. She'd been rambling on and on about whether or not to call her parents. She wondered if Helen thought they'd be mad at her for driving behind the ambulance in Helen's car. She wasn't allowed to drive via the highway without express permission.

"Where are you going, Mrs. Tobin? They told us to stay put. You're not supposed to go in there." She jumped up and tagged along until Helen stopped mid-hallway, outside Laura's door. Helen wanted to lash out at this girl with the odd sense of timing, choosing now to concern herself with rules of propriety.

"What's his name?" Helen lowered her voice and folded her arms across her chest. "I was unaware Laura had a boyfriend." She knew it couldn't be the Iverson boy. Whenever Pete tagged along with the girls, he was nothing but milquetoast staring at Candy.

Candy rolled and rerolled the bottom of her shirt, hiding then revealing the stains. "I promised Laurie I wouldn't tell you." She let the shirt be, dropping her arms at her sides. "I can't."

In an attic apartment on Proctor Street, Helen understood girlfriends and secrets about babies. But that was when she was one of the girls, and even at that she'd confided in her mother. "Where Laura is concerned, I have a right to know. I'm her mother, and she could be dying." Though her words came out clear enough, it was as if someone else were speaking them. They had the emotional weight of clouds or fog.

Dr. Sterling exited Laura's room before Candy could be persuaded to betray her friend's confidence.

"Good news," he said. "Your daughter will be fine. She's a bit groggy from a sedative I gave her, but you can go in now. Family only," he said, putting his arm out to stop Candy from entering the room.

"Why did she lose the child?" Helen asked. Even all these years and three miscarriages later, she knew she posed a question to which there was likely no answer.

"As much as I might like to share the details of your daughter's health with you, I'm obligated to respect her wishes. You'll need to discuss this with her. I suggest you wait until she's feeling stronger. She's been through a lot today."

His beeper chirped. He unclipped the small rectangular box from his belt; reading the number, he silenced the page. "I've got to answer this. Remember, keep the visit short, she needs her rest."

Taking a few backward steps away from them, he ran his hand through hair the color of wheat. "And you," he said, pointing to Candy, "are Laura's guardian angel. Your quick thinking saved your friend. Keep looking out for her, okay?" Candy visibly swooned as he took off down the hall.

Helen didn't have time to correct Dr. Sterling's theology; the Catholic Church never sanctioned the idea of guardian angels. And if they did exist, they certainly didn't come in the form of nattering adolescent girls.

Leaving Candy in the hallway, Helen entered Laura's hospital room. The shades were drawn, the shabbiness of the room illuminated by a single over-the-sink light. The absence of tubes, and monitors, and the rest of the paraphernalia associated with illness made Laura look like she was napping in an ordinary bed.

Who was the boy Laura had given herself to and where had they discovered each other? There was so much Helen wanted to know—and much she didn't. She didn't want to think about this faceless boy in her house, or in her daughter's bed on the few occasions each week when she left the house, trusting her girl to behave. She tried to shake the image of them entwined on the leeside of the dunes, where no one, including Helen, could see them. It would be best to leave the details alone. Helen would have to accept that Laura was no longer a child.

Helen had been distant from her daughter, always lost re-imagining how her life might have turned out, but Laura needed her now. Certainly her daughter had been wrong to disregard her religious upbringing, but no matter her age or her waywardness, Laura's atonement was complete the minute she lost her child. In this, Helen was convinced. So much so, she thought perhaps she'd be able to tell Laura about her siblings. The ones Laura never missed because she never knew they existed.

In a gesture she thought should be harder to accomplish than climbing the steepest wooden steps from the beach to Sea Escape, Helen forgave Laura her indiscretion. She swept her daughter's lovely hair from her forehead. Faded shades of pink became visible on her full cheeks. Laura reached for her mother's hand, her eyes fluttering open. All her movements slowed by the pills she'd been given to numb the pain of childbirth and child death.

"You're going to be fine, dear. Rest."

"You know, don't you?" Laura slurred her words. She rubbed her eyes the way she had as a girl on those occasions when Helen wouldn't budge on the extra cookie or the later bedtime.

"I can explain."

"Hush. We'll talk about everything later," Helen said.

With the noisy door handle giving her away, Candy—incapable of following any rule for long—entered the room. Helen gave her a disapproving look, partly because someone had to teach this girl to knock and partly because she wanted Laura all to herself.

"I needed to make sure she was all right," she said. "Laurie, I can't believe this happened. If only we had stayed at the clinic a little longer. I shouldn't have left you when you said you weren't feeling well. I thought you'd be okay."

"What clinic?" The rest of the truth washed over Helen like salt water over beach stone. "Oh, dear God, you didn't. Tell me you did not have an abortion." Helen made the sign of the cross and began chanting prayers.

Candy cocked her head and squinted. Something troubled her. But Laura's silence told Helen all she needed to know.

"Laurie, tell her," she said.

Helen clutched her purse and made for the door. The last thing she heard was Laura's voice. "Go ahead, hate me. I deserve it."

Out in the hallway, Helen collapsed against the door, dizzy from nurses and doctors and patients whizzing around in front of her. With all the children Helen had lost, she couldn't believe her daughter had killed a child.

Helen had to get away. Only then did she realize she didn't remember where the car was parked and Candy had the keys.

26

I ordered my day around meeting Henry and Claire at the bus
stop; we were heading to Sea Escape. The afternoon was moody,
like winter-into-spring days so often are in Magnolia. With a finicky sun feeding the roots, yards of tan grass weren't making any
promises to turn green.

Our inland home was protected from the windchill that would
surround my mother's oceanfront property, but exposure to bitter
cold was a small price to pay for even a few minutes beachside, no
matter the season. Sea Escape offered views of grassy swales, rocky
bluffs, and pristine sand. As much as we all loved it there, it was
Henry who would brave gale-force winds and pails of salt spray to
get just a second's glimpse of Anaskaket.

I suppose that's why it didn't worry me to see him ducking
paper airplanes or wincing when the bus driver shouted, "Everyone else get back in your seats," as he took his sweet time making
his way to the front of the bus. I knew I had the power to change
his mood with the landscape, and I couldn't wait to do it.

After successfully navigating the last step, Henry heaved his backpack onto his broad shoulders. It took him another few seconds to set one foot in front of the other, trudging toward home. I wanted to tell him to hurry. The sooner we got there, the more time they'd have to play before it got dark, and I needed to see if I could find more letters to read to my mother. I'd become more curious about my parents' life together—and apart. And slightly less concerned she'd mind my intrusion.

Henry finally saw me waiting at the end of our driveway when Claire ran ahead calling out, *"Mommy,"* waving a piece of paper in my face.

"Look! A one hundred and six on my spelling test," she said.

I took the paper from her, tapping the red number next to the "you're awesome" sticker. "You must be the smartest girl at Lynch. I didn't think you could get a grade higher than one hundred." I kissed her cheek and pulled her knit cap down over her ears, her silky hair trailing from the bottom of it.

"I getted all the bonus words this week. Auntie Luce made up a song to help me remember."

"You *got* all the bonus words." As soon as I corrected her, I wished I hadn't.

"That's what I said." Claire gave me an exasperated look and dropped her backpack on the driveway. Picking up a clump of snow left displaced on our lawn from the day's thaw, she rolled a poor excuse for a snowball and threw it out into the street.

"Honey, that's dirty. Leave it, okay?"

Henry hadn't picked up the pace from the bus stop to our house even after he saw me. I wondered if he was still missing Luce or if he was just worn-out from another day with Miss Ackart.

With my welcome missing the mark with Claire, I decided I would get Henry's right. I started off with what I knew he wanted to hear.

"Throw your backpacks in the car. We're going to Nana's."

"I hate that place," Claire said. "The lady with the doll is scary, and Nana doesn't talk."

"No, I'm taking you to Anaskaket. We'll go see Nana another day." It made me sad to think most of Claire's memories of my mother would likely involve the rehab center, since there hadn't been much remarkable about their connection before she landed there. Henry was the one upon whom my mother sprinkled what little attention she had to offer.

"I'll take a walk with you and let you play in the dunes, but then you need to let me get a couple of things done inside."

Henry's face didn't light up as I'd expected it would. He dropped his head, and even without seeing those big dark eyes, I knew something was wrong.

"She took my book. Miss Ackart said until I start paying attention, I can't have it back." He used the sleeve of his parka to wipe the tears from his face, but he wasn't thorough enough to catch them.

I squatted down to his level. "This isn't about a book, is it? You had a tough day with Miss Ackart and you're sad about Auntie Luce leaving. It's okay. We've got plenty of books." Even as I said it, I knew another book wouldn't do.

At the second mention of his teacher's name, he unzipped his backpack and pulled out a piece of paper. "Here's another note telling you I'm dumb." Henry didn't bother to zip his pack back up. He stood there expecting me to overreact like I'd been known to do.

I shoved the note in my parka pocket and lifted his chin so his eyes met mine.

"We are going to Sea Escape. We are not going to get worked up over books or notes right now. No worries, okay?"

Claire came up behind me and jumped on my back. "Hey, that's what Auntie Luce says."

I pulled her arms around my neck and hoisted her up piggyback style. "Sometimes you have to push your worries aside, and I know the perfect place to lose a few. Henry, you ready?"

He nodded his head and took one more swipe at his tears. He

seemed relieved I didn't get angry or question him further about his day. After zipping his bag, he made it halfway to the car when he stopped.

"Nana hasn't been home in a bunch of days. There won't be any food and I'm starved. I could go in quick and get something to take with us," he said.

"That's a great idea. I'll get Claire buckled and start the car." I wanted to reassure him that Miss Ackart had him all wrong. He was the most thoughtful ten-year-old boy ever. But I didn't dare bring up her name again. She had the power to pull anyone down, and we were in desperate need of being lifted up.

"I don't need no one to buckle me," Claire said.

"Anyone," I said, correcting her before I could stop myself.

In summer we had tourists, in winter, construction. Our town had a perpetual traffic problem. My children were patient on the longer-than-usual ride, but once the car started grinding the clamshell driveway, they unbuckled their seat belts and began forcing on their mittens.

"We're definitely going in after, right?" Henry asked.

The car barely came to a stop and before I got out my yes, they'd hopped out and made their way down the boardwalk leading to the beach. I shouted my usual edicts—"Stay away from the water. Don't go as far as the rock house. Wait for me." But like a boomerang the wind threw my words back to me. I looked at Sea Escape, empty, abandoned. I felt bad for the lonely old thing, a house that once held such hope and promise. Such love.

I could take freezing hands, but nothing was worse than the needles of cold that pierced my eardrums within minutes of a beach walk in winter. I picked up my pace, pulling on my own knit cap. Putting it on reminded me I still wore the mother-of-pearl prize Luce had given me that morning. Afraid to lose it, I took it from my hair and tucked it in the pocket of my jeans, right next to the key.

Born to be beach babies, Henry and Claire followed all the

rules. Chasing waves, they knew how much to taunt the surf without letting it get the best of them, wetting their shoes. They were content to draw hopscotch patterns on the sand, using stones as markers. They took turns without fighting about fairness. On a warmer day, they would have begged to take the longer trek to the jetty. A long cluster of boulders, alternating flat and round, at low tide you could play hide-and-seek. Tagged the "rock house" by my father, it was a wonderland for make-believe, though on windy, damp days, it was a treacherous place.

It was cold on Anaskaket, yet I felt more warmth with my children on that strip of beach than I'd felt in a long time.

If anyone had asked me which of my children would want to go inside first, I would have said Claire. She loved the beach, but when she'd had her fill of chasing seagulls and her brother was lulled away from her to his pensive place, she was done. On this day, she was different. I watched as she climbed the lifeguard chair, and once on top, she sat surveying the landscape. For a second I imagined her, a pretty seventeen-year-old lifeguard, with her hair pulled back, skin tanned—part Latina, part sunshine. She'd attract boys, no doubt; they'd literally gather at her feet. One special boy would look up at her and flirt. She'd keep her eyes on the waves, on her job, on the swimmers. Unlike her mother, she wouldn't be taken in by his promises. Christian was right about Claire. No one would be able to persuade her to do something she didn't want to do.

As I stood there lost, imagining summer, Henry brought me back. "Can we go in now?"

There was Claire, in no hurry to head inside, and Henry, pleading to. There wasn't much I could count on anymore.

After haggling with Claire over the number of Oreos she could eat and which cartoons she could watch, she came down from the lifeguard chair and we walked to the breezeway. Claire kicked off her shoes and dashed inside. Henry untied his and clapped out his sand. No matter your age, everyone's trained to stick to Sea Escape sand protocol. My mother's rule: no grainy shoes in the house.

"You can watch TV in Nana's room, but sit on the floor," I called after them as they scrambled up the winding stairs.

I turned up the heat and got down to the business of readying the place for my mother's return. She'd hate the idea of a handicapped ramp—Sea Escape altered, her infirmity made visible. It wouldn't help to remind her she lived on Cedar Point. There wasn't another house near her property for at least a half a mile. I would suffer the sighs and eye rolls as she made her disappointment known. Bringing her back, knowing she'd be happier home than in rehab, I would embrace her resistance. I kept making lists.

The contractor had given me a reasonable estimate. I just needed to tell him to go ahead and build the ramp. Once Holden arrived, I'd assign him the job of finding the old account and freeing up the money. He wouldn't complain about tracking down the funds in the passbook savings—money in my name, not his; money he'd want me to share. I wondered if, with the promise of cash, he'd be nice to me.

Giggles came from Claire, humming from the upstairs television. I guessed Henry still wasn't in the mood to laugh. With the children occupied, I took stock of the downstairs. If the butcher block island were removed from the kitchen—something Christian could easily do—and if I pulled up the carpeting, the entire first floor would be wheelchair accessible. As I neared her wing chair, I remembered Holden making some wisecrack about her always sitting there.

Turning from her chair, I noticed the secretary desk against the wall. Above it hung the prettiest picture of my grandmother. Maggie McIntyre. I wished I'd paid more attention to my mother's stories about her. I remembered how her death added more darkness to the gloomy life we led here after my father left us for good. There was no picture of my mother's father in any room in our house. Lee McIntyre. I loved his name before I knew why my mother had lost affection for him. If she ever had any to begin with. I'd asked my mother once why there were no photos of him, but she didn't bother to answer me. I wondered what awful thing he'd done to cross her and felt bad for this man I was related to. Now I knew. Yet I still loved the name. Lee.

Something about the secretary nagged me. Drawn to the keyhole, I tried the drop lid, and the desk opened. So much for the key I'd pulled from my pocket. I tried it anyway, to see if this were its home. It didn't fit. I toured the house in my mind, searching for other places where keys were required. I couldn't come up with anything with a lock downstairs. No doors. No safe. No cabinets.

I'd found the passbook and key in my mother's room; I should've started there. Taking the stairs, I went in the direction of her room. I wasn't halfway there when I knew where I should look, certain I finally knew what it was I'd been searching for. The most mysterious place in the house would hold the answer. My father's office.

I opened the door and felt like I was entering another time. The source of the house's staleness may well have come from that one room. The office smelled of old books, aged wallpaper, and distressed wood.

His desk, centered between side-by-side bay windows, had authority; its espresso-stained desktop was poised and tidy. The curtainless windows welcomed all manner of light into the room. The only shadow there was the presence of my father amid all the things he'd loved. Praised for the way he used his words, awards and citations in frames to match perched upon the walls. The only photograph in the office was of my mother holding me as an infant. Standing in the dunes, she wore a yellow dress and held me cheek to cheek. This was the favored photograph from that long-ago bunch taken with his tricky camera. He'd written about it in the second letter I'd read, telling her she was pure sunshine that day, and how glad he was it had turned out so fine. He thanked her for parting with it.

In the picture, her happiness was big and bright and genuine, her love for me exposed in fading color. Next to the photograph was a paperweight. A stone, painstakingly chosen by me from the beach below his window, painted fern green. I'd spent what seemed to a nine-year-old like hours sketching and resketching those seagulls. I didn't put more paint to the rock until I was certain I had them right. Back then, I felt I'd captured the appearance of birds flying high. As I held the Father's Day gift in my palm, I loved the fact that he'd placed it in such a prominent location. There were no visible reminders of Holden staking a claim in my father's room. I started to hunt for him there.

In drawers. On bookshelves. Nothing of Holden, from Holden. Pity for him was replaced with elation for me when, on the floor of the office closet, I found a fabric-covered lockbox. An ordinary container clearly embellished with my mother's artistry. Even before I hauled the box into the light, I knew the key would fit.

I wasn't prepared for how many there were, or how foolish I felt for thinking that he'd sent her only the ones I'd seen plus a few more. Curled up on the floor, I pulled out the stack of letters with postmarks reading 1951. Best to start at the beginning. Yet from the longer rows behind it, one confident corner poked up, urging me to read it first. Out of the tattered envelope, worn from repeated reading, the random letter upstaged the rest.

October 14, 1954
My dearest Helen,

I'm missing you like mad. I got that handkerchief covered with lipstick you mailed me. It's beside me here, reminding me of the last time we kissed. I'm down today, lost without your lithe body against mine as I try to find sleep. I should never have left to take this job. When I get home, you will never again be able to convince me to take one of these overseas assignments. This can't be

"Mommy, can I have more Oreos?"

Claire yelling from down the hall jerked me away from the letter. I tried to ignore my daughter, along with the feeling that I was intruding on my parents' private relationship. And I was stunned to find out my mother had encouraged him to leave us.

"Henry, give her one more, then that's it. You'll spoil your dinner."

"Henry isn't here," Claire said. "He went to the rock house."

27

Claire couldn't be right. Henry wouldn't go to the rock house without telling me. I tore around the corner into my mother's bedroom. Claire was alone. She sat cross-legged on the floor, drugged by the television. The evidence of Oreos painted around her mouth and over her teeth told me she hadn't listened to me either.

I peered out the bedroom window as I interrogated her. "What did he say? How long has he been gone?"

Precarious evening light made it impossible to see down the beach in the direction of the jetty. I didn't wait for her answer. Stepping over the package of cookies, I ran down the stairs with Claire at my heels.

At the foot of the stairs, I was panicked. "Stay right here. Don't move." I knew I shouldn't be shouting, but I needed her to do what I said. She predictably started sobbing. I made for the breezeway. The south side of the house was where the cold wind found me. Nature, too, was against me. I couldn't imagine why Henry had gone to the rock house when the airstream and the darkness told him not to. Never mind that I had. In seconds, I knew I'd never find him without a flashlight. My voice couldn't compete with the squall. The light might draw him to me if it turned out my shouting couldn't. I ran back to the breezeway to get the Maglite down from the shelf above the coatrack, and that's when I saw them.

Henry's sneakers lined up and sand-free sat on the plastic boot mat by the door. Either they'd been right there where he'd left them and I hadn't seen them in my rush or he'd put them there after I'd gone out.

"Henry Joseph Martinez."

His guilty face and slumped shoulders appeared in the doorway separating the breezeway from the kitchen. He didn't speak.

"Where were you? Claire said you went to the rock house."

"I didn't." He must have read the doubt on my face. "I was here the whole time."

"No, sir," Claire said, coming up behind him. "You said I couldn't come because it was dark." She wiped her tears on the sleeve of her sweater, smearing Oreo dust up the length of her arm. I closed my eyes to center myself. All the same, I came off harsh, like my mother.

"Mind your own business, young lady. Now go turn off the TV and collect your things. Do not eat one more cookie, understand?"

Claire stormed out of the kitchen. I don't know which was louder, her sobs or her stomping. Henry kept his eyes glued to the hole in his sock. I moved toward him, took his hand, and walked him into the kitchen. His hand was inside warm, not outside cold.

"I don't know what's going on with you. Did you go to the rock house? Tell the truth." Breathing regular. Cheeks, his usual citrus brown. He didn't look like a boy just in from the beach.

"I told Claire I was going there 'cause I wanted to be by myself. But then she wanted to come, so I told her it would be real scary."

"So you lied."

His bottom lip quivered. I expected tears that didn't come.

"I'm having a hard time believing you. Why did you say you were going to the rock house? You know never to go there alone. This is serious, Henry. What if Claire went looking for you?"

"I don't know. I need to be alone here."

"I know you love this place, and I know you miss Nana. But lying isn't going to help one bit. Not here or in school. Now tell me. What's going on?"

"I can't."

Henry picked at a corner of the Formica counter where a tiny portion had lifted free years ago. I covered his hand with mine to reassure, and to stop him from doing more damage.

I thought I was losing my mind when I heard a dog barking inside Sea Escape. It took me a minute to realize Claire must have changed my ring tone again.

"Where are you?" Christian asked, when I answered. "I took off early from work. The house is dark, and I tripped over Holden's suitcase. Is he with you?"

"I didn't know he was in." As I was telling Christian that I'd expected Holden to phone me when he got to our house, a call cut in. "I have to take this, it's probably him."

Everyone wanted a piece of me.

"Helen isn't doing well." Without saying hello or softening the blow, that somehow our mother had gotten worse between my lunchtime visit and dinner, Holden told me he was at Paxton Rehab Center. He needed me to come quickly. Part of me wanted to believe he was being needy because he wasn't comfortable being there alone with her. But I could tell he was worried. At least visiting her had been his first priority.

Two phone calls and twenty minutes stood between me and the rehab center. Christian met me at Sea Escape to pick up the kids so I could rush to my mother.

When I got there, I pushed through the heavy double doors of the center. Holden paced outside her room. Intent on thumbing his BlackBerry, he didn't look up as I passed him, heading right into my mother's room.

She was lying in bed, the sheet pulled up to her chest, her arms straight lines by her sides. Jenny, suddenly the epitome of professional, was sliding a twenty-three-gauge butterfly needle into a hand vein.

"Look, Helen, Laura's here." Without looking up, she plugged the tubing and saline into the catheter with one swift motion.

A doctor in his mid-fifties stood at the foot of the bed, poring over her chart. I'd met him only once, but something about him was more familiar. He probably felt he knew me too. By now the staff must have filled him in on the grievance I'd filed over her nursing home transfer. Aside from the newly inserted IV, my mother didn't look any different than she had when I'd left her sitting by the window, finishing her pudding. Standing on the opposite side of the bed from Jenny, I lowered the side rail and leaned in to get a closer look at the asymmetry of her face. The rail made a loud bang when it dropped down alongside the metal bed. My mother startled, but Jenny held tight to her hand and the needle. "Whoa. Wait a sec, Helen. Let me tape this down, okay?"

"No-hosp-tal," my mother said. She kept her hand still but shook her head back and forth.

"Can someone fill me in?" I looked to the doctor, but his head was down, his eyes shielded by his hair.

"She got pretty dizzy after a physical therapy session," he said as he continued to write things in her record.

"Blood pressure's a little low." Jenny prattled on as she adjusted the flow of drops and discarded her supplies.

"Sorry, I needed to finish my thought," the doctor said as he looked up. "Your mother is at the very least dehydrated. You really need to drink, Helen." He motioned for me to come down to the end of the bed. "Her physical therapist said she was staring off and it took a few seconds for her to respond to verbal commands.

I should probably transfer her to Memorial for another CT. She could be having what we call TIAs. I don't mean to alarm you, but simply put, they're mini-strokes."

I didn't tell him that blank stares and silence weren't always symptoms of a stroke when we were talking about my mother.

Holden finally came into the room. I wondered if he was worried now, thinking I was taking charge, though that certainly couldn't have bothered him for the last several weeks. Whether she knew what we were talking about or not, my mother kept repeating, "No hospital." Jenny didn't acknowledge her protest; neither did the doctor. Maybe they'd given up trying to make out what she was saying. Holden surprised me when he understood her, but he bowled me over with his insensitivity.

"If you're having another stroke, you have to go to the hospital. Let the doctor make the decision." He shouted from the other side of the room as if she were deaf. Adopting the posture he used whenever our family was getting to him, he planted his legs in a wide stance and started rubbing his arm.

"No one is going to transfer you to a hospital if you don't want to go," I said to my mother, giving Holden a look. "Close your eyes and rest. We'll be right outside." Smoothing a soft curl from her forehead, I caught my ring in her hair. Without her feeling the tug, I disentangled it. Like he was one of my children, I motioned for Holden to zip it and leave the room. I asked the doctor to join us.

"Nothing has changed about her wishes. She doesn't want extreme measures taken," I said, as if I had to remind Holden of that. "What good's another CT?"

"None, I suppose," the doctor said. "She's still on blood thinners. I could tweak the dose. Let's see what the IV fluids do for her blood pressure tonight. If she remains stable, she can stay. Tomorrow we'll need to address the appropriateness of her placement here. I apologize. We're just not staffed to manage acute care issues."

I knew I had a case against them pushing her out over money or the pace of her recovery. I didn't have justification to fight them moving her out because blood clots ricocheted around her brain during physical therapy.

Jenny emerged from the room. Without speaking to the doctor, she put out her hand to take my mother's chart. "Helen's asleep. As soon as you left, she was out. If you all want to talk some more, there's nothing going on in the conference room." As she expressed the hospitality that had curiously gone missing during our team meeting, the doctor took his cue to move on to the next patient.

"We'll talk tomorrow." He shook Holden's hand, the other he placed on my arm. "I'm told you're a godsend to your mother. I wish every patient here had someone like you in their corner. Whole darn medical system would be different, that's for sure."

I didn't believe the team was pleased with my role as my mother's benefactor, or that they sat behind the conference room door expressing altruistic wishes for every patient to have someone like me. His kindness was appreciated, though, mostly because he offered it in front of my brother. The man who'd never once thanked me for taking care of our mother when it should've been a team effort.

"Why don't we head to your house?" Holden asked after the doctor left. "She's in good hands and I could use a drink. You could whip us up something to eat and tell me more about her finances."

"Has anyone ever told you you're an ass?"

"Well, Saint Laura, I didn't know you knew the word."

"Look, Holden, I know you don't like me. And that's fine, I guess. But I didn't invite you here for a visit. I can't do this by myself. And I'm not going to wait on you or cook you dinner. I need help."

Right then I felt like I had less self-control to shout at him than Claire did with a box full of cookies. Everyone was being an obstacle. For once I claimed my right to be angry. Still, I didn't want to upset the patients, so I started walking toward the conference room. Holden followed me.

"It's no secret Helen and I are no longer close," he said.

Like you ever were, I thought.

"Don't expect me to wring my hands like you if anything happens. Practically speaking, she left me years ago. You know, she hasn't talked to me about anything important in decades. Look, I was willing to come here and help you out with this transfer nonsense, and now that's in a state of flux. Other than sorting out her finances, I can't think of what else you need me for."

He went right for a chair, stretching his legs out under the table, pulling his BlackBerry from his breast pocket.

I went to the picture window overlooking the bay. The beacon from the lighthouse rotated its light in a wide circle. Otherwise there was only darkness. I couldn't make out a single shrub or tree in Christian's garden surrounding the center.

"What's wrong with you?" I asked. "It wasn't her fault that our life fell apart after Daddy died. Why can't you love your own mother? She loves *you*. I have a right to struggle with her; she can't forgive me. To tell you the truth, I don't blame her. I can't forgive myself."

"Are you serious? What's with the two of you and your fairy tales? Next, you're going to tell me you never told Christian about your baby."

When I didn't say anything, he kept going.

"Well, the Tobins certainly have cornered the market on being the family of secrets."

"Of course I told him. What are you talking about?"

"I'm not about to fill you in on ancient history. It doesn't matter to me. If you want the truth about our so-called *perfect* family, read Joseph's letters." Holden laughed the kind of laugh that's a lot more pain than pleasure. "I guess I shouldn't be surprised you never have. You probably couldn't bring yourself to face things. You bought the fantasy she was peddling."

The letters. I didn't confess that I'd read some to our mother, and that just that afternoon, without her permission, I'd dipped into the rest. I hadn't thought twice about pulling the yellowed pages from the envelopes with the upside-down stamps. I'd already learned a few things—my grandfather cheated on my grandmother, he didn't approve of my parents' marriage, and my mother played a leading role in my father's disappearing act. I could tell by the way Holden stared at me there was more. Tied up in multicolored ribbons, organized by date, the truth lay all over the floor of my father's office.

28

❊

May 2000

Helen entered the darkened sewing room, duster and furniture polish in hand. After three labored pulls of the drapery cord, morning sharpened the outline of her sewing machine and cutting table. The once per month cleaning of this room involved nothing more than a cursory dusting. She would finish with time to spare before Laura and Christian arrived. If she were planning a longer stay in the room this morning, she might open the windows to let in spring air. She settled for the citrus punch of lemon Pledge.

It took mere minutes to dust off the surfaces of her lonesome apparatus. She ran her hand over the top of her sewing machine; the arm shaft and presser foot felt like a part of her. She missed them the way an amputee misses a limb.

Helen had been meticulous in creating Laura's layette after she'd been born. She didn't tempt fate like her pregnant daughter, who was busy buying up receiving blankets and hooded towels in the impartial colors of green, yellow, and cream. Laura's baby's things would be ordinary, not personal as her own had been.

Helen was most proud of the pink bed ruffle she'd sewn to circle the bottom of Laura's crib. Standing there with her dust-cloth in one hand, her mind on the past, Helen longed to touch it once more. She was drawn to her supply closet. The minute she unzipped the garment bag, she saw it hanging over the cloth hanger.

She remembered mere weeks postpartum, carting Holden and baby Laura to three fabric stores until she found the precise material she'd set her heart on. Scalloped eyelet, called galloon embroidery, had decorative edging on both sides of the fabric, great for a fuller skirt. With Laura asleep on her shoulder, she'd poked around the notions section of the well-stocked shop, finally deciding on rhubarb ball fringe trim. Yes, the three-quarter-inch pom-poms dangling to the floor would give the skirt exactly the whimsy she'd envisioned.

Helen pulled the eyelet dust ruffle from the closet. It had once looked so perfect, brightening Laura's nursery. That is until Holden, tired of his mother's long-standing distraction, had acted out—at either Helen or Laura, or both of them—drawing smiley faces with permanent marker on every round circle of the ball fringe that adorned Helen's creation. She was sure Holden had no idea what these handmade things meant to her, the comfort that making them provided. Life was busy for Helen then, with Joseph gone most of the time, leaving her to hold down the fort, which, for more reasons than she cared to think about, she'd come to mind less and less. She preferred to see Holden's misbehavior as merely impulsive, a thoughtless act born of boredom. So the eyelet ruffle, with its defiled trim, had landed here in the closet of keepsakes, along with a wedding gown, a hodgepodge of other long-ago fabrications, and later a funeral dress.

It would be easy enough—if Laura had a girl—to remove

the fringe from the ruffle and embellish it with another type of rickrack. It wouldn't do for a boy, all that pink. Holding the fabric, Helen felt a hint of desire to sew. She told herself she wouldn't be breaking her vow, as it wasn't for her, or Sea Escape, or Laura, for that matter. She would be sewing something for the new baby.

"Hello, Mother, are you up?" Laura's voice climbed the stairs and pulled Helen from her reverie. She hung the bed skirt back over the hanger, closed the drapes, and put away her cleaning supplies.

The two women met midway on the switchback stairs; Helen's aged body and Laura's pregnant one had them going at the same protracted pace.

"You're early," Helen said.

"Sorry, we were up and well—I'll help Christian get started on the porch. Are you going to get dressed?" Laura drew back against the railing in response to a doozy of a baby's kick. She held on to her abdomen while she caught her breath.

"You will do no such thing in your condition. I don't need the furniture out there. And for the love of all things holy, will you go downstairs and sit someplace."

Harsh water spray drowned out Laura saying something about being fine, and fit enough to walk the beach. She even took some sort of exercise class for mothers to be. Christian waved from outside, where he was power-washing winter from wood. A table, four chairs, and two chaise lounges stood in line on the grass, waiting to take their places in the sun.

Helen knew Laura would insist on lunch outside, so she dressed in a simple pair of wool slacks and a heavy sweater. After returning to the first floor, she made her way to the couple. She'd become quite fond of Christian, though she'd had her reservations about him in the beginning. They'd become so serious so quickly. But to his credit, he was a good Catholic, and he'd been more successful getting Laura inside a church than she had been.

His family was close-knit and charming, the few times she'd met them, though his sister was inordinately cheerful. As Helen sat in her wing chair, beach-gazing for almost an hour, Christian arranged the furniture and Laura the lunch. Helen realized she'd worried for no reason. It was true Christian had taken Laura from her physically. She'd moved out of Sea Escape and into a home of their own within weeks of their impromptu nuptials. But Laura had emotionally left the house and her mother long before. Aside from conversations about tides and household doings, Helen's own reminiscing was the only thing the two discussed. They hadn't dared broach the subject of the unborn baby.

Christian certainly had a good work ethic, Helen thought as she watched him struggle to secure the table's umbrella within its base. She'd like to think he did it all for her, to keep the overbearing light from her eyes. Then he stole a kiss from Laura as she deposited the fruit in its plastic tray alongside the deli-made salad on the table, his hand planted firm and low on her stomach. It was an intimate gesture Helen turned from, one that told her he was doing it all for her daughter.

She had to admit, Laura carried the pregnancy well. Like some sort of ball, she wore the child high. A clear indication the baby was a girl. Perhaps her incessant beach walking did have its benefits, but it could just as easily be jeopardizing her delicate condition. Helen wished she could tell Laura not to take any chances.

When at last they were all in their wrought-iron chairs circling the glass-topped table, one place empty where Joseph might have been, Christian raised his glass.

"To summer! I know it isn't official, but what do you say we kick this one off with a gift to you, Helen?"

"Oh, yes, I meant to thank you. The new cushions are quite good-looking." She smoothed a hand over the button-tufted cushion, drawn to three stray threads that hung from the cording, something commonly seen with assembly-line manufacturing.

"You will take them in for me before you go, won't you? I'd rather not have to lug them in if it rains," Helen said, stabbing a forkful of her lunch. Since when was it fashionable to put grapes in the chicken salad, and for heaven's sake where was the celery?

"I told you she'd like them. You worried for nothing," Christian said to Laura, before he got up and reached inside the sliding glass doors. Back out he came with a book larger than any scrapbook or photo album Helen had ever seen. He pushed his plate forward, and like a librarian reading to children, he showed the opening pages to Helen. Out of the corner of her eye, she saw Laura rip a hanging thread from her own cushion.

"We know you've wanted landscaping around Sea Escape for some time. I'd like to design it and supervise the crews. You can choose anything you like."

Helen stared at the renderings of shrubs, circular and bushy, plants, spiky and low. It took her a moment to process what he was saying. A garden?

"Maybe she doesn't want—" Laura avoided looking at her, pushing her own plate aside.

"Here are a few ideas to get us started," Christian went on. "Pick whatever you have your heart set on."

Helen had dreamed of a garden for years before Joseph died. She couldn't bring herself to dig one once he'd been taken from her. All interest in crafting her life within and outside Sea Escape had been lost to her. Perhaps the impending arrival of the child gave her strength to look forward, as she backpedaled, trying to convince Laura she was indeed grateful for the gift, not reluctant.

"Forgive me for being so quiet. I'm stunned by the thoughtfulness of your offer. Yes, plant the garden, please."

For nearly one month, the couple broke bread with Helen at least once per day. In the beginning, Helen and Christian surveyed the land around Sea Escape in evening light and pored over books. She shared her longings for salt myrtle, buckthorn, and the double pink blossoms of *Rosa rugosa*. Christian taught her about coastal soil, the plant life the land would accept or reject, and the best places to grow her seaside beauties. Though at first Helen objected, Laura left them to their visioning, taking strolls on Anaskaket before their simple supper. As the month progressed and the plants were at last in their homes, Laura's walks shortened. Negotiating the steep wooden steps became more difficult with her ever-increasing size.

Later in the life of her new garden, the meal they shared was a catch-as-catch-can lunch. Christian had mere minutes to stop in and scrutinize the work in progress. Inspecting the job and kissing his very pregnant wife, he assured Helen that the project was nearing completion. Yet she did not want the labor of love to be finished. She would be left with the landscape, which was indeed everything she'd dreamed it would be, but as breathtaking as it was, she would be alone again. Without easy conversation about plantings, all around her patio table with its store-bought cushions. Without Laura.

She knew when Laura's own child arrived, her daughter would become distant again, preoccupied with the burps and hiccups so consuming to a new mother. On an ordinary Tuesday, as she and her daughter sipped the iced tea they fancied, a sun-brewed dark blend garnished with fresh mint pulled from the place where herbs were planted, Helen saw the end of their special time approaching. The joyful anticipation of her grandchild's arrival would soon be replaced with the reality of it.

Laura repositioned herself in her patio chair and straightened her maternity top before gripping the table with both hands. She moved on to fidget with her glass, tearing the mint sprig into smaller and smaller pieces.

"Is something wrong?" Helen asked.

Laura looked away from her mother. "I have to tell you something about my baby."

Helen braced herself, clutching the arms of her chair. Laura's pained expression told her this might well be bad baby news.

"Hey, Mrs. Tobin," Candy said, as she came onto the deck. "Did you notice I came around? I knew you wouldn't hear me if I knocked." Candy winked at Helen and then bent down. Without hesitation, she planted a kiss on her cheek and a bakery box on the table. The girl remained an exasperation, though Helen had grown to like so much about her. She couldn't say exactly when that had happened.

"The landscaping looks fabulous. I love the roses by the weathered fence. And that bench with the container gardens. You might not be able to tear me away from here. It's paradise." Though they were intended for Helen, Candy spoke loud enough so the workmen could appreciate her compliments too.

She moved to where Laura was sitting. Stranded in her chair, Laura didn't move to get up. Her friend pulled her into a hug, getting as close as was possible given Laura's bulk.

"You're gonna go any day now, mark my words. I wasn't even that big with the twins."

"I'm hugely aware that I'm as big as Sea Escape, you don't have to remind me. Mother, were you this big with Holden and me?"

Helen waited, hoping something in the form of an answer would come to her. She wasn't one to lapse into idle chitchat, and she certainly wasn't likely to gab about pregnancies with these two. Such a hallmark of this generation it was, to open intimate details up for public consumption.

"It was a long time ago. Can I pour you some tea?" Helen asked.

Candy accepted the offer to quench her thirst as she opened the box of cookies. Helen wondered if anyone made anything with their own hands anymore.

"When I was in my last trimester, I ate four of these black and whites a day," Candy said. "Two for each kid. Now that the girls are in preschool, do you think I have to stop telling people I've got a postpartum weight problem?"

Laura and Candy laughed like they always had, their ease with each other sisterly. Laura's earlier nervousness vanished with the arrival of her longtime friend.

"Well, at least I'm not one of those mothers who whips out a boob when one of her three-year-olds says 'I'm thirsty.'"

The girls' laughter was higher and louder than the breakers on the beach below. One of the diligent crew members smirked at Candy's remark, though he kept his head down. Knowing he'd overheard them sent them into another fit, this one quieter than the last. Helen sipped her tea.

"Sorry, Mother. I know your generation didn't get into breast-feeding, but it really is the best thing for a newborn. Antibodies against illness, bonding and all that," Laura said.

Helen, lured into a discussion she should not have been having, lowered her voice and covered one side of her mouth with her hand. "Who says I object to it? I breast-fed you, Laura. I believe in discretion, that's all."

"You did? I didn't— Well—I assumed."

"So you were about to tell me about the baby before Candy arrived. Is there something the two of you are keeping from me?"

Candy's good manners, which had matured more than Helen gave her credit for, prompted her to place a cookie on a napkin and slide it in front of Helen. "Laura told me she had news too. Come on, I can't wait another minute."

"I had another ultrasound. This time Christian and I couldn't stand the suspense. We asked."

A girl, Helen thought. Named something special and strong, like Dianne or Julia, not one of those names everyone else was choosing, Jennifer or Sarah. Helen was silent at first, though in an effort to be polite, she offered a weak smile. "In my day," she said, "you waited until the birth. You were thankful for whatever God gave you."

Laura and Candy exchanged a look. Helen hadn't meant to color the day with her comment. She hadn't intended to open a wound. They'd taken it the wrong way. Candy reached out to hold her dearest friend's hand.

"Thanks for being excited," Laura said to her friend, ignoring Helen. She pushed her shoulders back, and taking her hand back from Candy, she placed both firm on her abdomen. "I love knowing. I didn't think I would, but I do," she said.

"It's a boy."

29

Saint James Church was spread out over a hill as if God Himself had placed it there. Fluted spires reached toward heaven; the sacred building begged to go home. Oval glass saints, stained bloody, wandered around the outside of it, promising redemption if only you'd go in and repent. Weeks after my mother had a stroke, I walked into the vestibule of my family's church. Not as a child looking for miracles. I hadn't gone there to wallow in my sadness over losing my father and my mother seemingly at once when I was a girl. I didn't go there to deposit my guilt over my teenage pregnancy at the foot of the crucifix.

I genuflected and made the sign of the cross, taking my seat far from the gaggle of women who'd gathered around the altar to chant the rosary. I bowed my head and begged Him, like I'd done so many times before, to bring my mother back to me. I'd loved her every minute of my forty-five years, and she'd once loved me too. I was in Saint James Church because I was running out of time for her to love me again and I didn't know how to set things right.

Kneeling there, I took in the church of my childhood, the place I went with my mother every Sunday and on holy days of obligation, like Ash Wednesday and the Feast of Saint Blaise. Silently, we'd walk in and take our regular seats midway up the aisle, off to the right. My mother would pull a small prayer book from her purse, plant herself on the kneeler, and begin to pray. Eyes closed, she'd leave me to my own version, rote prayers she'd taught me before I was old enough to read. I'd recite them, attaching most of my meaning to the ad-lib intentions I'd tack on at the end.

"Dear God, bless my mother. Make Holden play with me. Please keep my daddy safe in Vietnam. If you can, make him come home again real soon, Mommy misses him and so do I. Amen."

My early church memories included Holden sitting there with my mother and me. When I was five, he would've been sixteen. My mother sat between us, because Holden said I bugged him with all my moving around and nonstop whispering. He never sang, refusing even to hold a hymnal, and he wouldn't shake my hand at the sign of peace. Little by little he stopped coming with us. "Pay attention to your own affairs," my mother said, when I'd ask why he didn't have to go while I still did. I didn't really know what she meant, but it didn't matter since there was no real passion behind my protests over going to church. Secretly, I loved it there. Sacred mysteries and ancient ceremonies intrigued me. I was fascinated by the red light near the Tabernacle that announced *Jesus was in the building* and the cloudy incense that filled my head with holy dreams of all things possible.

After my father died, Saint James Church became a sad place. The last time I remember Holden sitting with us was at my father's funeral. Throngs of people I didn't know filled the pews and said "I'm sorry," as if they were the ones who threw him out of that plane without a parachute. The three of us—my mother, Holden, and I—did not sit in our regular pew that day; instead we sat and stood and kneeled in unfamiliar territory. We had front-row seats. It was in this place of honor that I saw my mother begin to vanish right before my eyes. Dressed in black, a rounded piece of lace tripped off the top of my mother's head, covering her face and her feelings. She looked so beautiful, wearing a dress she'd stayed up all night stitching. I surrendered to sleep on the edge of her sewing room, certain my father couldn't be dead because my mother was creating something special. But there we were, the three of us. All I really remember was my mother looking like a movie star, flanked by a ten-year-old girl and a twenty-one-year-old boy. Except who'd want to try out for the part of the widow.

It was on my eighteenth birthday that Saint James's became the place I went hoping what the saints tempted me with outside could truly be found inside. I was in need of being saved.

I no longer went to church at scheduled Mass times or because my mother made me, which was one of the many things we did and did not talk about. I'd slip in the back pew whenever I was overcome with my need to ask God's forgiveness for conceiving a baby with a boy I didn't love. A baby I hadn't wanted. His gift to me never fully appreciated until every last cell of my child had been scraped from inside me, when I was seven weeks along.

Daniel Rutland was a summer boy. He arrived every June, mid-month, walking onto the beach one day as if he'd materialized out of nowhere, and he would disappear sometime during Labor Day weekend. Everyone knew him, or at least of him. After his first week in Anaskaket, he was as golden brown as the rest of us. His hair was sun-streaked and wild. He was a frequent topic of conversation among my group of girlfriends. How could someone so cute be so quiet? Did he have a girlfriend back home? Couples like Candy and Pete were forever arguing about him. Pete would say it wasn't okay to stare at someone you weren't dating. Candy's famous line was "Just because I'm window-shopping doesn't mean I'm planning to buy." To me all she talked about was how adorable Daniel was and what a great couple we'd make. None of us really knew him. He stayed on the periphery of our bodysurfing by day and bonfires by night. Until the summer I was seventeen.

High above my friends, I took my assigned chair on the beach. Duets of beach towels and radios tuned to rock and roll stations striped the sand. By the end of June, Daniel had moved his things to the foot of my lifeguard tower. Conversations were painful at first; neither of us had Candy's knack for chatting. As if we were giving presentations in class, we blurted out the facts of our lives. His dad stayed in New York to work, coming to Anaskaket only a few weekends each summer. Mine was dead. His mother didn't like leaving her deck; she thought beach sand was best left by the water. My mother felt the same. Maybe they could be friends. But I never told my mother about his, or about him.

Though we never spoke of it, he and I felt the pressure to be a couple, especially as the sun lost its position in the tangerine sky and everyone else fastened their bodies to each other like barnacles to driftwood. At first, I wasn't comfortable with our lips and hips meeting. When Daniel's hands were laced in mine, my whole body tingled, and it frightened me. He was tense with me too, so we kept our timid kisses and caresses relegated to shadowy night. I was flattered having the beautiful boy's attention, yet still thankful for firelight and his closed eyes.

It took two weeks for Daniel to gain enough confidence to slide his fingertips up underneath my high school sweatshirt, one more for him to move them inside the waistband of my shorts. It wasn't long before his touch had more weight and it became obvious to me that I might have to repay the affection he was giving me. I knew not to go on that walk to the jetty. It should've taken more than one wine cooler and a gentle whisper in my ear to convince me to remove my clothes so we could enjoy the warm sensation of our bodies skin to skin. A drink and a promise certainly weren't enough to numb me to what I agreed to do in those dunes.

I was startled back to the present as the squeak and clap of kneelers returning to their upright position told me the rosary crowd had finished. Their whispering made its way to the vestibule. I rested my head on my folded hands, keeping my eyes down in case any of the women knew me. I didn't want to explain my tears or answer questions about my mother. Silence fell over the sanctuary and relief over me as one by one they left. I was certain I'd dodged giving a status report when a heavy hand came down on my shoulder.

Father Kelly, with his shock of white hair and round face, stood hunched over me. "God bless you and your mother." He paused near me long enough to let me know he was there to extend his priestly support but would be happy to leave if he'd interrupted deep meditation. He was an expert at taking cues from sinners.

"Thanks, Father. We can use your prayers. She's had a setback. It's so hard to know what she's thinking. Her speech is a huge frustration, for her and for me."

"Helen's always been a woman of few words. But her faith is strong, Laura. God is working within her, have no doubt." Father Kelly looked up to the gilded ceiling as he tapped his fist on his chest.

He was right about my mother's brand of faith. She wasn't one to talk about the depth of it. She wasn't a "holy roller," an expression she liked to use when she was annoyed with someone who dropped his or her religious persuasion into every sentence like a heavy Bible on a table. My mother's spirituality, like mine, was quiet and introspective, though her beliefs were more strongly held than mine. She was traditional church. No premarital sex. No birth control. No abortion. She said I was a menu Catholic. She believed I browsed the rules and chose only those that appealed to me. The truth was I was weak.

"How are you holding up?" Father Kelly asked.

Maybe it was because he was a priest or maybe it was because I was in church, but the minute he asked about me, I was overcome. Father Kelly motioned for me to push into the pew so he could sit down and console me. Midway to the wood seat, he plopped his aging body down.

"Life is a test. Life is a trial. My dear, you have been given a cross, but God and I have faith in you." He began to pray those simple prayers of my childhood. Whispered words as familiar to me as my name. *Our Father who art in heaven . . . Holy Mary, mother of God . . . pray for us.*

When he finished, I dabbed my eyes with a crumpled tissue I'd found stuffed in the pocket of my parka. He asked me if there was anything else he could do. He'd already offered a Mass for my mother that morning, he said.

"I bet if you stopped in at the rehab center, she'd appreciate it. My sister-in-law used to say the rosary with her before she went back to New York. She told me Mother looked really peaceful during it."

"Yes, I've met Luce, is it? I take it she's the one responsible for the colorful room decorations. Last time I was there I think I blessed more statues than patients."

I laughed, imagining Luce ecstatic in the presence of a priest, running around finding items that could use a good blessing.

"I didn't know you'd been to see her. That means a lot."

I paused. He didn't move a muscle. He must've known that a flinch here or there had the power to interrupt a confession. "Father, there are things I should've told her. I started to, a couple of times, but I knew she wouldn't listen. I don't know whether I should tell her now or pray He will forgive me for what I've done." I blew my nose again, then shoved the tissue back into my pocket.

"People change, Laura. The grace of God softens hard hearts, making them capable of hearing the truth. I've known your mother a long time. It's true she's not the woman she once was. In the midst of her great suffering, she's changed, not just in physical ways for the worse but in soul-searching ways for the better. Her body may be weak, but her transcendent heart is strong."

"So you think I should tell her, before it's too late. Even now, as sick as she is?"

"I can't tell you what to do. I believe He will give you the strength you need to discern what His will is for you. You need only ask."

Father Kelly stood, placing his hand on my shoulder again, this time less to console me and more to get his footing. As if this man got some benefit from leaning on the likes of me. "Call me if you want to talk or pray or if you want me to see her—even urgently. In the meantime, I'll drop in on her when I bring communion to the center next week."

Watching him walk away, up the aisle from me, I thought, he looked ageless. He'd been our parish priest for countless years, and only God knew the burdens he carried, the pain he shouldered for the rest of us.

Father Kelly bowed at the altar, straightened up, and then took the three steps to the sacristy. When he was gone, I was alone in the church. Then I saw the red light glowing from near the altar all the way back to where I sat, and I remembered, Jesus was in the building.

30

꧁꧂

Standing at the porch handrail, I surveyed the garden my husband had sketched, sculpted, and then had planted for my mother. The cool air hung low over the winter landscape. In one month or two, this room without walls would be serenity personified. There would be flowers everywhere in a rich palette of colors. The hydrangeas would be dressed in pink and blue bonnets. The prickly bushes would be adorned with crowns of yellow roses. Despite the racket made by the impending storm, the porch at Sea Escape was bliss on sand.

Fog lifted like a theater curtain, revealing the long arm of the jetty. The balusters on the porch railing partially shielded me from the draft coming off the ocean. A squall was definitely on its way. Different noises in different seasons clambered around Sea Escape. Warnings with a purpose, this commotion prepared a person for what was to come. Take in the furniture cushions and tie down the teak umbrella. Close the windows and protect the tender plants. It forced a change in afternoon plans, in favor of moving to a couch in front of windows facing east to get a better view of cloud formations and storm surge. And like an overture it began, tempting me to stay for the show.

Or maybe I was avoiding the letters.

Several of my father's letters lay spread out on his office floor, exactly where I'd left them two nights ago. The afternoon Henry and Claire and Christian and Holden and, finally, my mother pulled me away from them. Holden laid down a challenge for me to read, but as I watched the wind pick up over Anaskaket Beach, my conscience bothered me. Maybe I didn't want to know any more about our family. One letter reinforced what I thought I knew about one couple's perfect love story, while the others confirmed what Holden had been saying, that there was a lot more to my parents' past. According to him, I was the only Tobin still in the dark about our secret history.

I hadn't asked my mother for permission to read her communiqués with my father. And if I did, and she chose to answer, I wasn't sure what she would say. I sat on the couch, watching the swells, and as the jetty's outstretched arm faded from view, I knew I had no choice. I wrestled my legs out from under me and went to my father's office to retrieve the box. I wouldn't read them in his territory; I would open them in hers. In front of the east window, in the chair my mother lost herself in time and time again, I covered my lap with another of her handmade quilts. And once again I crept inside my parents' marriage.

Letter after letter, he expressed his love for her. My father was witty and adoring, charming and devoted. No wonder she kept every letter neatly arranged by date, each bundle tied up in one of her signature ribbons. I felt sad for my mother when I learned her wedding had been rushed to accommodate his orders to ship out to Korea. No wonder she'd seemed sullen the day of my simple ceremony, an intimate soiree held on the porch at Sea Escape. Christian's mother hadn't been thrilled either. Though Father Kelly was a guest, I knew our mothers were sad that we didn't exchange vows in either Christian's family church or mine.

I understood my mother's disdain for her father, having learned first of his infidelity and later about his gambling. When my father consoled her after my grandfather dismissed her grief over losing her quaint cottage in the Worcester tornado, I could see why Sea Escape became her place. In letters mourning the love nest my father never saw, he thanked her for all the time she'd spent choosing fabric and completing her handiwork. A perfect square of fabric slipped from one envelope, making me wish she would've told me about the Paradise Garden Sage bedroom curtains and the cornices recovered in red.

There was hope and longing written all over the early letters. It wasn't until I got to 1960 that I found out about my brothers, and why Holden was forever calling my mother Helen.

September 8, 1960
My dearest Helen,

No one but you knows how very hard it is to be back to work, away from you, after losing our son. I feel terrible tonight. I find myself wondering what the years ahead will hold for us. I wonder if they will be kind years or years of short previews of happiness but never the real show. I find myself growing so completely weary of this life, which keeps me so on edge, this life of kissing and running, this life of love but don't touch. If these are to be the best years of my life, then I hate to think of what the others will be like.

It's easier said than done to look ahead, I know, Helen. All we can do is try to imagine Mary Pat and Warren taking care of our Joey in Heaven, along with Paul, and our other little dear, while we take care of their Holden. I'm going to renew my commitment to treat him like my true son. And in that way, I will prove my love for you. Tell me it's not too late to set things right.

I read the letter again and again, as many times as my mother had lost and gained children. Holden was her best friend's child. Had there been clues in the stories she'd told me about the girl named Mary Pat? What happened to her? And why did she give him to my parents? Finding out about Holden unsettled me, but learning that my mother had given birth to a son named Joey blindsided me. No wonder she called Henry by that name. She wasn't just holding fast to her husband all these years; she was unable to let go of her boy. Reading my father's words, the way he implored her to talk to him about their children, in particular, their Joey—that name she'd used against my wishes for my son—I took solace in how hard it was for her to tell him how she felt. I knew about holding on to something so hard and for so long that letting go of it no longer felt like an option. Day after day, sitting in her familiar chair surrounded by glass, she wasn't being stoic. She missed a child she couldn't hold on to. I understood because I'd found my own way to do it.

I held the letter to my chest, grateful for the sign that told me what must be done with my own baby secret. I returned the letter back into its envelope and filed it by date in the box. Folding the quilt, I draped it over the back of my mother's chair as neatly as she would have. I didn't need to read any more letters to know that it was time.

I didn't expect to meet laughter as I approached the threshold of her room at Paxton Rehab Center, and never in a million years did I expect to find Holden painting her nails.

"Don't question my leanings, Mother. Once in a while I do this for Edwina. Keeps her from spending a week's salary at that damn day spa."

Her laugh had perfect pitch, like the wind chimes she'd hang outside in summer.

"Not-true. You-good-boy."

I'd stumbled onto a tender moment and felt the pinch of jealousy, though it didn't last. Catching a glimpse of their connection, I could see why she'd chased his affection for all those years. When I was at work in the nursery, each baby felt a little bit like my own, if only in some small way. Holden may not have shared her blood, but he was her son.

"Laur-a." My mother brightened as she looked at me standing by the door. Her silver hair was pulled off her forehead and, like mine, held back in an adornment from Luce. Her cheeks had natural color, her features soft and even. She was as relaxed as if she'd just finished an afternoon of sewing.

"You'll never let me live this down, will you?" Holden asked me as he placed my mother's right hand on the tray table and tightened the cap on the polish.

Moving toward them, I took the bottle from him and read its shade. "Nope. And to be honest, I didn't take you for Rosy Giggles. You strike me more like Bitter Plum."

Now all three of us were laughing, something that hadn't happened since long before my father died.

"You had us worried the other day, Mother. Today you seem so much better," I said. This time, I didn't hesitate to kiss the top of her head. Our hair clips made a tinkle when they met.

My mother raised one finger in a gesture that said, *Wait a minute.* She pointed to the walker parked behind Holden.

"If you wreck those nails, Laura will have to redo them. I'm going to deny to the death that I was the one to give you a manicure." Holden pulled the walker toward her.

All I did was move the tray table away from her chair, our mother did the rest. After getting her hands in the right position, she showed off how she could come to a full stand without any help.

"You're right, Laura. She's well on her way back to Sea Escape."

My mother looked away from her tedious job of standing, preparing to walk. The words *Sea Escape* had caused a distraction. I put a hand on her elbow to steady her. She eased back down into the chair.

"Why don't you two visit? I need something to eat," he said.

Without a second thought, Holden copied me and kissed her. As if frightened by being that close to her, he backed out of the room without waiting for an answer. Still a frequent flyer, this time I minded that he left, because I had no idea how to tell her what I'd come there to say.

She had every right to be incensed with me. Here was the lightest moment the three of us had shared in years and I was about to ruin it. She raised her right hand in a motion originating from her back and shoulder muscles. Her stroke-affected side reached out to me. I dragged the chair as close to her as was possible.

"I'm sor-ry I hap-pen-ed to-you," she said, cupping my chin and cheek with her hand. I rested there; the image of her holding me as a baby in our dunes passed through my mind. I didn't care that I was smudging her polish. I didn't care that I looked like a little girl accepting motherly affection.

"It's not your fault. The stroke. And look at you, now. You're doing great."

She worked hard to leave her hand on my face, her desire to comfort me as strong as mine to savor it. When her body said time was up, her hand went limp.

"I'm sorry—about a lot of things," I said, guiding her hand to her lap, reluctant to let it go. "I need to tell you something."

She sat there resigned. She didn't let out a deep sigh or roll her eyes. There was no cross look to change the elegance of her face.

"When you first got sick, I read some of your letters from Daddy. At first, out loud to you when you were sleeping. I did it because I know he was everything to you."

She moved her head like a pendulum, side to side. In whispers, she said my name.

"And I read more, by myself at Sea Escape today. I know about Holden. And your son Joey." I squeezed her hand, but it remained lifeless. Her nonreaction wasn't enough to stop me from forging ahead with my confession.

"I know you're angry with me about my baby too. I should've told you things. Important things. Back then, all you did was miss Daddy. Holden had moved out. And when Nana McIntyre died, you got even sadder. I couldn't tell you how awful I felt all the time. You had enough to deal with. I just needed someone to love me. Daniel paid attention to me, and it felt good. I'm not saying it was your fault. I'm the one who took that walk on Anaskaket that night. I'm the one who agreed to be with him."

My mother didn't move, and neither did I. We were mirror images of each other. Our soft, wavy hair, hers gray, mine the color of night. Tears streaming down our apple cheeks, middle-aged and old.

"I didn't think you could handle one more thing. And I couldn't imagine having a baby at seventeen, so I stole the passbook out of your drawer. My name was on it, and I only planned to take what I needed. Then the people at the bank wouldn't let me have the money. They said I couldn't withdraw any until I was eighteen. So Candy figured out a way to get it for me. She went to the clinic with me, that part's true. When I got there, a nurse took me by rows of pregnant women, each one with a hand resting on her bulging stomach. I couldn't breathe in that room. There wasn't a single chair left for the stupid girl who wasn't exactly sure how she got there in the first place. On the exam table, I heard the nurse say words like *fetus* and *vacuum aspiration,* but it wasn't until she handed me a consent form that I knew I couldn't do it."

I looked out the window, away from my mother, so afraid to see her reaction. The stroke left her with a tiny collection of words, it hadn't really touched what she could do with her face. What if she didn't believe me? It was safer to keep my eyes on the garden outside the center, to look at the flowers my husband had planted there. Christian, who never once judged me.

"In the beginning, I didn't tell you because I was angry with you for leaving me when Daddy died. You'd be sitting right there, but you were gone. I didn't mean to be so awful to you. I think mostly, I was punishing myself. I constantly thought about telling you I didn't have an abortion, but it was easier to let you hate me. Once, when I was pregnant with Henry, I started to, but you were happy then. With me and Christian. You finally had your garden, and I didn't want to wreck it for you."

When I turned back to her, both her arms were coming off her lap, the left one higher and more controlled than the right. Her uncoordinated message was unmistakable. She wanted to hold me. I accepted the embrace initiated by her, motivated by our shared understanding of miscarriage. In my ear, she spoke as clearly as she had before her stroke assailed us.

"Joey-Lee—" She struggled for breath. "Jos——"

"You still miss Daddy and your baby." I finally and fully understood her. It wasn't just that her speech was strong and clear. It was that secrets no longer had the power to create such space between us.

My mother pulled back from our hug. "Jos——" With all her energy, she continued to grip my hand. Once more her words came out garbled and thick with emotion.

"Dad-dy-girl."

I didn't need more words to know exactly what she meant. "That's the thing," I said. "I loved Daddy, you know that. But really, I was always your girl. All these years that you've been missing him, I've been missing you."

31

December

Helen straightened her wedding quilt, aligning the floral circles. She hated to see things askew. It certainly was difficult to get moving at this ungodly hour. She wouldn't have bothered to raise the shades to face the morning or plump her nest of pillows if Laura and the children weren't coming over. They didn't need to see the only room with a television in disarray. And today, even a set without cable would be a blessing. Joey was spending the day at Sea Escape.

Laura's hospital Christmas party for children didn't begin until noon. Leave it to her to volunteer to set up, serve, and clean up. Why she took on so much was puzzling. Perhaps Joey's unwillingness to be cooped up inside for hours was the reason he'd refused to attend it. Helen would make it perfectly clear to him at the outset: there would be no beach walk in this frigid weather. He would have to be content with her and boredom.

Moving to the bureau to tidy her hairbrush and hand mirror, and most important, to remove the prescription bottle from view, Helen counted back to when she'd started taking the nightly tablet. Even yesterday's phone call to old Doc Cohen hadn't been enough to convince her that any day now her energy level would lift. He didn't agree with her that her symptoms might not be amenable to this pharmaceutical. He tried to restore her confidence by telling her this medication was merely slow to do its business. Guarantees aside, Helen remained skeptical. She'd never wanted to step foot on the slippery slope many her age were already sliding down. But he'd insisted she start on it, certain her recent complaints couldn't be the result of anything else. He'd been saying she was depressed for years. Would she finally agree to give one pill a trial?

Over time, he claimed, the physical toll depression took became more prominent. All-day tiredness, joints that took turns throbbing, dizziness upon standing, an appetite gone missing. And those headaches. Helen called the overused diagnosis foolishness, but on her last visit, she'd been too fatigued to resist. Now he insisted she not come off it. *Give it time* was his refrain. She put the plastic vial in her drawer. No one need know she'd accepted her faulty constitution, especially since she really hadn't admitted to any such thing.

Helen wasn't thrilled with the idea of looking after Joey all day. He was such a busy child. Always flitting here and moving there. Though she did love the boy. Helen smiled at the thought of that single piece of hair that popped up in back, especially after he pulled off his winter cap. From the time he was an infant, she could see Christian in him. He was a lucky boy to look so much like his handsome father. She was pleased he didn't look anything like her son. Her heart, she was certain, couldn't have taken it.

Helen would rather have gotten dressed much later, but she didn't dare meet Laura at the door wearing her robe. Worried stares would precede her daughter's "good morning." During their last visit, she'd prattled on about how Joey didn't want to go to the party, something to do with a bully at school and not believing in Santa Claus. With Christian at a weekend conference and Candy visiting family, Laura wasn't left with many options. *Like it or not, he'll have to come with me,* she'd said. Then without thinking, Helen had volunteered to watch him. She couldn't say who was more surprised, her or her daughter. Helen sensed Laura's reluctance to let the boy stay at Sea Escape without her supervision, but once the offer was out there, Helen felt compelled to see it through. Perhaps she did have enough energy to dress and make a pot of coffee. Laura deserved to go off for the day untroubled. In fact, if she hurried, they could share a mug and muffin before Laura drove into Boston. Helen might just be able to put on a good show for her daughter this morning.

Laura was late as usual. In she hurried with an armload of groceries. Joey carried his own bulging bag. At least as the children got older, the amount of paraphernalia they lugged through the door had decreased.

"Claire's in the car, and I really need to fly. Henry will help you put these away. Are you sure this is okay with you?"

"Joey and I will be fine. For goodness' sake, I raised two children, practically on my own. And be careful. Running late is a recipe for recklessness."

Laura stiffened; the quick raise of her eyebrows told Helen one of her sentences contained offending words. This time, like every other, Helen was left to wonder which one. She didn't ask. Laura wouldn't say.

Joey pulled a stool over to the cabinet that held drinking glasses. A gallon of milk, cap already off, sat on the counter.

"No. No." Helen shot her impatient command from a distance, though she made no move to intervene, taking the boy from the counter.

"Let one of us do that." Laura's resigned tone and droopy

shoulders put her in competition with Helen for the woman with the least energy.

The boy stopped mid-motion, looking first at his mother and then at his grandmother, uncertain which would step in to tell him exactly what he'd done wrong.

"Run along," Helen said to Laura, sighing. This was going to be a very long day. She moved toward him, pulled a glass from the shelf, and poured. "What in the world will I do with this much milk?" she asked no one in particular.

"I'll be back around four." Without kissing her mother or her son, Laura walked toward the back door. "Henry, be good." And just like that, Helen was alone with the boy.

Joey drank a full glass one gulp after another without pausing to breathe.

"You certainly do things quickly," Helen said.

He pinned those big eyes on her and stared. The silence seemed long, but it could only have lasted a second or two. Then he was at it again, moving in and out of cabinets, opening and closing the refrigerator. He put away the single-serving containers of yogurt, stacked canned fruit, and froze the prepared meals considered healthy choices. Helen's groceries proclaimed her age. It was a wonder her meals didn't have wheels. The boy made short order of the task his mother had given him. Joey was meticulous in putting things exactly where they belonged.

Wondering what they would do next, Helen opened the cold oven and pulled out a box filled with muffins she'd ordered from the bakery on a whim. "Would you like one? I'd hate for them to go to waste. I thought your mother might be able to stay and visit."

"I'm always hungry. They look good." Joey reached toward the box to nip off a piece of a muffin top. Helen scowled and pulled the box back toward her body.

"Why don't you push the coffee table over between the two wing chairs? I'll toast these up, and we'll have breakfast oceanside."

Joey stared at Helen with a look that questioned whether she'd lost her mind.

"Yes, I know, but we'll make an exception. We'll eat in there this once. You were so thorough with the groceries, I'll bet if we drop a few crumbs, you can push a vacuum cleaner. It will be our little secret."

His face broke into one of his carefree smiles. His eyes twinkled with the prospect of breaking a rule, however inconsequential.

Helen split the muffins, hers bran and his blueberry, in half. After spreading butter on the tops and bottoms, she placed them directly on the oven rack under the broiler. Whatever happened to her baking sheet? From the open kitchen, Helen could see Joey carefully inching the coffee table between the two chairs. She kept an eye on him in case he was hasty in setting things up. He shouted to her from across the grand room. "Is this good?"

"Perfect. Now come help me dig out the napkins; it's a trick for me to bend down. Perhaps we could share a sliced banana."

He pulled forks from the top drawer and then squatted down to pull cloth napkins from the bottom one.

"When we get bakery muffins, we eat um cold," he said. "We only warm them up in the microwave if they're stale. We use paper napkins. These are kind of fancy. And wrinkly."

"Taking the extra time to toast the muffins and set a nice table is very important. We won't fuss over the wrinkles today. But in the future, you would iron these before your guests arrived."

"That's a lot of work for a muffin."

"It's not a lot of work, it's the appropriate work. In my day, a person who could set a pretty table and serve a delicious meal was considered an artist." Helen peeked into the oven to check the toasting.

"No, sir. Artists make things with paint or charcoal pencils and stuff. My dad's an artist."

"Your father is very talented. He designed Sea Escape's gardens, as you know. Some might argue that bringing a garden to life isn't art in the traditional sense either, but you and I both know it is. And what about your grandfather Joaquin's pastry? You need only take one bite to know he's a master. He wouldn't serve a cold muffin."

"I guess."

Moving in sync with her, Joey smoothed out the napkins, but then he tucked them under his arm, negating his efforts. He juggled the utensils in one hand and with the other reached for a freshly poured glass of milk. Helen predicted a disaster. "Leave the milk here. I'll bring it along with my coffee."

She pulled down three china dessert plates and placed them on the tray she'd retrieved from against the backsplash. With the muffins each to its own plate, she sliced a banana, arranging the coins in a circle on the third. They met in the grand room. Helen thought their breakfast contributions made for a pitiful table. Joey's ear-to-ear grin said he thought differently.

"We need to open the curtains. Otherwise it won't really be an oceanside breakfast," he said.

Helen rubbed her right arm as if the tray had weighed a ton. "You're right. Here, let me show you how this works."

She moved to the far wall and gently drew back the draperies. "Pull this." She pointed to the string that would open them.

"I can't. I'm not supposed to touch it, I'll break it."

"I'm giving you permission. Go on."

Joey pulled with all the gusto of a bell ringer in a tower cathedral. "Gently, gently. Use a smoother motion, like this," Helen said. "One, two, three. One, two, three."

Joey looked as if she'd scolded him. "Go on," she said again. "You are more than capable of doing it right."

Her confidence in him spurred him on. Tentative at first, he got the rhythm she'd insisted on. And the drapes began to sway, revealing Anaskaket Beach and the faint light typical of a December morning.

"A traverse rod requires a gentle but consistent touch. See

those tracks? It took me longer to mount the hardware than it did to make the draperies. I'm getting tired just thinking about the day I hung those." Helen took her seat and exaggerated catching her breath. Joey kept staring at the pulley rope and how it attached to the rod.

"You made this stuff?" He moved toward the breakfast table. Breaking off a piece of muffin, he looked at Helen as he leaned over his plate to pop it in his mouth. She nodded at him, a gesture meant to affirm his attention to crumb control. "Are you an artist?" he asked with a mouthful.

"Why, I guess you could say I was. Once upon a time." Helen took a sip of her coffee as she stared out to the lonely beach. Lonely being her familiar.

"I could never make those. I bet it takes a long time. It looks hard." Joey abandoned sitting in the chair; trying to lean over his plate must have been a chore. He kneeled up in front of the table at Helen's feet, and then it was obvious. He hadn't moved to make eating easier, he wanted a better view of the beach.

"What makes you think you couldn't learn?"

A pensive look came over his face. Helen wondered how it was that a ten-year-old boy could doubt his potential with such certainty.

"My teacher says I don't concentrate like I should. Plus Nicholas would say only girls sew stuff."

"Nonsense. You can do anything you set your mind to. You'd have to take your time is all. You mustn't rush cutting a pattern or stitching a seam. And what does this Nicholas know about window treatments? Just for girls? What rubbish."

"How come you don't do it anymore?" He got up to look more closely at the brocade fabric. Leaning in, he traced a silver thread up toward the ceiling until it was higher than he could reach.

My goodness, Joey asked a lot of questions. Helen certainly wasn't going to tell him that she'd made a vow never to sew again after the life she'd carefully crafted failed to come to fruition. "All the rooms already have curtains. There's no need for me to make any more," she said.

His ability to look at her so directly made Joey seem older than his years. But his milk mustache reminded her that he was merely a boy. "There aren't any curtains in the room with the big windows. Upstairs."

"And how would you know that, young man? Have you been snooping around without my permission?" She was forever telling Laura to keep an eye on the children. This was no longer her daughter's home. She should be teaching her children to respect other people's privacy. Helen kept the door to Joseph's office closed.

"You can tell from the beach. All the windows have um except that one."

The boy who spent every last minute when he visited on Anaskaket Beach probably knew the outside of Helen's home as well as she knew the inside.

"My mom says that was her daddy's office and that you won't change anything about it, even though it makes you sad."

"Does she now? What else does your mother say about me?" Helen put her coffee down and folded her arms across her chest.

"She says you can't love anybody real good because you're too busy missing Joseph."

"When did she tell you that?" Helen felt a tingling sensation travel down one of her arms, and a dull pain like a hand grabbed hold of the back of her head.

"She didn't say it to me. I heard her tell my dad. She said she doesn't know why you can't love her *and* Joseph. She loves Dad, and me, and Claire, and Lee, all at the same time."

"Lee?"

"The baby she had before me. It died when it was too little for the doctor to know if it was a boy or a girl. Lee is a name that works for both."

It was preposterous that Laura had named the child she'd had a hand in losing. Helen knew she felt remorse; Henry's reveal only confirmed it. Why on earth would she work in that newborn nursery, if not to punish herself? It was unbelievable to Helen that Laura had told her son there had been another child. How had her daughter found the courage to talk about the unwanted one?

"Can we go for a teeny little walk on the beach? We've been sitting here a long time." Joey pressed his face against the window. A steamy circle became visible on the glass. He looked longingly toward the jetty. Helen did the same.

Lost in thought, she saw her daughter in a new light. It was true, Laura's first child was the result of one mortal sin, the baby's death swaddled in another, but clearly she felt remorse. And like her, Laura had the courage to claim her child in the naming. Helen supposed she could overlook the one she'd picked. Laura couldn't have known about her grandfather's double-dealing.

Helen possessed neither the ability nor the energy to go back over the pain her desire to hold a baby in her arms had brought her through the years. And it was pointless to attempt to untangle the feelings associated with adopting a child not born to her. What good would it do to rehash the past or discuss these things with Laura? Being a woman of few words, Helen decided to do what she did best. She would *show* Laura her forgiveness, and she would do it by loving her boy.

"We won't be going outside today. There are more important things to do right here inside Sea Escape. Come, Joey, there's something I'd like to show you."

32

Babies didn't die in my newborn nursery. The unit director bragged about our better than average nurse-to-infant ratios, which afforded me the luxury of noticing a single labored breath or the most subtle change in skin tone, giving me plenty of time to alert a physician should a newborn get in trouble. Once they were transferred to the intensive care unit, I wasn't witness to the daily progress reports that went out to family and friends. *Grave, critical condition. Serious, but stable.* I had no firsthand exposure to the phenomena nurses in other areas of the hospital talked about. There was the septic man whose vital signs dramatically improved for no reason. The teenager who awoke from his coma. The woman whose cancer pain all but disappeared. And then, within hours of these miraculous recoveries, each patient lost the battle to heal. That's why it came as a complete shock when Dr. Sterling called me at home to tell me my mother was dead.

One day after she spoke fluently and stood under her own determination, just hours after she'd forgiven me, I learned that my mother had slipped away in the middle of the night like a gypsy.

Jenny was the one to find her. She'd entered the room singing, armed with towels for morning care. My mother lay still in her hospital bed, draped in the black mantilla and holding her rosary beads. Both gifts given to her by Luce.

"But I was just there." I shouted into the phone, my alarm bringing Christian, wet and dripping from the shower, into our bedroom. "I don't understand. She was doing so well."

The doctor paused at the right times, he comforted me in the right places. He had a knack for allowing turmoil while still effectively reminding me that my mother had plenty of clots waiting to break free from her plaque-lined blood vessels, bent on completing their collective mission: to take her out of this world. *At least she didn't suffer,* he said, though I wasn't sure how he could know this, if no one was with her when she passed. All I could do was be grateful it wasn't another huge stroke that robbed her of her newfound ability to walk and talk while leaving her awareness intact. My mother didn't deserve to go through everything all over again— taunted by losing function while holding on tight to faculty.

Christian took the phone from me and placed it back on our nightstand. Holding his towel with one hand, he rubbed my back with the other. He didn't say anything, and I didn't need to. He knew my mother was gone. I didn't cry at first. I sat on the edge of our unmade bed, a place where moments ago I'd been asleep, at peace with my confession, thankful for her absolution.

Two shadows filled our bedroom doorway. Henry and Claire didn't come to jump on our bed, giggling as I tried to make it around their happy feet. They didn't plead for extra hugs or beg for something sugary for breakfast. They'd abandoned each morning ritual, every delay tactic for not getting ready for school. My son and daughter knew something was wrong. There was only one thing harder than accepting that phone call, and that was telling my children that their grandmother now resided in heaven.

I reached out my arms to them in a fashion similar, though more coordinated than my mother had the day before to me.

My arms weren't fully wrapped around their warm bodies when Henry's tears came down.

"Nana was very sick—" I didn't get far. He knew the rest.

"No! You said she was getting better. She was going home. You lied!"

Henry backed away from me. Claire, having lost all the independence she'd found over the last few weeks, wrapped her legs around me, clinging like a koala does to a branch. The intensity of her grip prevented me from going to Henry. Christian readjusted his towel and got down on bended knee.

"Look, you've got to understand, Mom couldn't know. We thought Nana would get better."

Henry started to bang his head against the doorframe he leaned on. Once, then twice before Christian strong-armed him away from the wood.

I don't remember how Christian managed to calm Henry while peeling Claire off me. I didn't feel rage at my mother for leaving me, like I had for weeks after my father did. I didn't feel guilty asking Christian to wake Holden to tell him the news. I don't remember getting dressed or driving over to Paxton Rehab Center. All I could focus on was my need to be with her.

Passing clusters of narcissus and hyacinths bursting out of the dirt rows that lined the brick walkway, I brushed past two nurses coming out of the center. They were smiling. I wondered how it was that flowers could bloom and women could laugh when I was bereft. I didn't make it halfway to the unit when Jenny came out from behind the nurses' station. She took my hand like a child's and walked me into the dim room.

I searched my mother's face for subtle signs of life, but all I found was tranquillity. I didn't see her eyes flutter beneath her creaseless lids. Her nostrils didn't flare as even a single breath slipped in or inched its way back out. Every muscle in her face— the ones that had twisted as she struggled to speak, or grimaced as she fought to walk—was slack.

My mother looked peaceful pretty. But her essence wasn't on her face or in that room. I'd gotten there too late. She'd already left me to join my father and her sons.

"Is anyone else coming to see her?" Jenny smoothed out a wrinkle in the top sheet. To a nurse in this situation, presentation is everything. To any ordinary family member, Jenny would've been perceived as cordial—and in fairness, she was—but I knew she had work to do.

I shook my head, but the rest of me wouldn't move. I couldn't be rushed. I stared at my mother, memorizing every angle and line of her, knowing that when I left this room, I'd be closer to losing her once and for all. I cried the tears of a child, all gulpy and wet. After years of longing for her presence full and whole, I'd found her laugh, her touch, and her love. They were hidden behind my lie.

My tears went from a gentle rain to a downpour when I remembered Henry banging his head on my bedroom doorframe. Like my mother, I was called to soothe a child in mourning while tending to my own sorrow. An odd mother-child occupation. And with that one daunting thought, I forgave my mother for not doing a very good job with the impossible task of helping me cope with losing my father while she fought *not* to let go of everyone she'd ever loved.

I wiped my face and stood. It was my turn, and I would do things right. I leaned down and put my warm lips to her cool forehead. I touched the Spanish comb that held her hair in place, though now its purpose moot. "Make sure this is accounted for on the release form to the undertaker. We'll be using Miles Funeral Home. Tell them I want her to wear it."

"Consider it done. Tell me what you'd like me to do with her things and I'll take care of it." Jenny made a sweeping gesture around my mother's room, decorated like a chapel. I'd grown accustomed to the garish Mary statue and the picture of Jesus holding his heart.

"Do you think some of the other patients would want these?

They've been blessed by a priest, so you can't just throw them away. If you don't think anyone does, pack them up for me."

It felt strange deciding what to do with my mother's things when she was lying right there. In a weird way, it felt good to be there. I knew it would be hard to leave.

Henry decided to help me.

The gentle rap on the door turned out to be Maeve with a message for me to call Christian. Only then did I realize I'd left my house without a single thing except my keys.

"I'm so sorry about your mother," she said, trying to be all nice and kind. "Use the phone in my office." I wanted to be mad at her, but there seemed no point. Maeve hadn't succeeded in pushing my mother out of rehab. Helen Elisabeth Tobin left the place of her own accord.

Christian picked up after the first ring. "Is Henry there with you?" he asked, a hint of panic in his voice.

"What are you talking about? I didn't bring him here."

"He said he wanted to be alone, so I left him in his room. Can you hold on while I check to see if his bike's gone? He probably followed you. He would want to see her."

I didn't need Christian to come back on the line to know that Henry's bike wouldn't be found leaning against the wall of our shed. And I could've told him, he wouldn't come here either. He'd been upset for days back when my mother was in the ICU and he'd seen that deceased man on a stretcher traveling the hospital halls one final time, taking a trip to the morgue. Maybe later on, Henry would want to see my mother, his desire to convince his mind she was truly gone. But my son—overwhelmed and lonely—wouldn't want to be in a hospital room, closed in and dank. He would need his beach.

"I'll tell them to call you if he shows up here," I said. Jenny nodded her head, seemingly happy to help. "Stay there, in case he comes back. I'm done here. I'll call you when I get to Anaskaket."

I was sure. Henry went to Sea Escape.

33

Henry had to be devastated to race to Anaskaket without permission. The bike lay tossed on its side near the steps to the wraparound porch. It was both sad and sweet to see that my good boy took the time to find his helmet in the middle of the mess that was our shed. It was flung on the clamshell driveway, further evidence he was in a hurry. I made for the boardwalk that would take me down to the beach. He had to be at the rock house.

I whispered "thank you" for this day that promised a respite from wind and rain. I willed myself to see him sitting on the dry granite he called the "living room." It would be covered in a layer of cool sunshine. I scanned the beach but didn't see him. Parts of the rock house were visible from the top of the wooden steps; his favored rooms were not. Henry would be safe—I told myself—unless, in his anguish, he'd been enticed to lie down, as I once had.

I'd been discharged from the hospital after two days, home for one, when I took the steps to the beach, needing to get away from my mother's harsh stares and the oppressive silence that encased Sea Escape. I didn't make my way to the rock house with any sort of plan. Merely exhausted, I lay down on the damp stone, content to let the water caress me. At first it soothed as it rocked my empty body. Then the tide rose around me, lifting an arm and then a leg. The pain didn't register until it began tossing me back against the rock. Again and again it battered me, unrelenting in its desire to get me to feel something. Though part of me wanted him to, my friend the sea wouldn't take me that day. Instead he deposited me back on the jetty. Salty tears ran free as I finally wept for my baby. From that day on, the sea and my child were forever connected.

Standing there scouting for Henry, the vividness of that memory seized me. Thoughts of something horrible happening to him had their way with me. So I scrambled to the bottom, my feet landing on every second or third stair. I needed to find him.

Once beachside, I ran. Anaskaket was empty except for a couple making their way toward me. Their pace was dictated by her limp. Barefoot and holding a pair of sandals in one hand, she walked on one heel, as if something were lodged in the ball of her foot. She leaned on the arm of her handsome companion. Everything about him was silver. His cropped hair allowed the morning light to grab hold of his single diamond earring.

When I was nearly face-to-face with them, I slowed my pace, afraid to waste time coming to a complete stop. The emptiness in her eyes told me something hurt her more on the inside than any sea glass or shell could from the outside.

"Did you see a boy with black hair, about this tall?" I pointed to my upper arm and looked past them, scanning the rock house, willing Henry to come into view. "He would've stopped at the jetty."

"You won't find anybody there. I've been walking a long time; no one's come this way," she said.

Certain Henry would find his peace at the beach, I didn't want to believe this stranger, but then the man who sparkled glanced up to Sea Escape, his eyes coming to rest on the upstairs windows.

A voice with the timbre and tone of my mother's rang inside my head. *Go home.* I don't know why, but I trusted then that Henry wasn't at my father's rock house. He was in my mother's safe harbor.

I didn't take the time to thank the couple. Barely able to breathe from all my urgency, with a new and different certainty, I climbed the steep steps back up to Sea Escape. I ran through my mother's garden. The open door to the breezeway and my son's sneakers carefully lined up on the mat told me, long before the noise did, he was inside. Henry was safe.

I controlled my breathing so he wouldn't see me upset. I wouldn't say one word to wound him. As I made my way toward the din coming from upstairs, I could already imagine him sitting blank-faced in front of my mother's TV. He'd be on the floor, not on her bed. That was the rule.

A lump formed in my throat when, halfway up the stairs, I realized the whir and hum weren't coming from her television set without cable. I don't know what I expected to see when I rounded the corner, coming face-to-face with the open sewing room. A door forever closed, a room long silent.

Henry's back was to me. The drapes no longer drawn, he faced the ocean. But he wasn't concentrating on the view. Henry was running my mother's elderly sewing machine over brightly colored fabric. Raspberry on white, the print reminded me of coral.

I stood on the threshold I'd slept on a long time ago, when I was Henry's age and I was grieving too. I'd felt small and alone back then, watching my mother fill her spool with black thread, intent on piercing dark cotton. Still, I had faith that everything would be all right, because she would never leave me like my father had.

It was hard to believe, all these years later, with my mother suddenly and completely gone, there was life in that room. Henry was making curtains. He was perched on one of the old porch cushions I'd given to my mother before he was born. The tufted pillow seemed created for exactly this purpose. Henry was positioned eye to eye with the needle, one foot was squarely placed on the foot pedal.

I didn't want to startle him, so I stood still, waiting for him to sense me there. I'd never seen my son so single-minded. He was lost in the art of making something from nothing. He kept right on allowing the machine to do its magic under his power. I cleared my throat as quietly as I could and took a few steps into the room. He wasn't unsettled by my presence, once he realized I was there. He didn't pause the process until I bent down to kiss him. Little river tearstains covered his face.

"You have to take your time," he said, his voice shaky, his hands steady. "If you go too fast, the stitching will be crooked. You can use a seam ripper to pull out the thread, so you can try it again, but the needle leaves marks. See." Henry pointed to the cutting table, where a finished curtain identical to the one he was working on lay stretched out across the length of it.

"When did you learn to do this?" I feigned interest in the completed product, though even from a distance I could see rows and rows of zigzag needle punctures. The finished seam was straight-line perfection, proof my mother held him to her high standard.

"Nana started teaching me in December, the day you went to that party with Claire. These were supposed to be a surprise for you." The water works started again, fresh streaks traveled the length of his cheeks. "Nana says cotton's good to learn on. She says it's forgiving. That means even if you make a bunch of mistakes, it'll still turn out nice in the end." I turned his chair so I could hold him, the comfort I offered as much for me as it was for my dear boy. I felt his head rest heavy on my shoulder. His capable hands, warm on my back, kept me from falling apart.

"You've done a wonderful job. They'll look fantastic in our family room, where everyone will see them."

Henry broke our hold, and with care he smoothed out the fabric that had bunched up as a result of our hug.

"No, we're hanging them here at Sea Escape."

"Honey, Nana's not coming back. She's—"

I couldn't get out the word, *dead*. The four-letter word with the power to devastate, one syllable with the potential to change everything.

"Are you sure?" he asked. "How do you really know?"

"I went there. I saw her." Now I was the one crying, remembering her body lying on that bed while everything else about her went missing.

"Does it hurt to die? Do you think she was mad at me, because I didn't finish these in time?"

"The doctor said she died in her sleep, so it didn't hurt. And Henry, she could never be mad at you. You know, I think she loved you more than anyone. She never taught anyone else to sew."

He looked lovingly at his creation, his gift made visible in fabric and thread. "Really?"

"Really. When I was your age, she let me watch, but she never offered to teach me. I don't think I would have been any good at it anyway. But you—"

"That's kind of funny, because I told her the same thing. She said that was nonsense, I could do anything I put my mind on. So we came up here and she showed me all this stuff we could pick from to make curtains for the office. She was teaching me to be an artist."

Henry was quick on his feet, opening my mother's storage closet to reveal shelves filled with bolts of jacquard, tapestry, damask, and satin. "I said okay, I could try it."

"Not my father's office," I said. Like seeing old friends, I walked over to the rolls of fabric she'd stored there. As it had been since my father's death, everything remained tidy in this space. I unzipped a random garment bag. A baby blanket hung over one hanger, her wedding dress on another, both preserved in clear plastic. "You must have it wrong, honey. Nana would never change my father's office."

"Yes, sir. She told me not to tell you, because she wanted to show you when we were done that she loved Joseph *and* you. Look," he said, reaching farther into the closet to pull out a long, slender bag. "She even bought the curtain rods we'd need to put them on. It's called heartware."

I smiled at Henry and kissed his head. Right then I would've given anything to know what had made my mother ready to block out my father's light by hanging curtains from those windows. Why, out of the blue, she'd forgiven me. But she wasn't in her sewing room. She wasn't sitting in her wing chair, watching the plants come alive in her garden while the waves spilled over the sea floor. I'd never have the chance to ask her anything again. And to think I'd almost missed the chance to do my own talking. Now all I had left was a child's story made tangible in cloth.

"I'd love to know about that first day you learned. Did she say why she wanted to show you?"

"I don't really remember. It was a long time ago." He got teary again. Out of respect for the fabric and my mother's creations, he stepped back from the closet, wiping his face on his sleeve.

"Don't be sad, honey. You'll finish them." I couldn't tell him when he would. And I wouldn't pressure him to tell me more about her unexpected gift to me. Suddenly overwhelmed with everything I had to do—the decisions about the funeral, the phone calls to family and friends—I didn't tell Henry there was really no point in hanging them here. In this empty house, where no one would appreciate them.

"Don't be mad at me, Mom. I know you told me not to talk about him to her, but it slipped out."

I didn't see it coming, but when I understood what he meant, everything made sense.

"You were wrong when you said talking about your other kid would make her sad," he said. "It didn't. She told me that a long time ago she didn't like that name one bit. But talking about your baby, with me, made her love it."

"You told Nana about Lee?" It had been only yesterday that my mother held me, saying Joey-Lee, together in the same breath. I'd assumed the string was one name, her child's first and middle. But she'd known about my Lee. And because Henry had no ties to secrets deep, he'd told her the truth that allowed her to forgive me with both their names. The children, hers and mine.

34

Funerals, like birthdays, are celebrations of life. My mother's took place on a Tuesday in spring, and it was as tasteful and religious as she had been for seventy-seven years. Once again, I found myself sitting in the front pew in Saint James Church, saying good-bye to one of my parents. This time, I was determined to take in every detail.

Christian called in all kinds of favors, filling the church to brimming with urns of lilies: white, pink, and cream. Dressed in a navy blue suit and clutching two sheets of paper, Henry stood to my left. Claire wore a gray and white polka-dot dress. It was Josefina, the doll given to her by my mother, who brightened our pew with color, wearing a neon number. My daughter kicked her patent leathers against the kneeler until I put one hand on her thigh.

I looked back down the aisle to see Father Kelly leading the procession. Christian, Holden, Candy's husband, Pete, and my father-in-law, Joaquin, walked my mother's casket toward the altar. When it was time for me to join Holden to lay the pall, it took me a minute to disentangle myself from Claire. Christian slipped into my place, smiling when she welcomed his arms. A solemn hymn played in the background, and like a trumpet, Henry blew his nose.

Father Kelly hadn't objected when I told him I wanted to substitute the traditional white cloth Catholics lay over the casket to symbolize a return to one's baptismal promises with a creation of my mother's. Holden and I stood on opposite sides of her, taking our time to unfold the minky white mantle, with its swirly design, accented by tiny rosettes. Edged in white satin, the blanket my mother made for our brother looked striking draped over cherrywood.

Christian read from the Old Testament. I got misty when his gentle voice quoted Song of Songs. "The flowers appear on the earth, the time of pruning the vines has come, and the song of the dove is heard in our land."

When it was Holden's turn to read the responsorial psalm, I felt bad for him. He left all his usual swagger in his seat. I watched as he reluctantly let go of Edwina's hand. The paper he carried crinkled with nervousness. When he finally made it up to the lectern, he rubbed his left arm while he spoke. His voice quavered as he tried to get out the words, "Weeping may endure for a night, but joy cometh in the morning."

I'd been the one to choose the Gospel reading, one that honored my mother's devotion to God and her love of Sea Escape. Everyone who knew her understood the significance of John 14, which begins "In my Father's house there are many rooms."

My son, who seemed to have matured overnight, insisted that he have a job. He'd practiced the prayers of the faithful all morning, and again on the ride to the church in our hired town car. And though I'd told him he could change his mind, even right up to the last minute, I knew he wouldn't. He took his time walking up to the lectern. It didn't fluster him when the altar server forgot to move the standing box over for him to climb on. Henry didn't miss a beat. He moved it over himself, climbed on board, and once eye level with the crowd, he took the time to readjust the microphone and checked to be sure his papers were in order. Then he read.

Holding my breath for the first few intercessions, I felt like a stage mother, praying her star would steal the show. And then Henry came to the intentions I yearned for, and their names were bells ringing out inside the sanctuary.

"And for those who have died: Maggie McIntyre, Lee McIntyre, Mary Pat Finlayson, Warren O'Quinn, Paul William Tobin, Joseph 'Joey' Tobin, Lee Tobin, Joseph Robert Tobin, Helen Elisabeth Tobin, and all our deceased relatives and friends. We pray to the Lord."

Holden slapped a palm on his forehead. Lowering his head to his chest, he let go of Edwina's hand. I should've told him I'd intended to include all their names, each of them deserving of our prayers. It was new to me, needing to consider Holden's more sensitive side. He'd been different since he reconciled with her. I knew he had the first time I heard him call her Mother.

The Mass was almost over when it dawned on me to be nervous. It was my turn to get up in front of the congregation. I'd agreed to give the eulogy. If Henry could honor my mother without crying, so could I. I stood to step out of our pew and ran both hands down the length of my funeral dress. As I walked toward the altar, I wasn't so sure I could do it. Then I turned around and saw Candy dabbing her eyes with the linen handkerchief trimmed in Peony Sky in Jade fabric my mother made for her when we were in fifth grade. My mother-in-law, Ria, gave me a maternal nod; she'd always believed in me. And there was Luce, sitting up straight, eagerly awaiting my words. I could see her gauzy blouse bedecked in faux jewels. No one would tell her what not to wear to a funeral. My patchwork family gave me the courage to speak.

"I am not a writer," I began. Empathy for Holden's weak performance and pride in Henry's strong one spurred me on. "You all know my father was. What you may not know is that he wrote my mother letters throughout their married life. Beautiful letters. I'd like to read one.

My Dearest Helen,

I'm staring at your picture and I'm having one heck of a time putting my feelings to words today. You know, there was a time when I thought someday, after we were married, we would sit down and read over these letters and have a good laugh. I never want us to look back and say these letters sound silly. Surely they might amuse us, only because they're tame, trying to capture our love on the page, not because they seem like kids' stuff. I want them to bring back the feelings we had in the early days, the hope and promise of a beautiful life together. I want us to fully appreciate the misery we felt being apart and the ecstasy of coming back together.

Someday when we are old, yet still very much in love, I want these letters to help us recapture the love we felt in the beginning, to remind us of the memories the years tend to cloud. Wouldn't it be a remarkable life for us if someday we could sit down with our children to share these letters? The truth, the pain, and the joys of our love. Our separate lives joined to make one. We could sit in our cherished Sea Escape, with our children grown and married, maybe with children of their own, if we are so fortunate, and we'd tell them that if we could live our lives all over again, we wouldn't change a single thing. That would be worth more to me than all the wealth in the world.

I live now to see winter fade away to spring, and like you, Helen, I count the days until we will be together again.
All my love always,
Joseph

The inconsequential words I added at the end were uttered in a hurry. I knew I couldn't keep back the tears much longer. Even Holden rubbed his eyes. The organist began playing the song of farewell. Christian and I, each with a child's small hand in our own, walked back down the aisle behind her casket. We wept. Making that trip, by my friends, past my family—seeing Molly, Jenny, and Dr. Sterling, the people who'd cared for my mother in the end—made the finality of her death real to me.

Our driver led the way to the cemetery as my immediate family stared out opposite sides of the town car. Holden held tight to Edwina. Henry snuggled up against me. Claire sat on Christian's lap. No one spoke. The peaceful drive gave me a chance to take in the solemn grounds my mother wouldn't let me come to after my father's funeral. Holden and my mother had argued about it. I'd heard her tell him it was inappropriate to expect a girl my age to face such things. Funny how I'd never thought to come here any other time. Though I shouldn't have been surprised. It hadn't been a place where my mother found comfort, and obediently I took my cues from her. I found my place in and around Sea Escape, like she did.

It was beautiful, as cemeteries go, and I wanted to sear an image of it into my memory. The grave markers were chalk white against spring grass. Vertical stone statues rose above the cherry tree blossoms. My favorite was the one at the entrance to the memorial park, two lovers holding each other, their gaze cast upward, as if they longed to be somewhere other than where they were planted.

When the brief graveside service ended, the crowd dispersed, leaving Holden and me to say our final prayers, to shed our private tears. White petals left the rose I held, landing on top of her casket. A strange peace fell over me, knowing my parents were finally together. I imagined them holding hands, my mother young again, my father perpetually so. I wrapped my arms around my body, not sure if I was cold or if an otherworldly chill had taken hold. Holden stood unmoving by my side, never taking his eyes off the drifting petals.

"How old were you when she lost her Joey?" I asked.

"I was in first grade, so what's that, five, six? I used to come here in high school, and then again when I'd come home to visit. She refused to talk to me about him, so sometimes I'd come here, to see his name." Holden finally looked at me. "Their names," he said, searching my face for something. "You know, so I could be sure I wasn't making things up. That what I remembered really happened."

"I thought her other miscarriages were early. What do you mean, their names?"

"You didn't read the rest of the letters, did you?" Holden backed away from me, shaking his head. He laid out his hand in a deferential gesture, presenting me with a neighboring headstone a few feet from my parents' plot. I could make out their names even with my mother's casket separating me from truth etched in granite.

JOSEPH ROBERT TOBIN, JR.
AUGUST 18, 1960–AUGUST 18, 1960

TA LIEN
MARCH 20, 1964–APRIL 4, 1975

As I stood there trying to make sense of the connection, random images and garbled words collided until I understood. Lien was not my Vietnamese fairy tale. She was a real girl—the daddy's girl my mother had been trying to tell me about.

"She was his child? Why didn't she tell me? Why didn't you?"

"I told you to read the letters. You have no idea how hard I tried over the years to get her to let go of the lie she was living. Before and after he died. I couldn't go through it all over again with you."

"That's the date Daddy died. He was bringing her back here? To live?" I reached out my hand to lean on the headstone, trying to steady myself.

Holden didn't have to tell me my half sister was on that plane with our father because, before I finished asking the question, I remembered a room, named for a city. Saigon. My mother had decorated the special guest room for a child not her own, a child she'd found a way to welcome into her heart and our home.

"At first I thought the *perfect* funeral you orchestrated was just more denial, but then you left out her name," he said. "Admit it, you got sucked into believing Joseph walked on water. Helen was the master of painting us as the happiest family in Anaskaket, *until his tragic death*. But it wasn't that way. No matter how much she tried to convince herself. Or you."

I backed away from the stone and from Holden, my high heels sinking into the earth with each step. "Please stop. We should go. The kids are stuck in the car, and there are people waiting for us at Sea Escape."

"Don't bury it here, Laura. Don't be like her."

I dropped the rest of the rose on the ground as I made my way toward the limo. I wasn't mad at Holden, but I wanted to put it all together. I needed to understand.

I let Christian and the children think my silence was the result of deep sadness, which, in part, it was. Though if I were to be honest, my voice, reclaimed in the presence of a newborn, had been stolen from me once more, first by the ghosts of my brothers, and then by a sister I hadn't known existed. To say nothing of how lost I felt rifling through my memories of my mother and my father searching for clues, looking for pieces of the truth given to me in stories. At least in the end, my mother had wanted me to know. I would never forget the day she held me, as compromised as she was, and tried to tell me.

When we arrived back at Sea Escape, there were cars parked everywhere along the road out to Cedar Point. Christian's mother and father and Luce were already there, having insisted on providing the food for the collation. Henry and Claire scrambled from the car like they'd broken free from class, eager for an overdue recess. Christian whispered, "Take your time." I knew he needed to be with his parents and sister. Edwina kissed Holden and made her way inside.

When I stepped from the car, Holden touched the sleeve of my dress. "I meant to tell you it looks great on you."

I accepted his apology shrouded in a compliment. I suppose it must have been hard to be the keeper of all our secrets.

I smoothed out the wrinkles from my dress, though there were few. Artfully crafted, the fabric was well suited to the job of sitting, standing, and kneeling. I was glad Holden remembered the dress our mother made to attend our father's funeral.

"I didn't think it was right to wear it," I said. "But once I tried it on, it fit like she'd made it for me." I touched my mother-of-pearl hair clip to be sure the accent piece I'd chosen was still in place. I felt pretty and sophisticated. And I'd played my part even better than my mother had. On this, even she would've agreed.

"I don't understand why they were buried together." I said. "I would've thought that she wouldn't want to be with him forever after he betrayed her. That she'd want to be with the children."

"Don't you get it? Her life was all about appearances," he said, glancing up at Sea Escape sitting proud on Cedar Point.

Then I thought about Henry learning to make those curtains because my mother had wanted to surprise me. A fresh start to come by way of her hands, a needle, and some thread.

"Or maybe she forgave him," I said.

I linked my arm in Holden's. It wasn't his fault our family kept coming apart at funerals. We bypassed the crowds inside, choosing instead to walk the wraparound porch leading to the beach. Trays of Joaquin's sopaipillas, biscochitos, and my favorite, sweet bread, lined a banquet-size table pushed up against the railing. Henry, my little man, stood at attention at the far end of the porch. Miss Ackart was going on and on about what a wonderful job he'd done in church. Claire skipped up and down the boardwalk, her dressy shoes making a clickety-clack sound on the wood. Neither of my children had discovered the dessert table.

I reached into my clutch bag and pulled my mother's prayer book from it. The one she'd carried to Mass every Sunday throughout my childhood.

"I thought you might want this," I said, holding it out to Holden. I was about to say it belonged to his mother but was so overwrought I couldn't bring myself to.

"I'd like that." He took it from me, holding it like glass. Opening to the page with the inscription, we both took in her name, written in ballpoint pen, all kinds of flourishes gracing the page. There was one heart before *Mary* and another after *Pat*.

"She left a note behind. It's tucked in the back. All she writes about is how much she loves you."

He inhaled deeply, raising his chin. Holden was doing his best impression of his former self. The man who once did whatever he could to conceal his hurt was losing his resolve to hide it.

"I have something for you too," he said. As Holden reached inside his jacket pocket, Henry shrieked so loud old Miss Ackart slapped a hand to her chest. She looked like she was having a heart attack.

"Look!" He pointed to the top of the house in the direction of my father's office. I followed Henry's hand and Holden's gaze to find a window showcasing one of the curtains Henry made. Christian was waving down from above.

He threw open the window when he saw we'd noticed his surprise. "What do you think, pal? Aren't these going to look fantastic when you're finished?" Henry's face lit up the way it usually did when he was looking in the opposite direction, toward Anaskaket Beach.

"I don't know how he's going to deal with saying good-bye to this place," I said, the joylessness of our revelatory day starting to break me down.

"He'll be fine. Because that won't be necessary," Holden said, pulling the familiar savings account passbook and a legal-size document from inside his suit coat, impeccable worsted wool my mother would have loved.

"One final bombshell, though. There isn't any money in this account. Seems Grandfather McIntyre was a fox. But as soon as you sign this, I can get the process started. This place is yours for the taking. I'm renouncing my share."

"Holden, I can't. Keep the house, I mean. It wouldn't be right; it's as much yours as it is mine."

"I've got one house too many as it is," he said, letting his eyes wander from me to Edwina. She was right in the middle of a pack of Martinezes carrying large pans filled with steaming hot food to the table. She looked happy to be helping, and she didn't seem to care one bit about her nails.

"I want you to have it. On one condition. Don't be tied to her things." It was the first genuine expression I'd seen on his face since the last afternoon we'd spent together with our mother. "Make the place your own. Let the kids have friends over. Hell, let them wear their sandy shoes inside. This house was always meant for a real family. I know this much is true—she would want you to be happy here."

I ran my hand over the detailed stitching on the bodice of the pretty dress crafted by my mother. I shouted up to Christian and out to the garden my children danced in, "We're home."

And to myself I whispered two lines I remembered from one of my father's early letters, when I was certain their love was pure and honest.

Maybe someday we can afford our dream home by the ocean, our very own sea escape, where our life together will be perfect.

Acknowledgments

The faith waiting in the heart of a seed promises a miracle of life which it cannot prove at once.

—Rabindranath Tagore

In 2000, my mother had a devastating stroke, and as we said our good-byes she gave me a gift—the seed that would become this novel. Upon her death, I read letters written to her by my father, letters that further inspired me to write *Sea Escape*. Some plot points I've chosen surround historic events, and I've been as accurate as possible in depicting them. Some details from my life meandered their way into the story. Yet this is entirely a work of my imagination. Any resemblance to real events or people and their life stories is merely coincidence.

I'm beyond grateful to my parents for providing me those first principles, the little particulars from which everything else about this novel grew. I miss them dearly and hope I've done them proud by crafting this special kind of love story.

A special thank-you to George Esper, esteemed foreign correspondent and the author of *The Eyewitness History of the Vietnam War, 1961–1975,* for taking the time to share with me his experiences working for the Associated Press in Vietnam.

And thanks to Glen Schmidt, of Schmidt Design Group, Inc., for sharing his knowledge of landscape architecture design and planning.

I have deep appreciation for my amazing agent and friend, Elisabeth Weed. Choosing to work with her has been my single most brilliant career move. To have her keen editorial eye; her marketplace savvy; and her kind, thoughtful counsel is a true blessing in my life.

Thank you to my editor and this book's champion, Kerri Kolen, for believing in this story and for advocating for it at every turn. I'm thankful for the support offered to me by everyone at Simon & Schuster, especially Tracey Guest, Victoria Meyer, Aileen Boyle, and David Rosenthal.

There is no writer more fortunate than I to have such a fantastic cadre of trusted readers. Julie Basque, Lisa Marnell, Hannah Roveto, and Dianne Veale, your thoughtful feedback made this a far better story.

I will never know what I did to deserve a friend as true as Amy MacKinnon. Without her wise advice and fierce urging, I may still be searching for the heart of this story. She challenges me to be bold. I am forever indebted.

I'm a writer without words when it comes to expressing my gratitude to my daughter, Caitlin Griffin, and my son, Stephen Griffin. They believe in me, encourage me, and support me in everything I do. My love for them leaves me speechless.

Then there's my husband, Tom Griffin. My love. My best friend. Dear Tom, I'm holding you to your promise. I want you to know, I still wouldn't have missed the dance.

About the Author

LYNNE GRIFFIN is a nationally recognized expert on family life. She is the author of the novel *Life Without Summer* and the nonfiction parenting title *Negotiation Generation: Take Back Your Parental Authority Without Punishment*. Lynne teaches family studies at the graduate level and writing at the independent writing center, Grub Street. She lives outside Boston with her family.

Visit her online at www.LynneGriffin.com

Sea ESCAPE

Lynne Griffin's second novel is a thoughtful, deeply moving look
at the complicated love between a mother and daughter. Helen
and Laura are different women of different eras; a mother and
daughter alienated from each other yet bonded by love and loss.
Laura grows up in the shadow of her parents' love, and when her
father dies, it's as though she's lost both parents. For Helen, the
only way to cope with her grief is to retreat into the decades old
love letters from her husband, Joseph, the ones she's kept private
from her children. When Helen has a sudden and devastating
stroke, Laura's world is turned upside down. Now a mother herself, she must juggle her mother's care with her nursing career
and the needs of her own family. Laura is willing to do whatever
it takes to bring her mother back to health, and so she goes to Sea
Escape to search for the letters, hidden somewhere in her parents'
dream home by the sea. Along with the letters, Laura finds secrets
and lies filling the space between each line written. She uncov-
ers the patchwork details of her parents' marriage, discovering a
common thread: a secret that mother and daughter unknowingly
share.

For Discussion

1. In *Sea Escape* we are presented with three very different pictures of marriage: Maggie and Lee, Helen and Joseph, and Laura and Christian. Are there any similarities among these marriages? How does each woman's marriage shape her life and affect her relationships with her children?

2. Laura and Helen have an estranged relationship, even though they still see each other often. What does it mean to be estranged from someone? How does it differ physically and emotionally?

3. We see Helen and Laura in the roles of both mother and daughter. How does each woman's relationship with her mother differ from and influence the relationship she has with her children?

4. Helen never seems to forgive her father for all he put her and her mother through. Why do you think she's able to forgive Joseph's transgressions but not her father's? Do you believe she really forgave Joseph?

5. On page 210, rather than explaining to her mother what really happened at the clinic, Laura says, "Go ahead, hate me. I

deserve it." Why does Laura think she deserves to be hated? Why is it so hard for her to tell her mother a truth that it seems would only make things better between them?

6. Mourning is a theme throughout the book. How does each character grieve differently? In what ways can mourning be a selfish experience? What do the characters mourn besides the loss of a loved one?

7. Discuss the contrast between Helen's ability to accept other children into her home and Joseph's struggle to love Holden as his own son. Do you think it's easier for Helen to open her heart than it is for Joseph, and, if so, why?

8. Why do you think Helen reads Joseph's letters over and over again? Do you think it's comfort that she finds in them? Or is she looking for something else?

9. What does Joseph's office symbolize? Why do you think Helen finally feels ready to change it?

10. Helen had never been able to share the pain of her miscarriages with Laura. What do you think it says about Laura that she told Henry and Claire about losing baby Lee?

11. Each pair of siblings in the book includes a brother and a sister: Holden and Laura, and Henry and Claire. How do you think it would have changed the story if Laura had had a sister or if both Laura's children were the same sex?

12. Even though Helen guarded her secrets through most of her life, in the end, she wanted Laura to know the truth. What does understanding the truth do for Laura? How does it help her move on?

13. Sea Escape is supposed to be the ultimate dream home for Helen and Joseph. On page 285 Holden says, "Helen was the master of painting us as the happiest family in Anaskaket, *until his tragic death.* But it wasn't that way. No matter how much she tried to convince herself." Do you think the dream ever became a reality for Helen? Or was Holden right: Was all she created there an illusion, a facade?

A Conversation with Lynne Griffin

Sea Escape is inspired by letters your father wrote to your mother. Did anything else from your family history make it into the novel?

So many little particulars from my childhood and the relationship I had with my parents found their way into the novel. For example, I've included my parents' account of the Worcester tornado in one chapter and the way in which they met in another. Even the names of streets and other locales were borrowed from my family history to give authenticity to the novel. Though the story—what happens to Helen and Joseph—comes entirely from my imagination, friends and family will find a veritable hidden pictures experience as they read.

Did you find it difficult to create fiction out of something real in your life and not let the true story take over?

Yes, the experience of writing this novel was different and much harder than writing my first, its tenets more elusive. The fact that I'd written a novel already was irrelevant. My own mother-daughter story intruded as I wrote. The seeds I borrowed from my own life tended to obscure Helen's viewpoint and disrupt Laura's story.

It wasn't long before I realized I was in the way. Letting go, stepping aside to let these women do and say things my mother and I never did was the single hardest thing I've ever done.

You were working on another novel when the idea for *Life Without Summer* came to you. Was that other novel *Sea Escape*? Which book did you finish first? Did you work on them simultaneously?

When I found my parents' letters, after my mother's death, I went so far as to imagine excerpts of my father's beautiful writing shining within a novel I might write. In those musings, *Sea Escape* was born. Still I told myself: *You've never written fiction. You don't know the first thing about taking on such an ambitious project, weaving his words into your story.* No matter how much I dismissed it, the idea nagged me. For years it wouldn't leave me alone. Characters were named. Plot lines fleshed out. Twenty or so pages written—pages that would eventually become the last chapter of the novel.

Then the muse staged a coup, insisting she had a different plan for my literary life. One morning I woke from a restless night's sleep with a new story in my mind. From beginning to end, the whole plot was crystal clear. I knew the first line and the last line; and those words, in what is now *Life Without Summer,* remain unchanged.

So *Sea Escape* was pushed aside to make room for another story. Yet not for long. When my first novel went out on submission, I rolled up my sleeves and got back to what started it all: the story that compelled me to write fiction in the first place.

Both your books have themes of loss and mourning. Is this something that you deal with a lot in your career as a family life expert? Do you think your work has helped you to understand your characters better?

My father died suddenly of a heart attack when I was a sophomore in high school. He went on a business trip with my mother and only she returned from New Orleans. This event disrupted our family in unimaginable ways. I continue to grieve over that painful loss to this day. And until my mother passed away in 2000, twenty-five years after my father, she was never the same.

I began writing fiction at forty, after her death stirred up my fear of loss, the stabbing pain of it. Somehow writing to the heart of a story about a grieving woman and a lonely child gave me the chance to sort through things long buried, and to offer hope to others who may be afraid. It became my attempt to comfort those who know loss intimately as I do.

Whatever you call it, a hole, the missing piece, my soul wound, I accept even embrace my need to continually make sense of my profound losses. The stories I write, each unique in its way, highlight aspects of grief that are universal. While every person's journey toward healing is deeply personal, we're all tied to one another in the collective experience of it. At some point everyone will make its acquaintance. For those who do, I have a story.

Is there one character in the book that you relate to or sympathize with the most?

I'm asked this question a lot, and while I truly care deeply about all my characters—in all their shades of humanity—the one I love the most is Helen. Like my own mother, she struggles with what's called prolonged grief disorder. A specific kind of depression brought on by loss, that for some reason refuses to follow the typical trajectory of grief. In my years as a grief counselor, I've met countless people who simply cannot move through the grieving process. I empathize with Helen, stuck in the past, gripped by the pain. And I have enormous compassion for what my mother experienced after the death of my father. For this reason, *Sea Escape* is a very personal and deeply emotional novel for me, and Helen is a character I will be forever connected to.

You're from the Boston area, where the book is set. Was the setting important to you? How does it play a role in the story of these two women?

I grew up in Worcester and later in Holden. I've lived in and around Boston for most of my life. I live in a seaside town now. The familiarity of these settings made aspects of this challenging story easier to write. But the real reason portions of the novel take place south of Boston, on the Massachusetts coastline, is because my parents dreamed of having a home like Sea Escape. Placing the story there was my way of giving that to them.

Does Laura's story end for you where it does for us as readers? Do you have a future in mind for her beyond the pages of the book?

For me, the end of one of my novels is merely the end of the final scene. My characters are very real to me, so, yes, I believe Laura's story continues. I believe her grief work has just begun. The novel ends with her realizing that many things between her parents—and between her and her mother—were not as they seem. Still, she chooses to believe in love and commitment and dreams full of promise. It's who she is. So I imagine Laura will be just fine. She is a lot stronger than she gives herself credit for.

What's your next project? Are you working on a third novel?

I'm really excited about the next novel I'm working on. Once again, I'm digging to the heart of a family story with overtones of loss and a strong emphasis on the parent–child relationship. Stay tuned.

Enhance Your Book Club

1. Laura's favorite treat is the Martinez family's pan dulce, or sweet bread. Try making your own sweet bread for your book club meeting with this recipe: www.recipezaar.com/recipe/Pan-Dulce-Mexican-Sweet-Bread-285930.

2. Until Joseph's death, Helen was passionate about sewing. Bring in something that represents a passion or hobby of yours and turn your book club into show-and-tell.

3. Sea Escape is Helen's beachfront dream home, and it sounds like a piece of paradise. Describe what your dream home would look like and where you would build it.

4. Learn more about Lynne Griffin by visiting her website, www.lynnegriffin.com. And check out her blog at www.Family-Life-Stories.com.